THE SERPENT'S

EGG

A World War 2 Spy Story

by

JJ TONER

First published as an eBook July 14, 2016

First paperback edition published October 15, 2016 by JJ Toner Publishers PO Box 25, Greystones, Co Wicklow, Ireland

Second edition published April 2, 2017

Cover designer: Stephen Walker

ISBN 978-1-908519-36-8

This is a work of fiction. Names, characters, places and incidents are either the product of the author's imagination or are used fictitiously, and any resemblance to actual persons, business establishments, events or locales is entirely coincidental.

Other books by JJ Toner

The Black Orchestra, ISBN 978-1-908519-27-6
The Wings of the Eagle, ISBN 978-1-908519-18-4
A Postcard from Hamburg, ISBN 978-1-908519-30-6

These three books are also available as audio books

eBooks

Zugzwang, a Kommissar Saxon mystery
Queen Sacrifice, the second Kommissar Saxon story

Houdini's Handcuffs, a police thriller featuring DI Ben Jordan
Find Emily, the second DI Jordan thriller

Science Fiction

Ovolution and Other Stories
Murder by Android
Rogue Android

ACKNOWLEDGEMENTS

Thanks to all my proofreaders, Bonnie Toews, Lara Zielinski, Lesley Lodge, Paul T. Lynch, Karen Perkins, and Pam Toner. A special thank you to Marion Kummerow, who took time from the launch of her own book about the Red Orchestra, Unrelenting, to proofread the book from a German perspective. I am indebted to Stephen Walker for an inspired cover design.

JJ Toner lives in Co Wicklow, Ireland.
http://www.JJToner.net

THE SERPENT'S EGG

Part 1

Chapter 1

May 1938

Anna Weber completed her end-of-day chores in the food court at the department store, and punched her card. Stepping out through the main door, she merged with the Berlin crowds headed east into the wind and rain.

The Brandenburger Brauhaus in Kurfürstenstrasse was packed, ancient wood-paneled walls on all sides throbbing under a roar of speech and laughter. She looked at the crowd in bewilderment. How could she find him among this multitude? She needn't have worried. Max materialized from the throng like a magician, gripping a glass of beer.

He embraced her with his free arm and shouted in her ear. "What can I get you to drink?"

She tapped her watch. "There's no time."

"You have time for a small one."

Before she could object again he handed her his half-finished drink and disappeared back into the crowd.

Anna sipped Max's beer while she waited. The clock on the wall was five minutes fast, but still she watched nervously as it edged toward 6:15.

The wall clock showed 6:24 by the time Max re-emerged from the crowd, carrying a half-glass. She frowned at him and tapped her watch again.

"Drink up," he shouted.

She held onto Max's glass, lifting it to her lips. Max downed the half-liter in one long gulp. Max could drink for the Fatherland. If ever they made beer drinking an Olympic sport, he would surely win the gold medal! She set Max's glass on a shelf. He picked it up, finished it and wiped his mouth with the back of his hand. Then he linked her arm and they hurried from the beer cellar.

Madam Krauss had rooms in a townhouse a few doors from the Brauhaus. It wasn't far, but the rain had turned to a downpour. They ducked into Madam Krauss's porch, shaking the worst of the water from their coats. Max reached for the knocker, but before he could lift it the door opened and an officer in a Wehrmacht uniform emerged. The collar of his greatcoat was turned up, and he lifted his hat to his head as he brushed past, keeping his face hidden from them.

They stepped inside to a hallway with a steep staircase, the walls adorned with striped wallpaper from an earlier century. The Führer frowned at them from a picture on one wall.

A thin odor of damp straw filled Anna's nostrils. Not an unpleasant smell, it reminded her of the stables in Dresden where she used to take riding lessons as a child. She sneezed.

"*Gesundheit!*" from Max.

The cracked voice of an old woman emanated from a parlor beyond the staircase. "In here, children."

Madam Krauss was indeed an old woman. She sat behind a table, her head wrapped in a woolen shawl that matched the dark tablecloth. A meager fire flickered in the grate.

They moved forward and took the two seats available. Anna removed her hat and placed it in her lap.

Madam Krauss observed them with piercing eyes barely visible behind high cheekbones. Her wrinkled skin was the color of mud. Her hooked nose gave an impression of one of Grimm's witches.

She sat back and linked her bony hands across her belly. "Welcome to my home. You are Anna?"

"Yes, Madam, and this is my fiancé, Max-Christian."

"You are both welcome."

Madam Krauss placed a deck of Tarot cards on the table. "We'll start with you, young man. First, touch the cards. Shuffle them if you like."

Max picked up the cards and shuffled them energetically. He put the shuffled pack on the table.

"Thank you. Now I want you to close your eyes and concentrate on your dearest wish. Don't tell me what it is. Just keep it in your mind."

Max closed his eyes. Madam Krauss leaned forward, dealt five Tarot cards from the deck and placed them in a cross on the table, face down.

"You can open your eyes now, Max-Christian." She pointed to the center card. "Turn over this card first."

Max turned the card.

"Ah! The Wheel of Fortune. This shows me that you are a man of strong convictions, someone who always gets what he wants from life. Now turn over the rest of the cards."

He turned over the four remaining cards, and Anna drew in a sharp breath. The card on the right was the Grim Reaper, the one on the left a man hanging upside down, tied to a cross.

Chapter 2

May 1938

Madam Krauss stroked her chin while she examined the cards. She looked at Anna. "It's not what you think, child. The Death card often signifies marriage or a love affair. The Hanged Man could point to someone suffering an injury or something being broken."

Anna didn't believe her.

"The card below is The Pope, indicating travel or secrets, and the card above is the Popess, which speaks of passion, but also represents enlightenment or knowledge. The Pope and the Popess together gives us secret knowledge or enlightenment through travel."

Anna lifted her hat from her lap. She had flattened it under her fists. "But what does it all mean, Madam?"

Madam Krauss sat back in her chair again. She addressed her remarks to Anna. "Max-Christian is a man of strong convictions, convictions that will lead him into situations—perhaps in a foreign land—where his inner strength will be called upon to help him deal wisely with secrets. He may marry, but something will have to be broken first."

Like an engagement? Was she saying that Max would marry someone else? Anna didn't believe that. Surely the fortune teller was sugarcoating the truth. Max was going to die young.

"What does all that mean?" said Max.

"It means what it means, child. The cards cannot give us certainty. Every man and woman has a free will, freedom to make choices that determine how our lives develop. Without that we are no better than the animals, after all, are we not?"

Anna's fingers attempted to rebuild the shape of her hat. "And what about marriage?"

"Marriage is a possibility, but I would say not a certainty."

Max grunted. "So what use are the cards?"

How rude is that! Anna kicked his shin under the table.

"The cards do not lie. They have shown us your future. All I can do is interpret them as best I can." Madam Krauss gathered the cards and placed them in front of Anna. "Your turn now, young lady. Touch the cards, shuffle them if you like."

Anna placed a finger on the deck and withdrew it again.

"Thank you. Now close your eyes. Concentrate on your dearest wish. Don't tell me what it is. Just keep it in your mind."

Anna closed her eyes. She pictured herself in a white wedding dress with a long train, and Max beside her in a dark suit. They were in a church, exchanging rings. The priest raised his hand to bless them...

"Open your eyes, child." Anna opened her eyes. "Now turn over the center card."

When Anna saw the center card, her heart jumped in her chest.

The Lovers!

"Your center card is The Lovers. We know what that means."

"Marriage."

"Probably marriage, but love certainly. Now turn over the other cards."

Anna's hand trembled as she turned the cards.

"The card on the left is Justice, representing tenacity. This goes well with the card on the right, The Chariot, which represents victory. The card below is The Star. That is incapacity or hope. The card above is The Hermit or Wise Man."

Max snorted. "What does all that mean?"

She kicked at his shin again, but missed.

"Anna will be loved. She may marry. Her tenacity will ensure victory or justice, possibly with the help of a wise man with an incapacity or illness."

Anna sprang to her own interpretation straight away. "Could the wise man be a wise woman?"

Madam Krauss nodded. "Yes, that could be."

Anna smiled. "And could incapacity mean old age?"

"Oh yes, old age is a severe incapacity and no mistake." Madam Krauss chuckled.

The fortune teller put the cards away. She placed her hands on the table, palms up. "Take my hands, children." Anna took one hand, Max the other. "Make a circle." Max and Anna joined hands. "Close your eyes and concentrate."

"On what?" said Max.

"It doesn't matter. Just clear your mind."

A minute passed in silence. Anna opened one eye and closed it again.

"Yes, now I see it. I see your future. You will be married. You will be happy together. There is a child."

Anna's eyes sprang open. "A boy or a girl?"

"A girl."

Anna closed her eyes again.

"I see you traveling together on a train. There are mountains, snow-capped mountains." She released their hands.

Chapter 3

May 1938

In Max and Anna's studio apartment in Kolonnenstrasse, Anna stood by the window. The rain battered the glass, depositing droplets that quivered in the wind like frightened souls before coalescing to hurtle downward to collective annihilation. She shivered.

Max stirred in the bed behind her. He was the envy of all her friends. She was lucky to have him. There were so few young men that were not members of the dreaded SS, the thuggish SA, or the armed forces, the Wehrmacht.

She perched on the bed beside him. "Good morning, sleepyhead."

He ran a hand over his head and rubbed his eyes. "What time is it?"

"It's after nine." She touched his arm, grateful that he'd said nothing about the previous night's argument. "I thought you were going to sleep all day."

Max threw back the covers and leapt from the bed. "Make me some breakfast while I put some clothes on, Anna." The sound of her name from his lips sent a warm shiver through her body.

"As you command, Lord." She laughed. Her Max was a picture in his sleep, but he was so much more when he was awake, tall with a fine head of dark hair, lean and lissome—and naked!

Breakfast consisted of pan-fried eggs, coffee and light brown bread. They ate in silence, the argument hanging in the air between them like a bad smell. Anna had to say something to dispel it, and maybe to resolve the argument, one way or the other.

"I've been thinking about... what you said yesterday about your job—"

"Leave it for now, Anna. Let sleeping dogs lie."

"Yes, I will, but I just wanted to say that your situation would improve if we were married."

"You think so, Anna?"

How different the sound of her name now.

"Yes, of course. As long as we are unmarried it's obvious that we don't have authorization, and everybody knows what that means. If we were married there would be no obstacle to your promotion and I'd be more secure in my job."

"Since when does it affect your job?"

"Since the owners were forced to sell the store. Since all the Jews were sacked. There has been talk at work that half-Jews will be next."

"You're not half-Jewish."

"It's the thin edge of a wedge, Max. People talk. Rumors spread. If we were married all the rumors about me would cease."

He said nothing. The blank look on his face was not encouraging.

"Don't you want to get married, Max?"

"Of course I do. You know I do. I love you. I want for us to have children, but it's just not possible."

"It's not impossible. Others have managed it."

"Important people—rich people—can skirt the law, but not people like us. Now, let's leave the subject for the moment."

She jumped from the table, knocking over her coffee cup. A few drops fell on the tabletop before he grabbed the cup and righted it. "What gives the government the right to tell me who I can and cannot marry? Can't you see how unjust that is?"

"It's the law."

Anna's blood pressure rose a couple of notches. Max seemed to accept any injustice as long as it was 'the law.' Where was his fortitude, his conviction, his inner strength?

"And Madam Krauss —"

"— is an old witch."

"She's nothing of the sort. She's a gifted fortune teller and a psychic. And she offered to help us. Don't you think we should accept her offer?"

"You really believe that mumbo jumbo, don't you?"

"It's not mumbo jumbo. You heard what she said. She has friends in high places, friends who have been given permission to marry —"

"We have only her word for that." Max snorted. "Where are we going to get a hundred Reichsmarks?"

Anna made an exaggerated pout. "How much am I worth to you? You wouldn't pay a hundred marks to be able to marry me?"

"Of course I would, my love, but I don't believe this Madam Krauss can influence matters one way or the other. She's just trying to put her hand in our pockets."

"You don't know that. Why can't you open your mind? Some forces that cannot be seen are real."

He made an ugly face. "You mean like gravity or magnetism?"

"I mean like the force of the mind and the spirit world."

"My mother has a saying, the only person more foolish than a magician is his customer."

"And what makes your mother an expert on magicians?" She snatched his plate from the table and dropped it in the sink.

He stood up from the table and slipped his jacket on. "I'm going to be late for work. So are you. Can we agree to do nothing for the moment?"

"What will that achieve?"

"The law may change. The Nazis might lose power."

She frowned at him. "How likely is that within our lifetimes?"

Chapter 4

June 1938

Two weeks later, on Friday June 3, Max took a half-day from his holiday entitlement and paid a visit to Gestapo headquarters in Prinz-Albrecht-Strasse. He was directed to Department B (Race and Ethnic Affairs) on the third floor, where he had to wait an hour sitting on a wooden bench in a corridor, playing mind-games with the plaster cracks on the walls and watching men in uniform coming and going. When he was called, he presented an envelope containing his paperwork to a uniformed official behind a counter in a smoke-filled office.

"Name?"

"Max-Christian Noack."

The official placed his cigarette in an overflowing ashtray. "Your application fee?"

Max handed over 20 Reichsmarks. The official opened a cash box with a key and took out a pad of receipts. He signed a receipt, tore it off the pad and handed it to Max. Then he placed the money in the box and locked it. Max put the receipt in his wallet.

The official ran his eyes over Max's documents. The paperwork consisted of their two *Ariernachweise* together with 14 copies of birth certificates: his, Anna's, their parents' and their eight grandparents', as well as marriage certificates for all sets of parents and grandparents.

He scanned Anna's *Ariernachwies* before checking through the other documents. He stabbed a tar-stained finger at one of the marriage certificates. "These people are Jewish." It sounded like an accusation.

The official picked up his cigarette, filled his lungs and exhaled the smoke, his eyes never losing contact with Max's. "You are familiar with the Nuremberg Laws?"

The acrid smoke stung his eyes, but Max tried not to blink. "Of course, but I understand that exceptions can be made in some cases."

"In marginal cases, yes, where there is only one Jewish grandparent. Not in cases where there are two. This person is a second degree *Mischling*. I must warn you that making a fraudulent application is considered a waste of official time, which is a criminal offense." He handed the paperwork back. "You do, however, have the right to appeal to the Reich Committee for the Protection of German Blood."

"I've looked into that. There's a 2-year waiting list and very few cases are granted."

"Well, there you are, then. Let me see your personal papers."

Max handed over his identity card.

"You are employed in the Reich Labor Service?"

"Yes."

He clicked his fingers. "Show me your Party membership."

"I don't have that with me."

"Hasn't anyone ever told you, you must carry that at all times? As a member of the Party and an official of the Reich you should be fully aware of your duties. You would be well advised to familiarize yourself completely with the laws of the Reich." He handed back Max's papers. "You may go."

Chapter 5

June 1938

Max left Gestapo headquarters grumbling under his breath. He still had most of the afternoon free, so he took a tram to the Brauhaus in Kurfürstenstrasse and bought himself a fortifying liter of beer before making his way to Madam Krauss's home.

He knocked on the door and waited. Madam Krauss opened it a crack. "You don't have an appointment. What do you want?"

"I'm sorry, Madam. I need your help."

She let him in, but he had to wait in the front parlor for 30 minutes while she dealt with an existing client.

The front parlor was stuffed with furniture, old and heavy, like an antique shop. There was a bookcase full of dusty leather-bound books, a sideboard of Black Forest oak and various armchairs and sofas that nobody ever sat on. He stood with an ear pressed to the door. All he could hear was mumbling voices, Madam Krauss's and another, deeper voice. He couldn't catch anything that was said.

The parlor door opened and Madam Krauss came in, carrying a silver tray with tea and Danish pastries. She set the tray on a table.

"You remember me, Madam?"

"Of course. Anna Weber's sweetheart."

"Our marriage application was rejected by the Gestapo today. You will recall you offered to help us."

"I offered to do what I could. Tell me what happened with the Gestapo."

"I asked if they would make an exception for us. They refused."

"Anna's a Mischling?"

He hated the word, but passed no comment on it. "A quarter. Two grandparents on her mother's side were Jewish."

"How old are you?"

"I'm 25."

"I assume you've done your national service?"

"Yes."

"But you're not with the Wehrmacht. What do you do?"

"I have a government job."

"And are you happy in your job?"

He shrugged. "As content as the next man, I suppose."

"Are you a Party member?"

"Of course. Every government worker must carry a Party card."

"What does Anna do?"

"She's a waitress in the food court at the KaDeWe department store."

"How old is she?"

"She's 24. Will you be able to help us?"

She poured the tea and handed him a cup.

"You haven't answered my question."

Max thought he had. "Madam?"

"Tell me how you feel about working for the Nazis."

What a loaded question! To avoid answering and give himself time to frame a suitable reply, Max stuffed his mouth with apple pastry.

She fixed him with her gaze. "Well?"

He swallowed. "Can I be frank, Madam?"

"Everything you tell me is in strict confidence, child."

"The truth is I would never have joined the Party if I could have avoided it. I hate everything they stand for."

"I'm glad to hear it. I can see you are a young man who thinks for himself."

Madam Krauss raised her cup to her lips with a poised pinkie. "Far too many of our young people follow the Party line, these days, don't you think?"

Max took another bite of his pastry. If she was going to continue skirting subversion like this he might have to reach for a second one. He nodded. With a mouth full of pastry he was freed from the obligation to agree verbally.

"I thought so. I knew from the moment I saw you. I said to myself, here is a young man of independent thought, a man of conviction, who doesn't follow the crowd, a man of principle, who says what he believes and believes what he says." Max swallowed and opened his mouth to speak. What he had in mind was to introduce a note of moderation, but before he could say anything, his host continued to gild the lily. "A man of action. A true patriot who can be relied on to follow his own conscience. Am I right?"

Max shook his head.

"This is no time for modesty. Your young lady must be proud of you. And you make such a happy couple."

"Thank you. Madam."

"More tea? Help yourself to another pastry."

"No thank you, Madam."

Get on with it, woman!

She laughed. "When I was your age nothing would keep me from the pastry dish."

He suppressed an unkind rejoinder. "Will you help us, Madam?"

"You have the documents?"

Max gave her the two *Ariernachweise.*

"And my fee?"

Max handed over 100 Reichsmarks, a month's wages.

Her face cracked into a sort of smile. "I will be happy to pass these to a friend who will be able to help."

Max took a deep breath. "Thank you, Madam. When can we expect a result?"

"I would give it a week, perhaps two. Expect a visit from someone within the next two weeks."

#

When Max told Anna about his visit to the Gestapo office, and the outcome, she dropped one of her mother's precious cups. The willow pattern porcelain shattered on contact with the kitchen floor. "Oh Max-Christian, what did you do that for? Now that door has been firmly closed."

He helped her tidy up the shattered porcelain. "It was always closed, Anna. Maybe we have to accept that we will never marry. Our union is forbidden under Reich law."

"We agreed to do nothing and wait. You should have talked it over with me first. Now the Gestapo are aware of us, anything might happen."

He reached out for her. "Like what?"

She flapped at him to keep him off. "I don't know. I could lose my job at the department store. You could be kicked out of the ministry. The Gestapo might alert the Brownshirts and they could come and beat us. I don't know."

He managed to put an arm around her waist. "Don't give up so easily, Anna. I also went to see Madam Krauss."

She stared at him wide-eyed. "You paid her fee? But you said you never would. You said she was a confidence trickster."

"I know what I said, Anna. But I gave her the money and she's agreed to help us. She said we should hear something in about two weeks."

"What else did she say?"

"She asked me a lot of questions. I think she won't do anything to help Nazis or Nazi sympathizers."

"She suspects you of sympathizing with the Nazis?"

Max loved her in all her moods, but she was at her most attractive when she was angry, nostrils flared, blue eyes blazing, blond hair scattered about her face, and her fingers arched like talons.

"No, but she knows I'm a Party member."

"Only because you have to be."

"I think that's what she wanted to check out."

Anna's mood switched from anger to concern. Her brow furrowed. "What else did she say?"

"She decided I was a man of action, someone who thinks for himself."

She snorted. "And she claims to be psychic!"

"And someone who can't keep his hands from the pastries."

"She said that?"

"What she said was that she couldn't resist pastries when she was young."

Her eyes narrowed. "It shows."

He laughed. "I had the same thought."

"You didn't say anything! Tell me you didn't insult the woman in her own home."

"Of course not. I was very well behaved. We sipped tea in her front parlor. She said she would do her best, but she made no promises."

Anna stood on tiptoe and put her arms around his neck. "Thank you, Max." He kissed her. She responded eagerly. "I'm sure Madam Krauss will find a way."

"What makes you so sure?"

"Don't you remember, she foretold that I will achieve justice with my tenacity and with the help of a wise old woman."

"She said you'd have to break something first."

Anna's hand covered her mouth. "The cup!"

Chapter 6

June 1938

While Max and Anna were sleeping in their studio apartment in Kolonnenstrasse, the Anti-Nazi Resistance was busy in a secret location in a fashionable district in the west of the city. Adam Kuckhoff was putting the finishing touches to the editorial section of their latest leaflet. He handed it to Arvid Harnack who re-read the entire leaflet. A single broadsheet, it described several of the latest atrocities committed by the Nazi Brownshirts in the streets of Berlin and other German cities. The main article, written by Adam under the pseudonym 'Grock', warned of an approaching war in Europe.

Adam was 51, Arvid a mere stripling of 37, although Adam thought the age difference was not so obvious as he had a strong head of hair while Arvid's was receding fast.

Adam's editorial ended with a rallying cry. Arvid read it aloud. "Rise Up! Rise Up! Take a stand against the NSDAP regime. 'All that is necessary for evil to triumph is for good men to do nothing.' Edmund Burke (1729-1797)." He scratched his balding head. "Don't you think we should reverse those sentences, Adam? And 'Nazi regime' might be better than 'NSDAP regime.'"

Adam took the sheet from him. "You're right, my friend. Best to end with the call to action. Rise Up! Rise Up! Take a stand against the Nazis. I'll draft it again."

Adam was the creative member of the team, an experienced journalist with two novels to his name. Arvid, on the other hand, held a senior position in the Ministry of Economics. He was as intelligent as anyone Adam had ever met, but really, he was nothing more than a glorified civil servant.

Adam was happy to make the small changes. He had many friends in the theatre—playwrights, directors and actors—who would take umbrage if anyone interfered with their work, but compromise was the secret to successful collaboration, and this was Arvid's show, after all.

Adam greeted the world with an open, smiling countenance, unlike Arvid, whose neutral look always incorporated a permanent frown. Arvid's wife, Mildred, often mirrored her husband's earnest, concerned look, and Adam shared a private joke with his wife, Greta, that, without his spectacles and pipe, Arvid would be indistinguishable from Mildred. It was a tad cruel, but it carried a grain of truth, for Arvid and Mildred were like two sides of a coin. They dressed alike, and Mildred had an irritating habit of finishing Arvid's sentences.

Adam handed the final version of the leaflet to Arvid who checked the editorial for the last time. "I like it. Our most explicit leaflet yet. We must do a double print run."

"Good sentiment, Adam, but where are we going to get enough paper for that? We barely have enough for a normal run."

Mildred Harnack came in from the kitchen carrying the precious Hectograph plate cleared of ink and gelatin, ready to receive the new master. "Leave that to me, gentlemen. Herr Goebbels' office won't miss another couple of reams."

Arvid shook his head. "You've been pushing your luck as it is. I won't ask you for any more paper this month."

Adam held his tongue. Mildred Harnack had a history of depression. She had only recently returned from America where she'd undergone treatment. He wouldn't ask Arvid to put any more pressure on his wife.

"You can go home now, Adam. I'll work on the master plate overnight." Arvid rubbed his red-rimmed eyes. It had been a long night.

Adam reached for his jacket. "I'll get back in the morning early to give you a hand with the print run." He shook hands with Arvid before slipping out through the back door.

"Give my best to Greta and the baby," said Mildred.

It was dark outside, and windy, but mercifully the rain had eased.

Adam headed east. Mildred was a rock. Weighed down with worries about the failing health of her mother in the United States and her own insidious depression, she still had time to consider others.

#

Baby Ule was exercising his lungs on Greta's shoulder.

Adam barely had time to take off his coat before Greta was barking orders at him. "Get me a towel. He's dribbling all over my blouse. Check the bottle. It should be warm enough now. And find me a fresh diaper."

Adam did as he was told. "What's wrong with him?"

"I don't know. He's been screaming the place down for about thirty minutes. What kept you?"

"We finalized a broadsheet." There was too much noise to say any more. He checked the temperature of the milk on the back of his hand, as she'd taught him to, and passed it to her.

Greta offered it to the baby and the screaming stopped abruptly.

Adam shook his head in amazement. "He must have been hungry."

"He can't have been hungry. I fed him an hour ago."

"He seems to have a healthy appetite."

Greta rolled her eyes. "He should be sleeping. Look at him."

Ule's eyes were wide open, watching Greta, listening to every word.

#

Later, they lay together in bed and shared a cigarette.

"You're more energetic than you look, old man."

"Thanks. You're not too sluggish yourself."

She laughed. Adam melted at the sound. He framed his next statement with care. "We have a new source."

"Tell me."

"You'll laugh when I tell you, but I think she will have a lot to give us."

"Her? A female? Who is she?"

"Her name is Frau Krauss. I'd like you to visit her as soon as you can."

"Where is she based? One of the big ministries?"

"Not officially."

She propped herself on an elbow to look at him. "Enough of the mystery. Who is this Frau Krauss?"

"Her professional name is Madam Krauss. She's a psychic, a fortune teller and a palmist."

Greta nearly dropped her cigarette on his chest. "Tell me you're joking."

"It's no joke."

"Are we really that desperate?"

"Don't dismiss the idea, Greta. Madam Krauss's clients come from every level of government, the Wehrmacht, perhaps even the Gestapo. You'd be surprised how many of our leaders are superstitious enough to share their plans with a fortune teller. I am convinced she will be a treasure trove of useful intelligence."

"Arvid has gone along with this?"

"Indeed. Mildred found her. You know how superstitious Mildred is."

Chapter 7

June 1938

Max took an Autobus the 110 km to his family home in the medieval town of Lutherstadt Wittenberg, recently renamed in honor of its most distinguished 16th Century resident.

The Noack family residence was situated at the edge of town, a terraced house built over two centuries earlier that still retained many of its original leaded windows. His mother lived alone. She followed a strict routine that permitted Max just four visits per year. This was his second scheduled visit of the year.

He had a key, but in deference to his mother, he knocked on the door and waited. She opened the door, then turned on her heels without a word and went back inside. He followed her into the front parlor and found her sitting on the sofa reading a book.

"Hello, Mother, how are you?"

No answer.

"Are you all right? Is everything all right?"

She waved a hand at him. "Listen to this. 'Peoples deprived of democracy have to suffer dictators for which they carry no blame. Societies with a free vote get the rulers they deserve.' What do you think of that?"

"Very insightful, Mother. What are you reading?"

She set the book aside. "Sit. Tell me what your life has been like since I last saw you."

He moved to join her on the sofa.

"Not here. Sit over there." She pointed to the upright piano. Max pulled out the piano stool and perched on it.

He told her about Anna's determination to get married and their visit to Madam Krauss. At the mention of a fortune teller, Frau Noack launched into a long story about how a visit to a fortune teller had changed her life. At least the story had some connection to the conversation.

That story came to a halt half-told. And then she answered his original question. "I'm well. The town council keeps me busy, and my mind active. Is that the only suit you have? You know they finally agreed to rename the town."

"I heard that, yes. I have another suit for work."

He stopped by a Brauhaus for a quick beer before taking the autobus back to Berlin. She had offered him neither food nor drink. She would give him anything he asked for, of course, but it would never occur to her to offer. His visit had lasted less than an hour. Nothing of substance was discussed. And no emotions were displayed. A childhood memory bubbled up. He'd fallen from his bicycle, grazed his knees. His mother's reaction: "Big boys don't cry." His childhood was peppered with small incidents like that. Displays of emotion were strictly taboo in that house.

Chapter 8

June 1938

The distance from Adam and Greta's apartment to Kurfürstenstrasse was a little over two kilometers. Greta was happy to push Ule there in his pram. The weather was fine and the exercise would do her good. Since giving birth in January, she was having difficulty getting back to her ideal weight.

She made two stops along the way at the houses of friends, taking the pram inside on each occasion. At each stop, she extracted a few copies of the latest leaflet from their hiding place in a secret compartment in the base of Ule's pram, and handed them over. Her friends were eager to read the uncensored news and some to help with further distribution.

Upon her arrival at Kurfürstenstrasse, she took a table outside the Brauhaus, ordered a half-glass of beer, and observed a succession of Madam Krauss's visitors come and go. Several of her visitors wore uniforms. It seemed Arvid was right. This woman could be a source of valuable intelligence.

Lulled by the motion of the pram, baby Ule had slept all the way there. He began to stir. Greta rocked the pram and he drifted off again.

Observing a lull in the fortune teller's traffic Greta finished her drink and set off to Madam Krauss's house. She knocked on the door. When there was no response, she pushed it. The door swung open. She backed into the house, pulling the pram inside.

"Come in, come in," called a voice from a room at the back of the house. "Leave the pram in the hall. Come to the back parlor."

Greta could see no one. She assumed Madam Krauss had an

arrangement of hidden mirrors that allowed her to see into the hall. She checked Ule. The infant was sleeping peacefully.

The back parlor was dimly lit, a log fire in the grate casting flickering shadows around the room. Madam Krauss sat behind a table wrapped in a dark shawl. She waved a spindly hand to invite Greta to take a seat at the table.

"I have been expecting you. You are Frau Kuckhoff?" The voice, though cracked by age, carried authority.

"Greta Kuckhoff, yes."

The old woman placed a deck of cards on the table. "Touch the cards, Greta. Shuffle them if you like."

"I'm not here for a reading, Madam. Adam said you might have some information...?"

"I have a few snippets for you, but first, the reading. Shuffle the cards, child."

Greta shuffled the cards. Madam Krauss picked them up and dealt out the top five cards, arranging them in a cross on the table.

#

Greta thanked Madam Krauss for the reading. It was composed of generalities for the most part, but there were a few grains of truth mixed in that planted a seed of doubt in Greta's skeptical mind. How did she know that Greta's birth sign was Sagittarius, that Greta's marriage to Adam was his third, and that his first two wives were sisters?

Madam Krauss listed a number of her regular customers. There was a colonel from the First Cavalry Division, a high-ranking Kriegsmarine officer and a Luftwaffe major, both stationed in the office of the Supreme Command of the Wehrmacht, the OKW, in Bendlerstrasse. Her clients also numbered government workers from several ministries. A rich pool indeed!

"These men and women tell you things about their work?"

"Not usually, no. But if I can gain their trust they will often give me glimpses into their working lives, and sometimes if I'm lucky they may include sensitive military information."

A scream from the hallway signaled that Ule had woken. Greta ran to him. She picked him up and rocked him on her shoulder. He continued to cry. Greta took a bottle from the pram and asked Madam Krauss if she could heat it. The old woman directed Greta to the kitchen. While waiting for the bottle to heat Greta placed the baby on a blanket on the kitchen table and changed his diaper. Warm and clean and with a fresh bottle to suck on, Ule was soon content.

Madam Krauss admired the boy. "He's a big baby. He'll make his mark some day."

A warm glow of pride filled Greta's chest. "How can you tell? He's only six months old."

"See the way he watches you while he sucks. That's a sure sign of intelligence. And you and your husband are writers, are you not?"

"Yes, my husband is a writer and a journalist. I'm a journalist."

"There you have it. A creative, intelligent child. He will make his mark, certain as night follows day."

Once Greta had settled Ule in his pram again, Madam Krauss offered her a sheet of paper containing several pieces of minor intelligence that she'd collected from her clients.

Greta handed it back. "Never put anything in writing, Madam. Surely you realize how dangerous it is to write anything down. You must memorize anything you think might be of value and pass it to me by mouth."

"I'm not sure I can manage that. My memory's not as good as it used to be."

"Practice makes perfect. You'll soon get used to it. Now read me what you have there and I'll commit it to memory."

Madam Krauss had little enough to offer. Most of it was petty gossip or uninformed speculation. Greta selected a few items and absorbed them. When she was happy that she had everything that might be of value to the network, Madam Krauss threw the paper into the fire and they watched it burn.

Chapter 9

June 1938

Greta stood up and bid Madam Krauss goodbye.

"Before you go, Greta, I have something else for you." Madam Krauss handed over Max and Anna's *Ariernachweise*. "These two young people want to get married, but they've been turned down by the Ethnic and Racial people. I believe you have friends that have helped others in similar situations. Can you help them?"

Greta examined the documents. She could see why their marriage application had been turned down. The young woman was not fully Aryan. "What can you tell me about the couple?"

"The girl is a waitress in the KaDeWe department store. The boy works for the government. I would say they are a devoted couple. Max-Christian is a young man with a mind of his own."

"Meaning?"

"Meaning he's not a committed Party member. He could be useful to the network."

#

Greta thanked the fortune teller. She tucked the two *Ariernachweise* in the hidden compartment in Ule's pram and set off in an easterly direction to deliver leaflets to two more of her friends.

The second house was the last on her list. Frau Matilde Rosen gave her a warm hug in the hallway of her apartment. Alvensleberstrasse had once been an upmarket area of the city with apartments fit for a king. But, since the depression of the early 30's, the district had fallen into decline.

Greta wheeled Ule inside. Sophie, Matilde's 7-year-old daughter, came bounding down the stairs, pigtails flying. She peered into the pram.

"He's sleeping." Sophie made a long face.

Greta laughed at Sophie's expression. "He had an extra bottle of milk about an hour ago. He'll probably sleep for the rest of the afternoon."

Matilde said, "And keep you awake half the night."

"Most likely."

Sophie pouted. "I want to play with him."

Her mama wagged a finger at her. "Well you can't. If we wake him up he will be angry and scream the house down."

Sophie pouted some more. She frowned, and crossed her arms.

Greta put an arm on Sophie's shoulder. "I need to speak with your mama for a few minutes. Would you keep a watchful eye on Ule for me?"

Sophie's face broke into a smile. "I'll read him a story from my book if you like."

Matilde nodded at her daughter. "That's a good idea, Sophie, but be sure to keep your voice down. We don't want to wake him, do we?"

Sophie ran upstairs to fetch her book. Greta extracted the last leaflet from the pram's secret compartment and handed it to Matilde.

"I brought these for Sophie." Greta gave Matilde two children's reading books with colorful pictures. "I wasn't sure how advanced she is. If they're too childish for her I can bring something better on my next visit."

Greta and Matilde went into the kitchen where Matilde hid the leaflet in a jar marked 'pasta.' She put a kettle on. The Rosens' apartment was always the last call on Greta's route, and the two women usually shared a cup of tea.

Matilde glanced through the books. "They look perfect. Thank you."

Greta said, "Sophie's growing up fast."

Matilde smiled. "You've no idea. She's a little madam. She reminds me so much of Pauletta at her age, it's uncanny."

"How's her reading coming along?"

"Very well. The books you've given her have been a great help.

Her father has been teaching her numbers, and I tell her stories about distant lands and peoples."

"That takes care of geography. What about history?"

"She knows the history of her people going right back to the Exodus. That's all I've covered so far."

Greta glanced around the kitchen. The cupboards looked bare. "I wondered if you'd like to visit me one of these days, Matilde. My apartment is not far. You could bring Sophie and she could spent an afternoon playing with Ule."

"Thank you, Greta, but I don't feel safe on the streets anymore after what happened to David."

Greta braced herself for bad news. "Why, what happened?"

"Someone painted *Juden* on the outside of the shop. David scrubbed it off. But then a couple of Brownshirt thugs came into the shop and threatened him. They said the next customer who came through the door would receive a beating. He had to close the shop."

"That's terrible!"

"He came home, but then when he was half-way home they —"

"Oh no, Matilde."

Matilde eyes filled. "They ambushed him. They beat him. Then they followed him. He was terrified of what they might do if they find out where we live. He had to go into the city to lose them in the crowds."

"Is he all right? Where is he?"

"He's upstairs, sleeping. He's not badly injured, but he's terrified that they'll beat him again. They said they'd break his bones the next time. They could easily kill him. I'm not sure he'll ever open the shop again."

"How will you live? Do you have savings?"

Matilde shook her head. "We have a little put by. I don't know what will become of us when that's all gone."

"I will come by tomorrow with some food. Make a list of what you need."

"Oh, I couldn't ask you to do that, Greta."

"Nonsense. Find a pen. Make a list."

As Greta was leaving, Matilde gave Sophie the new books. Sophie gave Greta a hug and thanked her. Ule was still sleeping.

Chapter 10

July 1938

One thousand kilometers to the west, the War Office building in Whitehall was shrouded in mist. In a smoke-filled meeting room on the third floor, seven men sat around a table. These were the members of the Joint Forces Contingency Committee, their brief to consider and evaluate any and all threats to Britain and her empire. Six of those present were senior military advisors from the three arms of His Majesty's Defence Forces. All six were of high rank, as indicated by the scrambled egg on their uniforms. The seventh man was dressed as a civilian, his understated double-breasted pinstripe a reminder to everyone in the room of his special status. This was the Assistant Director of Military Intelligence, Sidney Blenkinsop-Smythe, known to everyone as 'B-S.'

The meeting was drawing to a close, the participants gathering their papers together, the table littered with empty water jugs, half-empty glasses, and overflowing ashtrays.

At the head of the table, Air Commodore Frank Scott, spoke in a stentorian tone. "Unless there's any other business, gentlemen…?"

A royal navy admiral slid one of the windows open to expel the foul air.

"Shouldn't we be discussing Hitler's invasion of Austria? It seems to me that he's far too big for his britches and if we don't do something about the man soon we will have a full-scale war on our hands." The speaker was the youngest man in the room, a colonel wearing a cap decorated with the dark tartan of the Black Watch (Royal Highlanders).

The air commodore responded, "We are all aware of the fall of

Austria, Colonel, but that is not a matter for discussion here. No doubt the Foreign Office will react to this news. Need I remind you, the focus of this committee is on possible future contingencies, not on military exigencies and certainly not on diplomacy?"

B-S rose to his feet. "There is just one more item that I would like to raise, if I may, Air Commodore."

The air commodore ceded the floor to the Assistant Director of Military Intelligence with a wave of his fingers.

"We have discussed ad nauseam the vexing questions of the United States and Japan. I think the committee should consider the likely disposition of the Soviets in the event of a war with Germany. The military might of that vast country should not be overlooked."

Air Commodore Scott looked at his watch, "We discussed this six months ago, B-S. Unless you have new intelligence to shed light on Stalin's intentions...?"

"We have reports of ongoing diplomatic activity between Ribbentrop's Foreign Office and the Soviets, yes."

"Probably a lot of saber-rattling. Herr Hitler makes his intentions toward the Bolsheviks abundantly clear in his book, and the mutual animosity between Communism and Fascism has been well documented."

"I agree, sir, but in light of our terms of reference, I feel it would be prudent to consider what our response should be in the event of the various scenarios that might arise."

A red-faced general coughed. "If I might make a suggestion, Air Commodore, I believe we should consider two contingent scenarios. The first, a hostile action by the Soviets against the Germans and Stalin's other east European neighbors, and second the reverse scenario of a military engagement by Hitler's forces to the East. An examination of the possible downstream effects of those two scenarios could be illuminating to everyone around this table."

The air commodore gave the proposition a moment's thought. "Very well, I shall include it on the agenda for next month. Assemble a small team, B-S, and prepare a brief report for the next meeting. Now, if there's nothing else..."

Chapter 11

August 1938

Saturday afternoon, August 6, Max and Anna were preparing to go to the grocery shop. There was a sharp rap on the apartment door.

Max answered, "Who's there?"

"Madam Krauss sent me." A woman's voice.

Anna took off her coat and patted her hair in front of the mirror that hung over the mantel. "This is it, Max." She crossed herself. "Please God, let it be good news. Let her in."

Max slid the bolt and opened the door.

The woman introduced herself as Greta—no surname—and explained that she needed some further details to help with their marriage application.

Max offered her a seat in an armchair. He sat on the sofa. Anna perched beside him, hands in her lap.

Greta started with a question. "Madam Krauss tells me you work for the Government, Max-Christian. Where do you work?"

"Please call me Max, Frau Greta. I'm with the Reich Labor Service, the RAD. Anna works at the KaDeWe department store."

"In the food court," said Anna.

"What do you do in the Labor Service, Max?"

"My job is to make arrangements with the railway company to move workers from building site to building site, wherever they're needed around the Reich."

"By workers you mean…?"

"Forced labor from the labor camps, mainly, and some engineers. There are big developments going on all over Germany, you know."

"How do you feel about your work?"

Max shrugged. "It's a job. Sometimes it can be a little overwhelming…"

"Overwhelming in what way?"

He reached for Anna's hand. "I have to work extra hours sometimes, when we have to move large numbers of workers around the country."

"How do you *feel* about moving workers from one end of the country to the other against their will?"

This was the same as Madam Krauss's line of questioning. It was political dynamite. The Party line was clear. These workers were all criminals or undesirables of one sort or another. They had forfeited their right to choose by their anti-government infractions. His personal feelings on the matter were entirely another matter. In fact it could be argued that German citizens no longer had the freedom for personal opinions. Since the Enabling Act of 1933, the Reichstag was a single party assembly. All opposition had been outlawed. How did that leave any leeway for independent thought?

Greta's use of the term 'against their will' clearly suggested a dissenting point of view, but was she to be trusted? It could be an elaborate trap.

Max steered a middle course. "Whenever I think about it, I have to feel sorry for those unfortunate people, but I try not to dwell on it. I hope to minimize their discomfort by doing my job as well as I can."

"How does that help?"

"By reducing unnecessary delays between train journeys, scheduling water stops—that sort of thing."

"So you have some sympathy for those unfortunate souls?"

There it was again—the nonconformist note.

"Yes, I suppose you could say that."

Greta smiled at him warmly. "You sound to me like a thoughtful, caring individual. Your sympathetic feelings toward those workers do you much credit."

"Thank you."

"Madam Krauss said you have no love for the Nazi Party. Is that right?"

There it was again. These people had some sort of subversive agenda—no doubt about it. Max had no love for the Führer or the Party, but he had no intention of getting involved in subversion.

"That is correct." Given the effect that the Nuremberg Laws were having on their lives, it could be no surprise that he felt that way.

Anna squeezed Max's hand. "What does all this have to do with our marriage application, Frau Greta? Has anything been done about that?"

"Yes, Anna, your papers are in the hands of the right people."

"What people are those?"

"They are the people—friends of mine—who have the power to help."

Anna's face was turning red, her eyes blazing. Max pulled his hand from Anna's and stood up. "Where are our manners? We should offer our visitor a drink. We have Schnapps."

Greta waved an arm. "No thank you. I must get home."

Anna leapt to her feet. "How long will all this take? It's been two whole months since we gave our *Ariernachweise* to Madam Krauss."

"These things cannot be rushed, Anna. It could take several more weeks."

"Several weeks!"

"Or months, even. You must be patient."

Chapter 12

August 1938

Twice each week without fail, Greta visited the Rosen family. She brought them food for their larder, newspapers and library books and reading material for young Sophie. It was clear that they never left their apartment. As a Jew, Sophie was excluded from attending school. Matilde did her best to provide her with an education. Greta helped by bringing reading trainers for Sophie and even sharing her knowledge of simple mathematics, geography and history with the child from time to time.

At first Sophie's papa, David, offered to pay for the food, but Greta refused; the family needed to hold on to whatever financial resources they had. Then he stopped offering and surrendered to an all-consuming depression. He stopped shaving. Soon he had a dark beard lined with gray. It suited him, but made him look even more miserable and more like the stereotypical Jew. Matilde did her best to remain cheerful, but her efforts were akin to those of Sisyphus and his boulder.

Their only contact with the outside world was through listening to a DKE *Kleinempfänger* cheap radio that could pick up nothing but music, anodyne family entertainment programs, and Nazi propaganda. The library books were some help, but the newspapers were full of sabre rattling and anti-Semitic ranting. Even the family entertainment was tinged with slurs against the Jews, the Communists and other 'undesirable' groups. Without Greta's underground leaflets they would have had no idea what was going on in the world outside.

Sophie was not happy with her papa. He seemed to have lost the will to live. She couldn't understand why they had to stay indoors all the time and why she wasn't allowed to play with other children. Baby Ule's visits became ever more important to her, and Greta let her do more and more with the baby.

Little Ule adored Sophie. He smiled at her a lot. She crawled about with him on the floor. She tickled him to make him laugh. And her lifelike doll, Aschenputtel, was included in all their games together.

Greta often stayed with the family for a couple of hours. On one occasion, when Ule and Sophie had fallen asleep together on the sofa, Greta asked Sophie's parents if they had considered leaving Germany.

David Rosen scowled at her. "We are Germans. Why should we have to leave?"

Before Greta could respond, Matilde said, "Be realistic, husband. There is no future for us in this country, husband. The Nuremberg Laws..." Her voice drifted away.

Greta said, "Those laws are just the beginning. Things will get a lot worse for families like yours."

David snorted. "You're probably right, but we don't want to leave. Where would we go?"

"Anywhere. It doesn't matter. France or Belgium, maybe, or England. Anywhere there are lots of Jews, but not Austria. The Nazis are strong there. "

Matilde said, "We could go to Poland. I have an uncle and a distant cousin living there."

David's face contorted as if he'd tasted a lemon. "Not Poland. Hitler hates Poland and the Poles."

Chapter 13

August 1938

Greta skirted around a shiny Daimler-Benz car in the driveway and presented herself at the door of the Schulze-Boysen residence in Pankow. She rang the bell.

It was the third week of August. All along the road the plane trees were in flower and the chestnuts were bristling with small green spiked balls.

Pauletta the maid opened the door and showed Greta in to the study. She whispered, "Have you seen my sister and her family recently?"

"Yes, I visited them two days ago. They are all well."

"Thank you, Frau Kuckhoff. I feel so guilty for not visiting them, but Herr Schulze-Boysen is not happy when I do."

Greta had heard this story before. She gave Pauletta a reassuring smile. "Matilde is well. She sends her best wishes."

Libertas appeared dressed in a black gown patterned with large pink and blue flowers. "Greta, my darling, so glad you could come." They embraced. "I hear you've been looking after Matilde and her daughter. How are they?"

"They are well, but their future looks uncertain."

"I told Pauletta not to let her sister marry a Jew. I warned Matilde. But no one ever listens to me." She rolled her eyes.

Libertas Schulze-Boysen was Greta's best friend, but there were times when Greta could have strangled her. An acclaimed actress at the height of her career, she was the darling of the theatre-going public of Berlin. Petite of frame but larger than life, she wore flowing gowns and expansive millinery creations and waved her arms about a lot while she spoke in loud, almost masculine tones. Among her friends she numbered all the major actors and actresses of the day as well as every theatre director, producer and playwright in Germany. The up and coming young writer, Berthold Brecht was a particular favorite of hers, as was Greta's husband, Adam and Adam's friends, the German-American couple, Arvid and Mildred Harnack.

The study was Libertas's favorite room. Filled with period furniture, its walls were lined on three sides by bookcases crammed with books.

"Hello, Greta." Hidden behind the high back of a leather armchair, Greta discovered Mildred Harnack seated by the fireplace. Greta hadn't seen Mildred for several months. The last definite news she'd had about her was that she was suffering with 'her nerves' and had spent some time in a sanatorium in Maryland. Her husband, Arvid, never gave anything away about her health.

Of the three of them, Mildred was the prettiest, with well-defined features and an engaging smile. Greta was under no illusion about her own looks—her lank hair and sharp nose. Libertas's favorite look was a juvenile pose that suited her miniature, doll-like figure. Greta knew she was the brightest of the three. She was certainly the most qualified, with degrees from German and American colleges. Mildred was an academic writer, very much minor league. Her most recent attempts to acquire grants from various American foundations had all been turned down. Libertas was from an aristocratic Prussian family and had no need of academic qualifications. Her mental powers were something of an unknown quantity.

Mildred shook Greta's hand warmly. They exchanged a few pleasantries, and Greta took a matching high-backed armchair on the opposite side of the fireplace. Libertas pulled up a Queen Anne chair and sat between them. Greta offered to change places, but Libertas dismissed the idea with a wave of her hand.

"I've asked you both here to discuss the case of Anna Weber and Max-Christian Noack. I've explained to Mildred, Greta, why you passed their papers to me.

Greta interrupted Libertas's flow. "And have you been able to do anything for them?"

"I'll come to that later. I thought we should discuss the prospect of Max-Christian's making a contribution to our husbands' activities. The young man is employed with the RAD in some capacity or other. As I understand it, the questions are whether he could provide intelligence of any real value to the Resistance movement, and if so, which of our networks should attempt to recruit him."

Mildred added, "And would he be amenable to our advances."

Greta ground her teeth. Libertas was holding court as only Libertas could, and Mildred was playing her game. These were questions that would be considered and decided by the men in their lives. The secrecy with which Arvid ran his network was legendary. He would be unlikely to welcome any new source. The addition of Madam Krauss had been a major surprise. On the other hand, Libertas's husband, Harro Schulze-Boysen, was totally open to any and all advances if they offered new intelligence sources. Harro held a high position in the Air Ministry. Of all the members of the Resistance, he was the best placed to gather valuable intelligence. But Arvid considered Harro's behavior the height of indiscretion and kept as much distance as he could between the two networks.

Greta turned her face to the fire to hide her contempt for Libertas's pretentiousness. "I'm pretty sure Adam won't be interested."

Mildred agreed. "Arvid won't jeopardize his operation for a young man from the labor ministry. I think I can speak for Arvid."

"Well, I know Harro will jump at the prospect." It seemed this was the outcome Libertas had been expecting. It left the field open for her to hand Max to Harro like a cat delivering a dead mouse.

Greta returned to her earlier question. "Have you been able to get their marriage application sanctioned?"

Libertas beamed. "But of course, darling. Would we be having this discussion otherwise? I spoke with my friend Emmy and she had a word in Hermann's ear. In spite of their obvious difficulty, it has all been arranged. You can tell Max-Christian he will soon be able to re-apply to department B. When he does, his application will be sanctioned."

Once again Greta marveled at the ease with which Libertas could influence Hermann Göring, head of the Luftwaffe, by manipulating Emmy, his devoted wife.

Greta asked for the return of the young couple's papers.

Libertas's smile turned to cracked porcelain. "I don't have them. Emmy forgot to return them. I will collect them from her the next time I visit."

Greta ground her teeth again. There was no point asking when that was likely to be. Libertas would be summoned if and when it suited Frau Göring, and the whole thing could easily fall apart before then.

#

They had tea, served on silverware by the portly maid in a tight outfit. When the maid had left the room Mildred suppressed a smile.

Libertas looked down her long nose at her "I know. She has a constant battle with her weight. But Pauletta is a good girl. I wouldn't replace her, not for the world."

Before they left, Libertas had one more card to play. "I've been thinking. Our two networks are doing more or less the same thing. We must be wasting precious resources by not working together. Harro has suggested that we might cooperate more closely. We might even consider merging."

Mildred looked at her, blankly. "Merging. The two networks?"

"Yes, why not? We should be producing a single leaflet between us and we should surely combine our distribution networks. That way we could minimize the risks. One joint network would be so much more efficient. Don't you think?"

Mildred took a handkerchief from her handbag and blew her nose loudly. "I doubt that Arvid would consider such a move."

"But tell me you'll put it to him."

"I'll ask him…"

"That's all I ask. Put it to him. See how he reacts. And maybe we could set up a meeting."

Chapter 14

September 1938

At Libertas's request, a member of the German Communist Party found them a disused warehouse close to the airport at Tempelhof. Harro had set up a small project in the Air Ministry to locate empty buildings to store spare parts for Luftwaffe aircraft. This gave him a perfect excuse to visit the warehouse openly. Arvid, on the other hand, took extreme measures to ensure that no one followed him to the venue. He arrived 30 minutes late.

They shook hands.

Arvid looked around, but could find nowhere to sit. The place was completely empty. The air temperature felt close to the boiling point of human blood, and there was a strong smell that he couldn't identify.

Harro opened proceedings. "My wife has established contact with a young man in the Reich Labor Service. His name is Max-Christian Noack. I think he may be a useful source of information. Unless you object, I propose to approach him and see if he is willing to join my network."

"Why should I object? I'm sure you will approach this man whatever I say."

Harro shook his head. "If you're interested in the guy, I'm happy to let you have him. I'm quite sure we can trust him. He's under an obligation to Libertas. She has arranged to have his marriage application approved by the Race and Ethnic Affairs people."

"I'm not interested. You have him. Was there something else you wanted to talk about?"

"Libertas suggested we should talk about closer cooperation between our two networks."

Libertas, thought Arvid. I knew she was behind this! He looked at Harro sharply. "What do you have to offer?"

"Well, it seems crazy to be running two print operations and two separate distribution networks. We could save ourselves a lot of work and time if we worked more closely together."

Arvid jammed his hands into his jacket pockets. It was as hot at the pit of hell and what was that stench? Rust? "I hope you're not suggesting a merger."

"Not a merger, perhaps, but maybe we could start by combining our creative efforts. I'd be happy to reprint whatever you print..."

"Giving editorial control to us?"

Harro paused before answering. "To Adam Kuckhoff, yes. Printing the same material in two locations would reduce the chances of the Gestapo closing us down. Then maybe you could think about using some or all of our distribution network. I estimate that we send out about twice as many broadsheet leaflets as you do each month."

Arvid couldn't argue with Harro's arithmetic. "I'm happy with our delivery methods, but I would like to send out more product, certainly. What else did you have in mind?"

Harro crossed his arms high on his chest. "I thought you were the one with the proposal."

Arvid snorted. "You've got me here under false pretenses. Is this some sort of trap?"

Harro smiled. "No one's trying to trap you. I think we can thank our scheming wives for getting us together."

Arvid exploded. "Your scheming wife, not mine. Mildred said that Libertas made her promise to get me to come to this meeting. Libertas gave her the idea that you had a proposition to discuss."

Harro held out a hand toward Arvid. "Take it easy, man. Libertas gave me the same story. She said you had a proposal."

Arvid took a step toward the door. "This whole meeting has been a waste of time."

"Perhaps not. I'm sure our wives acted in good faith. There is a lot of good sense in cooperation between our networks, don't you agree?"

"No, I don't. Your operation is too loose, too indiscreet. In my opinion it'll be only a matter of time before the whole thing crumbles and we all end up in the hands of the Gestapo."

Harro put a hand on Arvid's arm. "Before you go, Arvid, let's agree on one thing. If I can get this RAD man to join us, I'd be willing to share his intelligence. We can use Greta as go between. She is familiar with both networks and the baby gives her excellent cover."

"I'm happy dealing through Greta, but you'd have to promise to keep the new man at arm's length from everyone else in my network."

"Agreed."

"What is that smell? Is it rust?"

"I think it's dried blood. The warehouse was used as a 'wild camp' in the early days of the Brownshirts."

Chapter 15

September 1938

It was time for Max's third visit of the year to see his mother. He took the Autobus to Lutherstadt Wittenberg.

He might have expected questions about his plans to marry, but his mother's mind didn't work like that.

She was bursting to tell him a story about a neighbor, one Frau Magda Dallerbruch whose son, Karl, had followed his father into the Kriegsmarine. Karl had drowned in a training accident. Max had vague memories of a young boy of that name. His mother seemed unaffected by the tragedy, although she had attended the boy's funeral. Max wondered if he detected a slight trace of *Schadenfreude*, but dismissed the notion as unlikely. His mother lacked the natural empathy needed to feel another's pain and the self-knowledge necessary to take pleasure from it.

After that they settled into a stuttering conversation full of non sequiturs, tangents and deviations. Max kept track, making sure they covered everything on his list, and picking up her fragments of important news.

He returned to Berlin drained of emotion.

#

Madam Krauss had a visit from a Wehrmacht officer waiting to be shipped out to Czechoslovakia. Leaving a young family behind and facing the very real prospect of military action, he needed to know that he would survive. While providing the necessary reassurance, Madam Krauss gently extracted details of the date and strength of the planned military incursion. Breathlessly, she passed the information to Greta, and Greta passed it to Arvid.

Encrypting the information took an hour of concentrated work. The result was 244 characters arranged in groups of four on a single page. These he transcribed onto a piece of rice paper no bigger than a stamp, using a fine pen and a magnifying glass. Finally, the rice paper carrying the coded message was rolled into a narrow tube and inserted into a cigarette. The cigarette was placed in a pack with about 12 others, and the pack was carried by a courier for transfer to his contact at the Soviet Embassy, a cultural attaché called Alexander Korotkov.

#

Arvid also arranged to meet his contact at the American Embassy. Donald Heath, First Secretary at the embassy, carried a brief for the nascent US Intelligence service. When they met at an Embassy reception on New Year's Eve, Arvid had found a willing outlet for his intelligence. Born in Germany, Arvid had studied in the United States. His wife, Mildred, was a US citizen. As a committed Marxist his first loyalty was to the Soviets, but he was happy to share any intelligence he could gather with the Americans—or anyone else for that matter—as long as it helped to hasten the downfall of Adolf Hitler and the Third Reich.

Both men were thin, weedy individuals, Heath more so than Arvid. Both had receding hairlines, Heath's the more advanced of the two. Heath was not one to tolerate stupidity, his thin lips and the line of his mouth creating an expression of distrust, if not outright hostility. They preferred to meet in the open, as both men were heavy pipe smokers. On this occasion they met in Heath's office. The room was soon full of aromatic smoke.

Heath listened with interest to Arvid's information. "How solid is this, Arvid?"

"Rock solid."

"I'll pass it on. You know I appreciate every morsel you give me. And everything you've given me so far has been priceless. It's golden. Washington is more than grateful…"

Arvid sensed a 'but.'

"But I'm concerned about your other activities." He pulled a leaflet from his briefcase and placed it on his desk. "Is this one of yours?"

"Yes. Do you like it?"

"You do realize these are all over Berlin? They're everywhere. If you'd dropped a ton of them from an airplane you couldn't have done a better job of spreading them around. And what's this nonsense about Hitler's niece?"

"It's a story. She died in mysterious circumstances. Mud sticks. There may even be a grain of truth in it. The point of the story is to shake the people out of their complacency. Life is too soft, and everything seems to fall into their laps since Hitler took over as Chancellor. We want them to think for themselves and not swallow every feel-good story published in the national press."

"Well, I'd like to ask you, in the strongest possible terms, to put a stop to these activities. They raise the stakes enormously, drawing attention to your network when you should be keeping as low a profile as possible, collecting valuable Intel. That's the most effective way you can fight for Germany. This..." He stabbed at the leaflet with the stem of his pipe. "This rubbish is not helping anyone."

Arvid took a deep breath. "The broadsheet leaflets are the most direct way that I can strike a blow against the Nazis. This is my country, Donald. I can't sit on my hands and do nothing while insidious Nazi propaganda worms its way into the minds of our young people."

Chapter 16

September 1938

Greta saw very little of Adam during September, and when she did see him he never had time to talk to her. Something important was afoot, but she couldn't find out what it was. She paid a visit to Libertas's mansion to see if she knew what was going on.

Libertas shrugged a shoulder. "I've hardly seen Harro these last three weeks. I'm pretty sure it has something to do with Hitler's negotiations with the British and the French over the Sudetenland. All I can tell you is that we had a visit from Hans Oster and Walther von Brauchitsch a few days ago."

Greta knew who von Brauchitsch was. Everybody did. He was supreme commander of the German Army. "Who's Hans Oster?"

"Generalmajor Hans Oster is deputy head of Military Intelligence, the Abwehr."

"And you've no idea what this is about?"

"None. Have you spoken to Mildred? She might have picked up something from Arvid."

#

Mildred Harnack had little enough to add. Arvid had been spending so much time at the Economics Ministry that she had jokingly suggested he should have a bed put in his office. He had done exactly that, and now she never saw him from one end of the week to the next.

Mildred was sinking back into depression. Arvid had made promises to her when she left the sanatorium, promises that he had failed to keep. Greta did her best to cheer her up, but Mildred's problems were deep-seated and stemmed from homesickness. She needed to be in Maryland with her elderly mother, whose health was declining.

And then one day toward the end of September, Adam swore Greta to secrecy and told her what was happening. The British were taking a firm stance on the Sudetenland. They had threatened a war if Hitler moved against any part of Czechoslovakia. The French and Italians had sided with the British and Neville Chamberlain was to attend a conference in Munich to copper-fasten the British position. Generalmajor Oster and a wide grouping of senior Wehrmacht figures were planning to remove Hitler from power. As soon as the conference ended the Army would storm the Chancellery and arrest Hitler. A subgroup of the more militant conspirators wanted to have him executed. The SS would be neutralized and the armed forces would run the country until a new government could be elected.

Adam finished by saying, "I want you and Ule out of Berlin when all this happens. Take Ule away somewhere, anywhere. I'll contact you when it's safe to return."

Greta took Ule to Düsseldorf for a week.

#

On September 30, the conference in Munich broke up. Neville Chamberlain emerged waving a piece of paper that guaranteed "peace for our time." As the price of peace, key parts of Czechoslovakia had been ceded to the Third Reich. Hitler emerged from the talks as the world's greatest negotiator, and without the support of the British, the planned coup was doomed to failure.

Chapter 17

October 1938

On October 6, Pauletta, the maid from the Schulze-Boysen household, delivered a package to the Kuckhoffs' apartment. While Greta opened the package the maid played peekaboo with Ule.

Inside the package Greta found Anna and Max's two *Ariernachweise* and a short note from Libertas.

"Greta: Sorry for the delay. Emmy has set everything up. Tell the lovebirds to make a new application to the Ethnic and Racial Affairs department without delay. They should ask for an official called Kurt Framzl. He'll be expecting them. Tell them not to offer any more than the standard application fee (RM 20). The SS are now very strict about bribery. Corruption is considered one of the worst crimes against the Reich and they are determined to stamp it out in the lower ranks. We must have another get together soon, the three of us.

Affectionately, L."

The following day Greta set off for the young couple's apartment in Kolonnenstrasse, pushing the pram. The wind blew, but there was warmth in the patchy sunshine. Greta enjoyed the journey.

She found the apartment building, parked the pram, and carried a sleeping infant up the stairs to the second floor.

Anna opened the apartment door and invited Greta inside.

Greta said, "I thought you might both be at work."

"Max is at work, but I haven't been feeling well for a couple of days. You have news for us?" Anna looked terrified that Greta might have bad news.

Greta took a seat on an old sofa, settled Ule on her lap and handed Libertas's package to Anna.

Anna dropped it on the table as if it was too hot to handle. "What is it?"

"Open it."

Anna tore the package open. She read the note, the smile on her face growing wider and wider. "Who's this L?"

"She's a friend."

Anna read the note again. She squealed. "I can't believe it. It's fantastic. We can get married and it won't cost us a pfennig more."

"You'll have to pay the marriage application fee again."

"I meant it won't cost us any more than the fee we paid to Madam Krauss."

"You paid Madam Krauss a fee?" Ule began to cry. "He's teething." Greta put him on her knee and rubbed his gums. The crying reduced to a gurgling whimper.

Anna read the note for a third time, tears of joy rolling down her face. "I still can't believe it."

"How much did you pay Madam Krauss?"

"Oh, she charged us 100 Reichsmarks. I was glad to pay it. Max wasn't convinced that she would succeed. She said she'd try, but we shouldn't get our hopes up too high. This is wonderful! I can't wait to tell him. You must thank Madam Krauss for us."

Greta smiled. She said nothing. Madam Krauss had some questions to answer.

Greta lowered her wriggling infant onto the floor. He crawled across to Anna and stood up, holding her knees. He looked over his shoulder, grinning at his mother. Anna lifted him onto her lap and he stuffed a fist into his mouth.

"He likes you," said Greta.

Anna beamed. "He's big. He's heavy. How old is he?"

"Ten months. He's an eating machine."

"He's gorgeous. You must be very proud." She handed the infant back.

Greta asked if there was somewhere to change his diaper. Anna cleared a space on the table and watched the whole procedure with interest. Then Anna was struck by a thought. "I should call my parents and tell them."

"Don't do that yet. Wait until you have the marriage authorization in your hands. Something could still go wrong."

#

In the evening, Greta fed the baby and got him off to sleep. She served a meal for Adam. While he was eating she put on her coat.

Adam looked up from his plate. "Where are you going, Greta? It's late."

"The Rosens. It's been four days since my last visit. They must be running low on supplies."

"The Rosens are not your responsibility, Greta. They need to stand on their own feet, like everyone else."

"And how would you suggest they do that?"

"I don't know. It's not our problem. David Rosen has his antiques shop."

"I explained about that. The Brownshirts, the intimidation."

"It's really not your problem. I wish you'd drop it."

Greta took a deep breath. She loved Adam, but she hated it when he told her what to do. She wasn't a child. "Keep an eye on Ule. I shouldn't be gone more than a couple of hours."

She picked up her basket and left the apartment before he had a chance to object again. She set off toward the Rosens' home at a brisk walk. She had loved Adam since she met him as a student in America, and she respected his courageous stance against the Nazis, but his attitude on the subject of the Rosens was so wrong, so out of character. She couldn't understand it.

A beaming Matilde Rosen opened the door. She led Greta into the kitchen and poured her a glass of sherry.

Greta took a sip. The sherry warmed her as it went down. "What are we celebrating, Matilde?"

"David has gone back to work. He opened the shop three days ago. He's had some customers and brought home some money. I've been out to the grocery shop for the first time in a month."

"That's wonderful, Matilde. How is David?"

"He's almost back to his old self, making plans. He has started believing in a future for us again. He's convinced the bad times are at an end."

"Is that what you think?"

"You know what I think. Things will be much worse for us as long as this government is in power."

"And Sophie?"

"Sophie's happy that her old papa is back."

Greta looked up the staircase on the way to the front door, and caught a glimpse of Sophie and her doll, Aschenputtel, listening at the top of the stairs.

Chapter 18

October 1938

Once again Max found himself on that familiar bench on the third floor of the Gestapo building. A finger of sweat ran down the back of his neck. Anna was ecstatic. She was already working on her wedding plans. But something could still go wrong. His mind ran through all sorts of wild possibilities. It was so easy for things to turn sour in government work, for apparent racing certainties to fall at the last fence. The government worker who made the arrangements could be less influential then he thought; someone higher up the chain of command might have vetoed the whole thing. Or whoever he was could have met with an accident. He could be lying in a coma in a hospital bed, unable to sign the final document. He could be dead. Sudden, unexplained deaths were commonplace in Germany nowadays.

He ran a finger under his collar. No, it would be a mere formality now that Frau Greta had made the arrangements. He just needed to keep calm, present his documents to this Kurt Framzl and all would be well.

Framzl was a tall, fresh-faced individual wearing an SS uniform with the SS death's head on his cap. Max handed over the two *Ariernachweise*. Framzl frowned when he saw Anna's card. "Your fiancée is part-Jewish, I see."

"Everything has been arranged, Herr Framzl. I was told to ask for you by name."

"Indeed? I see nothing here. Oh, wait a moment. Your name is Noack? I have a note here somewhere." He rummaged through a bundle of papers in a tray. "Yes, here it is. I have been asked to consider granting special approval to you and this *Mischling*. What was her name again?"

Asked to consider?

"Anna Weber."

Framzl positioned the completed marriage application on the counter pad. "You have the application fee, Herr Noack?"

Max placed 20 Reichsmarks on the counter with a trembling hand.

Framzl opened the cash box, signed a receipt and handed it over. Max tucked it into his wallet with the first one.

Framzl placed the notes in the box. "You have something else for me?"

The implication was clear. This was the trap that they had been warned about. Offer a bribe and Anna could wave her wedding goodbye. "No, I don't think so."

Framzl locked the cash box. "Very well. I am willing to approve your marriage application. You will not be eligible for the 1,000 Reichsmarks marriage loan and there is just one other matter to be attended to." Framzl reached under the counter and pulled out another piece of paper. He unfolded it and placed it on top of Max's application. "Do you recognize this?"

Max examined it. It looked like a leaflet, crudely printed. "I've never seen it before. What is it?"

"Read it."

Max picked up the leaflet and scanned it. It was anti-Nazi, anti-government, clearly a subversive document. It ended with the words:

'All that is necessary for evil to triumph is for good men to do nothing.' Edmund Burke (1729-1797)
Rise Up! Rise Up! Take a stand against the Nazis.

A vague rallying cry, thought Max, and not at all realistic. The Gestapo had a way of dealing with anyone who took a stand against them.

"What is it?"

Framzl grabbed the leaflet from him, folded it, and put it back under the counter. "It's a broadsheet leaflet, one of many printed by the Communists, the so-called Red Orchestra. What do you think of it?"

"It's subversive. Surely it's not legal."

"Of course it's not legal. What do you think should be done about it?"

Where was this leading?

"The Communists should be arrested."

"And they will be as soon as we can catch them. Would you like to help us with this?"

What did this have to do with a marriage application?

"I know nothing of police matters, Herr Framzl. I would have no notion how to find these people."

"And yet you already know some of them."

Max was horrified. "No, I don't know these people."

"Frau Schulze-Boysen, the actress, you know her. She was the one who interceded on your behalf."

"I never heard of her."

Framzl curled his lip. "We have had our eyes on Frau Schulze-Boysen and her husband for some time. We haven't managed to locate their printer, but when we do, they will be arrested. You can help us with this task." He handed the marriage application to Max. "Your marriage application is approved in principle. All you require now is the official Reich stamp and my signature. However, it will be recorded as a black mark against you on your employment record. That black mark will mean that you will never be eligible for promotion. Do you understand?"

"Yes."

"You can redeem yourself and the black mark may be removed if you carry out one valuable service for the Reich."

"What sort of service?"

"You will join the Red Orchestra and work from within to help unmask the Communist subversives behind these leaflets. Bring me the location of the printer. Complete this task and I will stamp and sign your application, and the black mark may be removed from your employment record."

Max's heart rate doubled. "I couldn't do that, Herr Framzl. I have no desire to join the Communist Party."

"You must play the part like an actor. You must let these people know that you hate the Führer and the Nazi Party with a passion. You live and breathe to bring down the democratically elected government of the Fatherland by any means at your disposal. You can do that, can't you?"

"I don't know, Herr Framzl…"

"I know you can do it. Be passionate and they will believe you. I have every faith in you."

Part 2

Chapter 19

October 1938

Max took the long way back to the apartment. This Gestapo man was mad! How was he going to worm his way into the Communist Resistance, the Red Orchestra? Be passionate! Framzl was under the mistaken impression that Max was acquainted with an actress, an actress that he'd never heard of, and whose name he couldn't recall. He had no wish to be a Gestapo informer. They were the lowest of the low. And even if he did manage somehow to join the Red Orchestra, how could he report back to the Gestapo without getting himself killed by the Communists?

What would become of him if he failed? Refusal to approve his marriage application could be the least of his worries.

What was he going to tell Anna? He couldn't tell her the truth. He'd have to make something up to explain why their application was still not approved. Maybe he could persuade Framzl to stamp and sign the document without completing the impossible task, and they could still get married. If not, and he had to complete the task, Anna need never know the price he had to pay for her happiness.

He caught a tram. Leaving the tram a couple of stops from the apartment, he called into one of his favorite watering holes and drained a liter of beer to fortify himself for the battle to come. Good beer is supposed to stimulate the brain cells, but by the time he arrived at the apartment, he still hadn't worked out what he was going to say.

#

Anna was waiting for him at the door to the apartment. "How did you get on? Do you have it?"

Max waved the document. "I have it."

"Great! Why so glum? Is there some problem?"

"Not really."

"What does that mean?"

She took the document from him and examined it under the light. It consisted of two sheets: the top sheet was white and bore the heading 'Registrar's Copy.' The second sheet was green. It was headed 'Applicants' copy.' She saw the word *genehmigt* 'approved' on both copies. Max held his breath. He was sure she would notice the blank spaces where the official Reich stamp should be. But she didn't.

She beamed at him. "I'd like a January wedding."

"That's too early, Anna. I won't be able to take any more time off work until much later, and your employers wouldn't be happy if you took time off during the winter season."

"You're right. The spring, then. March?"

"March should be fine."

She picked up the telephone. "I'll ring Mother and talk to her about it. I told her you would prefer to get married in Berlin. Was I wrong?"

"You were not wrong, Anna, but if they want us to marry in Dresden and it's what you want, I won't object."

"A Berlin wedding will suit your mother." Anna dialed the number. "We should thank Madam Krauss. And Frau Greta. Madam Krauss will know where we can find Frau Greta."

And Frau Greta will know how I can contact the actress. If only I could remember her name.

#

The next day a major new exercise began in the Reich Labor Service. The head of Max's department, Gunnar Schnerpf, handed him a bundle of executive orders.

"We've had word from Albert Speer's office. Work on the Chancellery building is to be massively accelerated. They need engineers and an additional 2,000 workers per day for the next 12 months. I've identified several other projects that could lose some labor, but you'll have to find the rest. See to it." He ran a finger across his moustache and left.

Schnerpf, a decorated hero from the Great War, was short, rotund, with little hair on his head, and a stern look. His waxed handlebar moustache made up for his lack of stature. Without the moustache everybody reckoned he would have been unable to retain any control over the men in his department. His nickname was 'the bush.'

Schnerpf had identified five construction sites that could lose 300 workers between them. Max got to work.

Schnerpf appeared by his desk again at midday. "How are you getting on, Noack?"

Max was feeling pleased with his morning's work. He had located 1,500 of the workers required, 1,100 new labor from the camps, the rest from existing building sites. "I have most of the workers, sir. I'm just starting to trawl the records for civil engineers."

"I have another more urgent job for you. The OKW has made a demand for 50 able-bodied workers for a special secret task overseas."

"Where are they to be assigned?"

"I do not have that information, and if I did I couldn't tell you." Schnerpf scuttled back into his office.

By the end of the day, he had identified 50 workers for the secret job overseas and a list of well-qualified engineers for the Chancellery project. He completed the documentation and left it on Schnerpf's desk to be signed and approved in the morning, adding a short note to say that he was taking another day from his holiday entitlement. He would complete the labor search later in the week.

#

The following morning he went straight to Kurfürstenstrasse. Madam Krauss opened the door dressed in a housecoat and waved him inside.

"Anna and I are most grateful for your help, Madam."

"You have the approval?"

"Yes. You've made us both very happy."

"It was nothing, child. Show me your left hand."

He held out his left hand and she read his palm. "You and Anna will have a long and happy life together, and I see three children."

Max took his hand back. "I'd like to thank Frau Greta, too. Can you tell me where she lives?"

Madam Krauss fixed him with eyes like rivets. "I don't know where she lives, but the next time she visits me I will ask her to contact you."

Chapter 20

October 1938

Next, Max took an Autobus to his family home in Lutherstadt Wittenberg, arriving in mid-afternoon. His last scheduled visit had been in September, his next was not until Christmas. Concerned about how his mother might react to an unscheduled visit, he knocked on the door and waited. When no one came, he opened the door with his key and stepped inside.

"Hello, Mother. It's me, Max."

No answer.

There was no one in the front parlor. He found his mother in the kitchen, standing on a chair, reaching into a kitchen cupboard.

She pointed to a biscuit tin on the table. "Hand me up that tin, will you."

No surprise to see him walk into her kitchen on an unscheduled date. Typical Mother! He had expected some sort of negative reaction, but the one thing you could rely on was her unpredictability.

Max handed her the tin. She placed it in the cupboard and he helped her down.

She held him at arm's length and looked him over. "You're a bit thin. Have they been feeding you properly in Berlin?"

They?

"Yes, Mother. There's nothing wrong with my diet. How've you been?"

"Weren't you here just a couple of weeks ago?"

"Nearly three weeks, yes. I came because I have news. I would have used the telephone if you had one."

"Wait for me in the front parlor. I'll make tea."

Max was still uncertain how she might react to his unscheduled visit. It wasn't even a Saturday! She had a mercurial temperament. His childhood memories were littered with her screaming fits triggered by his actions. His most vivid recollection was of the day she found him trimming his fingernails in the kitchen. He was ten. He paid dearly for that mistake. She worked herself into such a state that she had to be sedated and taken to hospital.

He needn't have worried. She seemed unfazed by his unscheduled visit. Nor was she concerned that he might have bad news. Upon her return from the kitchen she spent 15 minutes telling him about the comings and goings at the women's guild and a hotly contested flower-arranging competition. The promised tea never materialized.

Eventually, the conversation got around to his private life.

"How's Anna?"

"She's well, thank you, Mother. It's Anna I came to talk to you about."

Her hand flew to her mouth. "Oh, Max-Christian! Didn't I warn you about taking precautions? Oh, you young people—"

"It's nothing like that, Mother. She's not pregnant. We've decided to get married."

She frowned. "She's part-Jewish isn't she? Isn't that illegal now?"

"Yes, but we've been granted special permission."

She held up her hands. "I don't want to know any more about that. But I hope you'll both be very happy. Have you picked a date?"

"We don't have a date. We're planning a spring wedding. The department store won't give Anna any time off until after the winter season."

"Where will the wedding be? She's not Lutheran, I think."

"She's Roman Catholic. We thought we might get married in Berlin. It's not far for you to come and Anna's parents won't mind traveling from Dresden."

She grabbed his hand and held on to it. "It's a pity your father's not here. Wait here for a minute." She left him and went upstairs.

He laughed. He couldn't remember the last time they'd had an exchange so free of sidetracks. He waited a few minutes. When she failed to return, he followed her upstairs. He found her in one of the spare bedrooms surrounded by old family photographs. She laughed. "Look at this one. This is you and me in Nuremberg at a rally. Do you remember?"

They spent an hour going through the photographs together. When Max said he had to leave she reached into the pocket in her apron and handed him a cigarette lighter. "This was your father's. I want you to have it."

He examined the lighter. It was steel, shaped like a tiny book, engraved with the date: May 1916. He had never seen it before.

"I can't take this, mother. You have so little to remember him by."

"Nonsense. Keep it."

He examined the lighter again on the autobus. The thought that his father had handled it before his death sent shivers up and down his spine. Wilhelm Noack had gone to fight in the War in 1916. He lost his life in the Battle of the Somme. His body was never recovered. If this was his lighter why had he not taken it with him?

Chapter 21

October 1938

The following day when he arrived at work, 'the bush' Schnerpf was standing by Max's desk clutching a bundle of requisition orders, his moustache twitching on his face like an eel on a hook.

"Where were you yesterday, Noack?"

"I took a day's leave. I left a note on your desk, sir."

"Did I not impress on you the urgency of the task in hand? Rebuilding the Chancellery must be the most important construction job ever undertaken in the Reich."

"I have located most of the labor and nearly all the engineers for the Chancellery job, and I have compiled a list of 50 able-bodied men for the secret mission overseas. I left the paperwork on your desk."

He wagged a finger as if admonishing a child. "You have been taking a lot of unscheduled leave recently. Is there something I should know about your private life?"

Max explained that he had been trying to obtain approval to marry.

"And do you have it?"

"I received it last week."

His boss frowned. "I thought your girlfriend was Jewish."

"No, sir, she's Roman Catholic."

Schnerpf handed him the requisitions, all duly stamped and signed. His mustache twitched. "When are you planning to get married?"

"Not until March at the earliest, sir."

#

Anna tended the tables in the food court of the KaWeDe department store. Closing time was approaching. She had been on her feet all day. They ached, but still she maintained her good humor, her bright smile.

"You're amazing," said her friend, Ebba. "I don't know how you do it. Don't you ever get tired?"

Anna laughed. "Smiles cost nothing."

Two smartly dressed young men came into the food court and took a table by the door. Anna gave them a few moments to read the menu. Then she went across to take their order. One of the men was heavy-set, overweight, the other was blond with well-defined musculature and deep blue eyes, wearing a modern double-breasted suit. She estimated his age at 22 or 23, perhaps a year or two younger than Max.

They ordered coffee and Strudel pastries. She smiled at them.

As she was placing the food on the table the younger man held her wrist. "My name's Jürgen. What's your name, darling?" There was something unpleasant in the tone of his voice.

"Anna." She gave him her blank smile, pulled her arm away, and hurried back behind the counter.

She spoke to Ebba. "Do you see those two men near the door?"

"The two in the Hugo Boss suits? What about them?"

"One of them made a pass at me."

Ebba laughed. "Serves you right for smiling at everyone."

The kitchen closed up shortly after that and the last few customers left. The two young men remained where they were.

Anna cleared their table. "The food court is closing now."

"Where do you live?" said the younger man. "Can I walk you home?"

"No, thank you. That won't be necessary."

She was shaking, now. She found Ebba in the staff room. "Those two men haven't gone. I'm sure they're SS. I'm not leaving here until they go."

Ebba took a look outside. "They've gone. The food court is empty."

Anna left the department store by a rear door that evening, and took a circuitous route home.

Feeling vaguely guilty about what happened, she decided to say nothing to Max about the encounter.

#

When he arrived home from work, Max found Frau Greta sitting on the sofa sipping tea with Anna.

Anna waved a bundle of Reichsmarks in his face. "Frau Greta has returned our 100 Reichsmarks. Isn't that wonderful?"

Max looked to Greta for an explanation.

Greta waved her free hand. "Madam Krauss should never have demanded a fee for what we did. I know that you will need the money for the wedding."

What 'we' did. She must be referring to the actress.

"Thank you, Frau Greta. What a pleasant surprise."

"I'm delighted that we could help you."

"When you say 'we' who do you mean? If there are others that helped us I would like to meet them so that I can thank them in person."

Greta laughed. "It was a team effort. I believe one or two of the others would like to meet you, too. Give me your telephone number. I'll see what I can arrange."

Chapter 22

October 1938

A week later Max took the S-Bahn north to the exclusive Pankow quarter of Berlin. Soft October showers had given way to weak sunshine, and the Mitte was alive with smiling pedestrians. He had to change trains once to reach his destination, a magnificent mansion surrounded by mature trees and protected by 3-meter high walls and massive iron gates. He pushed the gates. They swung open. Walking slowly around a gleaming Daimler-Benz saloon car, he knocked on the front door. It was opened by a plump maid who took him to a study.

Max had never seen so many books in one place. That and the elaborate, expensive furniture, the pictures on the walls, all told him that whoever lived in this household was wealthy and cultured.

A woman approached and introduced herself as Libertas Schulze-Boysen.

This must surely be the actress that Kurt Framzl had named.

Max shook her hand warmly. "I wanted to thank you for your help with our marriage application."

"That was nothing. I played a minor role in the matter." The contrast between her deep voice and short stature was striking. The immediate impression was of a pocket dynamo, someone in control of her surroundings. She invited Max to sit and took a seat facing him.

Without realizing it, Max's hand slipped into his pants pocket and emerged with his father's cigarette lighter.

"I'm pleased to meet you, Max-Christian. I've heard so many good things about you."

Max raised an eyebrow. "What have you heard?"

"Greta tells me you are a man of principle. And I've heard that you are not one to follow the crowd, that you have a mind of your own." She crossed her legs. Max noted her sheer stockings, her trim figure. "Greta was particularly impressed by your concern for the unfortunate souls that you are required to transport from place to place. You are a Humanist, I think. No?"

Max wasn't sure what that meant, but he wasn't going to argue with the woman in her own home. "Yes, I suppose so." The lighter turned in his hand.

"You will be familiar with the egalitarian ideas developed in the East?"

What did she mean by that? "I have heard of Confucius."

Libertas laughed. The transformation of her countenance was like the sun coming out from behind a cloud, sending ripples of pleasure through his body. "Not that far east, Max-Christian. I was thinking of Karl Marx and Friedrich Engels. You've heard of them?"

Communism. He'd hit 'pay dirt'! The lighter spun in his fingers.

"I am aware of their work. I have long admired Communism as a system, but I must confess I have never read any of their writings."

She nodded toward the lighter in his hands. "I hope you're not planning to smoke."

"Oh no, I don't. This was my father's. Forgive me." He slipped it back into his pocket.

She got to her feet, took a book from one of the shelves and handed it to him. Max read the title, written in gold on the spine, 'Das Kapital.'

"And how do you feel about Fascism?"

"Really, Frau Schulze-Boysen, I have no time for the Nazis."

"Call me Libertas. Everyone does." She pulled a bell rope. The maid appeared. Libertas took the book back and asked the maid to wrap it in brown paper. The maid scurried off with the book. "Remind me to give it to you before you go. You may take it with you, but you must keep it hidden. It's on the list of banned books as I'm sure you are aware."

"Thank you, Libertas." Max wasn't at all sure that he wanted to read the book.

"Now, tell me all about Anna and your marriage plans."

#

67

As soon as the maid had closed the front door behind Max, Harro Schulze-Boysen stepped into the study.

Libertas smiled at him. "Well, what did you think?"

"I think you're going to have to work on your technique. Your approach was crude, heavy-handed and far too obvious."

She frowned. "Never mind my technique. What did you think of Max-Christian? Will we be able to use him?"

"We may use him, but we'll have to check his background first. He could be a plant."

She snorted. "He's a young man with obvious Humanist principles and a fiancée who's half-Jewish. He's under an obligation to us—to me and Greta—for his marriage approval. Why do you have to complicate everything, Harro?"

#

Max unwrapped the book and showed it to Anna.

She shied away from it as if it were a venomous spider that would bite her. "That's the Communist book, Max. It's banned. Where did you get it? Get rid of it."

"A friend lent it to me."

She flapped her hands. "Well, keep it hidden. I don't want anyone to know that we have banned books in the apartment."

Every night for a week, he waded through the book before sleeping. Much to Anna's disgust. Soon his head was spinning with Marx's theories of the value of labor. The more he read the more he felt he needed to go back and re-read what went before, and the more he became convinced that the book should be mandatory reading for everyone working in the Reich Labor Service. By the end of the second week his mind was grappling with serious ethical questions around the use of unpaid forced labor.

Chapter 23

November 1938

Max lived in a constant state of fear. He tried to lead a normal life, to give the appearance that nothing was troubling him, but the Gestapo was always in his thoughts. Germany was like a hospital patient emerging from a coma. The Nazis had injected new life into the country, but she had a new sickness—a patriotic fever that infected everyone. Brownshirts roamed the streets of Berlin. Armed with sticks and cudgels they hunted in groups of four or five, picking on anyone they considered weak, foreign, politically deviant or Jewish. Max's nights were infested with bad dreams. He spent his days in a trancelike state that was the only way he could live with his unrelenting anxiety.

And then one day, while he was out of the office, a coworker took a telephone call for him. Herr Framzl would like him to call into his office tomorrow morning at 8:30.

Max's heart skipped a beat. This was what he had been dreading. Framzl would be looking for answers and Max hadn't crossed the first hurdle yet. He had heard nothing more from Frau Greta or Libertas the actress since she'd given him the Communist Manifesto. Should he have made it more obvious that he wanted to join the Red Orchestra? Should he have called back to the actress's mansion?

It was November 2, All Souls Day. Max felt kinship with the dearly departed. Surely he would be joining them soon.

Framzl kept him waiting for 30 minutes before taking him into an office with a glass panel in the door. 'Department B Race and Ethnic Affairs' was stenciled on the panel in gothic script. Framed between two limp Swastika standards, an oversized picture of the Führer hung on the wall behind Framzl's desk.

"How long has it been since we spoke?"

"A couple of weeks. Herr Framzl—"

"It's been four weeks. I'm disappointed not to have heard from you in all that time. I trust you've made some progress."

"I have spoken with the actress. I made it plain that I wished to join the organization, but I'm afraid they haven't come back to me."

"You made your intentions clear? You played the part of a disillusioned subversive, hell-bent on destroying the Reich? You played the part with passion?"

"Yes, Herr Framzl. I did as you told me, but they don't seem to have taken the bait."

"I'm disappointed in you, Noack. A person more cynical than me might wonder if you really wanted to marry your *Mischling* sweetheart. What was her name again?"

"Anna Weber."

Framzl left the room. Max spent an unpleasant quarter of an hour under the critical gaze of the Führer on the wall.

Framzl returned clutching a folder. Max detected a gleam in the Gestapo man's eyes.

"You will approach them again." He handed the folder to Max. "Read the note in there. It contains some solid intelligence to trade. Give it to them. You will surely be admitted to the Red Orchestra after that."

Max read the note. It bore the Wehrmacht insignia at the top, and was stamped 'Top Secret.' The typescript ran to no more than seven lines. It contained an order to withdraw the entire 'Condor Legion' from Spain. The Kriegsmarine were to evacuate the army units, the Luftwaffe were to return to their bases in Germany. Germany's support of General Franco's Nationalists was coming to an end! Max's heart was racing by the time he reached the signature at the end: Wilhelm Keitel, Supreme Commander, *Oberkommando der Wehrmacht* (OKW).

"Is this real?"

"Of course."

"How am I supposed to have found this? They'll want an explanation. It's not the sort of thing that the Labor Service deals with."

Framzl frowned. "You recently received orders to find 50 workers for a secret mission overseas, did you not?"

"Yes, but I don't see the connection."

"Those workers are needed for vital maintenance work on the airbase runways in Spain."

Chapter 24

November 1938

Greta received a telephone call from Max Noack on November 3. "Could we meet? I have something for you."

They agreed to meet at noon in Hartmann's restaurant in Nollendorf Platz, famous for its fresh fish. She wrapped Ule in his warmest blanket, put him in his pram and set off. She slipped a few leaflets into the pram. She could drop them off on the way back.

A police patrol in Winterfeldtstrasse stopped her. They checked her papers.

"Where are you going?"

She gave the young policeman her warmest smile. "I'm walking the baby. He should be sleeping but, as you can see, he's wide awake."

"Pick him up while we check the pram."

Greta lifted Ule from the pram and the policeman searched it. "What are you looking for?"

She got no answer.

When he was satisfied that there was nothing to find in the pram, the policeman straightened his back. "Thank you for your cooperation, Frau Kuckhoff. You may go."

She replaced Ule in the pram. "What on earth did you think I was hiding?"

The policemen blew on his hands and then waved her on impatiently.

Hartmann's had an extended patio area planted with young trees, popular for *al fresco* eating in the summer. The tables were deserted, the trees bare. They found a table inside, in a quiet corner.

Max ordered a platter of white fish freshly caught in one of the Berlin lakes. Greta ordered a simple ham omelet that she could share with the baby.

Max was unusually animated. He whispered news of an imminent withdrawal of all German fighting units from Spain.

"How did you come by this information?" It was common knowledge that a German infantry unit and several squadrons of Luftwaffe bombers, collectively called the Condor Legion, was fighting on Franco's side, but it seemed unlikely that they would withdraw before the outcome of the civil war was assured.

"We have been given the task of repairing the runways in Spain. I found a top secret OKW order on my boss's desk."

#

Arvid was highly skeptical of Max's information. "Why would Hitler move the Condor Legion out of Spain when the outcome of the civil war is still in the balance? It makes no sense."

"So you propose to ignore the information?"

"I'll speak with Schulze-Boysen. And I'll check it out at work. That level of activity would surely generate some waves in the Economics Ministry."

To Greta's surprise, Harro Schulze-Boysen was able to confirm the intelligence within 24-hours. The Wehrmacht did indeed have a plan to pull out of the civil war in Spain. Franco's forces would have to fight on without further assistance from Germany. A Kriegsmarine vessel was standing by in the Mediterranean to evacuate the ground forces.

Arvid encoded the information in the usual way on a roll of rice paper hidden inside a cigarette, and arranged for one of his couriers to pass the cigarette pack to Alexander Korotkov, his contact at the Soviet Embassy. The Soviets, who were actively supporting the Spanish Republicans, would devour this information.

#

That evening after Ule had settled, Greta spoke to Adam. "Arvid seemed pleased with Max's information."

"He was, but it's not clear how he came by it. The Reich Labor Service is hardly an obvious place for information about large troop movements."

"I thought he explained that."

Adam nodded. "He did, but I wasn't entirely convinced."

He fetched a bottle of wine and two glasses from the kitchen.

"What are you suggesting, Adam? Arvid has asked me to sign him up. You think he might be a Gestapo plant?"

"I didn't say that, Greta, but you know it is possible. Set up a meeting. I'd like to talk to him."

Greta sipped her wine. "Perhaps you could get him and his fiancée an invitation to the Thanksgiving party at the American Embassy."

Chapter 25

November 1938

On November 10 Greta made her way to the Rosens' apartment building. She'd slept badly. The Brownshirts had been active in the streets all night. A smell of burning lingered in the air and plumes of smoke rose into the sky over the center and east of the city. She knocked on the door of the Rosens' apartment, waited a minute and tried again. Ule was crying in his pram.

"Who's there?" Matilde's voice from behind the door.

"It's Greta Kuckhoff."

The door opened. Greta wheeled the pram inside, put the brake on and lifted Ule out. The expression on Matilde's face told Greta that something was seriously wrong. "What's happened?"

"The shop was looted last night. David went in to check on the stock and found the place burnt out. He was attacked again on the way home. They broke…" Matilde broke down.

Oh god! "What? Where is he?"

"He's upstairs, in bed. The Brownshirts broke his arm. He was lucky. He could have been killed or transported to a labor camp. We're finished now, Greta. There's nothing left."

Ule was exercising his lungs. Matilde gave him a weak smile that did nothing to improve his mood. "What's the matter with little Ule? He looks feverish."

"He is. I have a bottle for him, and I'm sure he needs a new diaper."

They moved into the kitchen to attend to the baby's needs. Within five minutes Ule was back in his pram wearing a clean diaper and enjoying a bottle of milk.

Greta said, "Will you leave the country?"

Matilde ran a hand across her eyes. "You know how David feels about that. He says it's unpatriotic."

"How can it be unpatriotic when the government want you to leave, when marauding gangs are killing your people?"

"I know. I've tried talking to him, but he's so stubborn."

"Where's Sophie?"

"She's gone to a friend's house. She kept pestering me. I couldn't keep her cooped up any longer. She passes for Aryan when she's on her own. She should be all right."

Greta bit her lip. "Let me talk to David."

Matilde took her upstairs. David lay in bed facing the wall. The air in the room was foul.

Matilde opened a window. "David darling, Greta's here."

A grunt from David indicated that he had heard, but he made no move to emerge from under the bedclothes.

"Darling?"

The bedclothes stirred. A bleary-eyed David Rosen stuck a head out. "What does she want?"

"She would like to talk to you. Please be polite."

David rubbed his eyes. He sat up in the bed. He looked terrible. He hadn't shaved or washed his hair for a week, and his arm was in a splint.

"Good morning, Herr Rosen. Matilde has told me the bad news. You were attacked again?"

David coughed. Matilde handed him a handkerchief. He wiped his mouth.

"You found someone to set your arm, I see."

Matilde fluffed up the pillows behind her husband's head. "We went to our doctor. He's one of us, one of the few still practicing in Berlin."

"Matilde tells me you've decided to sell up. I would like to help if I can. If you decide to leave the country you should consider France. I know many people who have moved there. It's a good country. You could apply for visas."

"We're not leaving Germany." David's voice was more gravelly than usual. "Now leave us alone."

"There's no future for you in Germany. Surely you can see that?"

"What business is it of yours? You're not one of us." He slid back under the covers until only his nose and the top of his head was visible.

Greta strode back to the bedroom door. "Think about it, David. You and your family could build a new life in France."

When they reached the bottom of the stairs, Matilde held Greta's arm. "Do you think the French Embassy would help us?"

"I'm sure they would. And I'm sure David will come to realize that it's the best course of action. For Sophie's sake, I hope he doesn't leave it too long."

Matilde gave Greta a steely look. "I'll talk to him."

#

Greta parked the pram in the hallway and carried Ule up the stairs to the apartment.

Adam was waiting for her. He opened the door and immediately began to harangue her again about her visits to the Rosen family. "Have you any idea what happened last night? The Brownshirts attacked Jewish businesses all over the country. They're calling it *Kristallnacht*."

The blood drained from Greta's face. "David Rosen's shop was targeted."

"I told you associating with them is not a good idea."

"What are you suggesting? The Rosens are under siege from the Brownshirts. They deserve our support. What are you saying?"

"I'm saying you should be more careful where you take our son."

"The Rosens are a family, just like ours. David Rosen has been attacked. The Brownshirts looted his stock and burned down his shop. They broke his arm. Matilde is desperately worried. She has no idea how they can survive. They need my help now more than ever."

"I'm sorry to hear that, but it's too dangerous. Every time you visit them you risk attack yourself. And drawing attention to yourself puts our work at risk. Can't you see that? We have much more important work to do than supporting a family of Jews."

A wide-eyed Ule had been watching the exchange. He burst into tears. Greta picked him up to comfort him. Adam left the room.

Later, when Ule was asleep in his cot, Adam turned the radio on and tuned in to the BBC, barely audible above the crackle.

Greta leapt from her chair and switched it off. "What gives you the right to tell me what to do? Do I tell you what to write in your miserable leaflets?"

Adam raised an eyebrow. "Miserable?" He turned the radio on again. "I need to listen to the news from London."

Greta ignored him. "And what happened to joint editorial input? Since Ule was born, I can count on the fingers of one hand the number of times you have consulted me on any of the leaflets' content."

"I've been trying to shield you and Ule from danger. I thought you understood that, Greta."

She placed both fists on her hips. "Hah! Editorial input is too dangerous, visiting the Rosens is too dangerous. What about carrying your ridiculous leaflets around the streets of Berlin in the pram in broad daylight, that's not dangerous at all, I suppose?"

Three bleeps cut through the crackle. Adam turned up the volume. "This is the BBC Overseas Service. Here is the nine o'clock news, and this is Alvar Lidell reading it…"

Chapter 26

November 1938

The following Monday Greta called Max at work and arranged to meet for lunch again at the same fish restaurant in Nollendorf Platz.

Max ordered a bucket of mussels and a glass of Bavarian Helles beer. Greta ordered a pasta dish with extra tomato sauce that she could share with Ule.

Greta shoveled the sauce into Ule's mouth. "I've arranged an invitation for Anna and you to attend a party at the American Embassy."

"That's very kind, Frau Greta. When is it?" Max was struggling with a mussel.

"Thanksgiving, November 24 at eight o'clock for nine. It's black tie, of course."

"Of course. I'm sure Anna will be delighted." The mussel shot across the floor. A passing waiter picked it up without breaking stride.

Ule was blowing red bubbles. Greta used a napkin to wipe his mouth. He blew some more. "We'd like you to join our Orchestra. Your Bass Alpenhorn is just what we need."

Max looked around nervously at the other diners. No one was showing any interest in him or Greta.

"Thank you, Frau. When is the first concert?"

"There are certain preliminaries to attend to first, Max. You will have to be fitted for a costume. I will alert the tailor and send him to your apartment. Would this evening at seven o'clock be a good time?"

"I would prefer Wednesday evening, Frau Greta, and could you make it earlier? Say six o'clock? Anna works late on Wednesdays, you understand."

#

When he told Anna that they were invited to a party at the American Embassy, she squealed in delight. Five seconds later she spotted the hair in her soup. "I have nothing to wear!"

The following day Anna and her best friend, Ebba, went shopping. Within an hour Anna had found the dress she wanted. Made from fine wool in cream, decorated with gold thread, it swept to the floor in a long, flared hemline. It had a plunging neckline. Ebba was entranced when Anna tried it on. "Oh, Anna, it's stunning."

The shop assistant agreed, saying the fit was almost perfect. It would require only minor alterations by the in-house seamstresses. She inserted some pins around the bust and waist and marked it with a piece of tailor's chalk. "When will the gown be needed?"

"Thursday November 24," Anna replied.

"For the Thanksgiving ball at the American Embassy," said Ebba in a sing-song voice.

"That's very short notice, but I'm sure we can get the work done in time. Slip it off, and we'll sort out the details."

The 'details' turned out to be 90 Reichsmarks for the dress and another 12 for the alterations. Between them Anna and Ebba scraped the money together. Anna's clothing ration for two months was not enough to cover the purchase, and Ebba had to come to the rescue again.

Ebba was happy to help. She laughed. "You'll be the belle of the ball. Poor Cinderella won't stand a chance."

Chapter 27

November 1938

On Wednesday on the stroke of 6:00 p.m., Greta called to the apartment. Anna was working late at the department store. Greta was accompanied by a rough-looking man in his fifties carrying a leather briefcase whom she introduced as 'Bruno.'

She shook Max's hand. "That information you gave us was very helpful. We were able to confirm it and pass it on to our friends. Welcome to our group and the fight for freedom against the Nazis and justice for the people of Germany."

What am I doing? thought Max, but he nodded. "I am with you, Frau Greta. What do I have to do?"

"There will be many ways that you can help, but you will have to prove yourself first. To start with you can help with the distribution of our leaflets. You will need false papers, and that's Bruno's department."

Bruno opened his briefcase and took out two blank identity cards. He asked Max for his date of birth and added that to each of the cards. Then he pulled an inkpad from his briefcase, took Max's fingerprints and applied them to each of the cards.

Max's heartbeat rose a notch. "Why do you need two copies?"

"The extra copy is insurance. In case our card man has problems. Your cover name will be Gunther Schlurr."

Bruno placed one of the cards in his briefcase. Max signed the second card with his new name. It was not one he would have chosen.

Next, Bruno removed a camera from his briefcase and took pictures of Max. As he worked, he said, "You are not yet a member of the KPD, Comrade. Have you considered joining?"

Max was alarmed at the suggestion and the word 'Comrade.' His nightly bouts with Karl Marx had colored his thinking a weak shade of red, but he was far from joining the KPD, the Communist Party. "Is that necessary?"

"No, not at all," said Greta. She jerked her head at Bruno. He packed up his briefcase and left the apartment.

Greta leaned on the bathroom wall behind Max as he scrubbed the ink from his fingers. "You must never use your real name when you are engaged on Orchestra work. You must use only the name Gunther Schlurr. Is that clear?"

"I understand, Frau Greta."

"I've set up an appointment for you with a dentist," she checked her watch, "in 40 minutes." She gave him a business card: Dr. Helmut Himpel, Dental Surgeon Lehderstrasse 5.

"Why do I need a dentist?"

"He will explain. Trust me."

#

The dentist's surgery was near Weissensee on the far side of the city. Max left a note for Anna and set out right away. He needed to take two trams and arrived 10 minutes late. November had turned bitterly cold. Clouds of steam rose from the bodies of the passengers huddled together in the trams.

Dr. Himpel's assistant checked his cover name, his real name and his address. Then she took his coat and escorted him into the surgery. Max sat up on the chair.

"Open wide." Dr. Himpel was tall, slim and tanned with deep-set eyes. He wore a Lange wristwatch that probably cost the equivalent of Max's salary for five years. He poked around in Max's mouth. "Hmm, very good, very nice. You have an excellent set of teeth. I can see you look after them well. Now which one would you prefer me to extract?" He exited Max's mouth.

Max blinked. "I beg your pardon?"

"Well, usually we can find a tooth in need of repair, but not in your case. Open wide again and I'll tap the ones that I would suggest. Then you can choose."

"You want to extract one of my teeth?"

"Of course. It will be replaced with the capsule."

"What capsule?"

"The suicide pill. Didn't they explain all this to you?"

Max shook his head.

"I'm sorry. Well, as long as you are working with the Communist Resistance you will be at risk of arrest by the Gestapo. I will place a cyanide capsule hidden inside your mouth to give you the opportunity to end your life rather than betray your friends under interrogation."

Max broke into a cold sweat. He swung his legs from the chair. "I never agreed to that."

"If you refuse you will have to leave the Resistance."

Max thought about that for a few moments. If he failed to remain in the Red Orchestra, the Gestapo would never stamp and sign his marriage application. He had no choice. He got back onto the chair...

#

By the time he arrived back at the apartment, the Novocain had lost almost all its strength and Max was in agony.

Anna asked him where he'd been, and when she saw the look on his face, she said, "What's the matter with you, Max?"

"Toothache. I've been to the dentist. He removed a tooth."

She put a plate of cottage pie on the table. Max couldn't touch it. He took to his bed.

Chapter 28

November 1938

ℰight days later, Karl Marx was gathering dust on top of the wardrobe. Max's mouth and jaw were still in pain, and he was having difficulty keeping his tongue from poking around in the cavity.

He received a telephone call at work.

"Herr Noack?" He recognized Greta's voice. "This is Sister Bernadina from St. Angar's Church in Klopstockstrasse. I'm delighted to tell you that your application to join the choir has been granted. The next rehearsal is at six-thirty tonight."

Max's singing voice was like a goose sitting on a rusty nail. "Who should I contact at this rehearsal?"

"Ask for Vigo." She hung up.

He punched his card early, took some aspirin for the toothache, and hurried to the church at Klopstockstrasse. The tram was full to overflowing with shoppers.

The church doors were open, but the place was deserted. He wandered around, looking at the elaborately painted statues and the relief panels on the walls depicting Christ's journey to his crucifixion. He had been taught in school about the Roman Church's fondness for graven images of their saints and Anna had explained the role played at Easter by the 'Stations of the Cross' relief panels.

The echo of a scratching sound alerted him to the presence of another soul. And he caught a glimpse of a dark-clad figure entering the vestry to the right of the main altar.

"Excuse me, Father…"

An old priest emerged. "Can I help you?"

"I'm looking for Vigo."

The priest pointed to one of the two confessional boxes near the back of the church. "He's in there."

Max thanked the old priest. He tapped on the box.

"Hello. What's your name, sinner?"

Max objected to the word 'sinner', but he replied. "Max."

"Enter the box, Max. I will hear your confession."

Max opened one of the side doors and entered the box. It was dark inside. A panel slid open. A disembodied voice said, "You must kneel."

Max discovered a padded hassock at his feet. He knelt down and came face to face with someone through a grille half-lit in the dim light.

"You seek absolution from your sins, Max?"

"No, Father, I'm not Catholic. I am here to meet someone called Vigo."

"I am Father Vigo. What can I do for you?"

"I'm not sure, Father, I was hoping for some guidance from you. I've recently joined a group, but I've yet to discover my role."

"You have joined the choir of the Red Orchestra, I think. I am also in that choir. Let me give you absolution and we can leave these cramped quarters. Are you truly sorry for your sins?"

"I am, Father."

"Then I absolve you. *Absolvo te*." He made the sign of the cross in Max's face.

They left the confession box together and Max got his first real look at the man: about 10 years older than Max, sallow-skinned, with a bald head surrounded by jet black hair in the shape of a tonsure. A strong stubble accentuated the lower half of his face. He was dressed in a clerical collar and cassock. "Are you really a priest?"

Vigo laughed. "What gave it away?"

"I thought it might be a disguise."

"No disguise. I really am a priest. But I'm also a member of the group."

"A Communist?"

"Now that would be a step too far, even for me. Not many of the group are members of the KPD, you know. You've met some of them, I believe."

"A couple of women and a man with a camera called Bruno."

"Strange name for a camera." Vigo flashed his teeth in a grin. "Bruno is a Communist, the ladies are not. What about you?"

Max shook his head. "Can you tell me what will be expected of me, Father?"

"Call me Vigo. It helps me to remember who's Catholic and who's not."

"It's an unusual name. Not one I've come across before."

"My father was Italian." Vigo laughed. "I suppose you could have guessed that from my looks."

Now that he mentioned it, Vigo's origins were obvious, but Max had no time for such racial stereotyping.

Chapter 29

November 1938

They sat side by side on a pew. Max palmed his father's lighter, turning it over in his hand. "What will the Resistance expect me to do?"

"Call them 'the Orchestra.' Ears are flapping from every window. I expect they will ask you to carry messages to our friends in cities outside Germany."

"What sort of messages, and what cities?"

"I can't tell you what's in the messages, Max. I've no idea. They're always written in code, and honestly, I'd rather not know. As for the cities, we have friends in Paris, Prague and Brussels."

Secret messages in code! Framzl had said nothing about that.

"Isn't it difficult to obtain travel permits?"

Vigo smiled. "The Communists can arrange those. They have a man who works for the railway company. Your main task will be helping with the distribution of anti-Nazi information by delivering broadsheet leaflets. You've seen the sort of thing the group prints?"

Max nearly said yes. Then he remembered that the only leaflet he'd seen had been the one Framzl showed him at Gestapo headquarters. He shook his head.

Vigo led the way to the vestry. The old priest had gone. Vigo opened a wardrobe containing vestments elaborately embroidered in every color. He used a key to unlock a file cabinet built into the bottom of the wardrobe and took out a bundle of leaflets. "These are for delivery. You must come with me to learn the route so that you can share my burden. We will split the route between us."

"How often are they printed?"

"Roughly once a month."

Max ran his eyes over the leaflet. The rallying cry was more subdued but just as unrealistic as the last one:

'Do what you can to obstruct the Nazis. Refuse to work. If you cannot refuse, work slower, make mistakes.'

"Where are these printed?"

"Sorry, I can't tell you. That's a closely guarded secret that you're better off not knowing."

Vigo pulled an overcoat from the wardrobe. The coat had wide pockets sewn on the inside. He tucked a bundle of leaflets into each pocket.

They set out together on the delivery route, knocking on doors along the way and handing over one or two leaflets at each stop. Max made a careful mental note of the route and the houses where Vigo dropped off his leaflets. There were 35 of them.

They passed a 2-man uniformed police patrol along the way. Both men tipped their hats to the priest. Obviously, the priestly garb was an effective barrier against personal searches.

Max said, "I'll have to get pockets like yours sewn into my coat, Father."

"That's Vigo, remember. If we stagger our journeys, you can borrow this coat."

Max gave a rueful grunt. "Could I borrow your dog collar as well?"

"But of course." Vigo flashed a toothy smile at him.

Max was amused at the thought of a Lutheran dressing up as a Roman priest.

The route was arranged in a figure of eight, starting and ending at the church. At each stop on the second half of the route, Vigo introduced Max as Gunther Schlurr. The sound of his alias was comforting to hear. Vigo was fully informed. He must be a trusted member of the Red Orchestra.

Max did his best to remember everyone that he met, but by the end of the run, he had to admit he'd forgotten half of them. Vigo slapped him on the back. "Never mind, Gunther. When the time comes I'll give you a list of names and addresses."

As they approached the church, Vigo reached into his robe and pulled out a packet of cigarettes. He offered the pack to Max.

"I don't smoke."

"And yet you carry a cigarette lighter?"

"It was my father's. It's all I have of him. He died when I was a young boy."

Vigo held out his hand, and Max handed him the lighter. The priest examined it. "A memento from the war, I see. Very pretty." He flipped it open and thumbed the wheel. It sprang to life with a smooth orange flame. Vigo lit a cigarette. He flipped it closed and handed it back. Max put it in his pocket.

In the tram on the way home, Max decided he liked Vigo. The man had spirit and a sharp sense of humor. He was surprised that the lighter had worked for Vigo. It probably hadn't been used since his father left, over 20 years ago. He took it out and tried it. It lit first time.

Chapter 30

November 1938

November 24 arrived at last. While Max slipped into his rented evening suit, Anna put on her gown. Ebba was there to help her.

Anna wriggled her hips. "It feels tight here, here and all along here."

"It looks fine. It probably feels strange because it's not what you're used to."

"I have the feeling that I'll burst out of it if I breathe normally, and I'm not sure I'll be able to sit."

"I don't think they do much sitting at these balls. Everybody stands around with glasses in one hand and long cigarette holders in the other. Breathe slowly, evenly. Here, try these on." Ebba pulled a pair of white gloves from her handbag.

Anna tried them on. They reached her elbows. Anna picked up her tiny golden bag and struck a Marlene Dietrich pose. "How do I look?"

"You look like a million Reichsmarks."

"I just wish I had some shoes to go with the outfit."

"What you're wearing is perfect. And no one's going to see them. Just remember to walk slowly. Try to glide about."

Anna practiced gliding.

Max looked ridiculous in his evening jacket and matching pants. Ebba tied his bowtie.

"How do I look?"

"Walk around for me," said Anna.

Max walked around the room, stiff-legged.

"Bend your knees, Max."

"The pants are scratching my legs."

"You look like a man of means," said Ebba.

You look like an arthritic penguin, thought Anna.

#

Max was acutely aware that, apart from Frau Greta, Anna knew no one at the embassy party. About half the guests were Americans and many spoke no German. He introduced the dentist, Dr. Himpel. Anna spent a few minutes chatting to his assistant before they drifted away. Max pointed out Libertas, the actress, flitting about the various rooms, but Anna never managed to meet her.

They spent some time with Frau Greta. She admired Anna's gown. Anna returned the compliment and thanked her for arranging the invitation. Greta responded, "That was not my doing. That was my husband, Adam. Let me see if I can find him."

Frau Greta left them, and they stood together sipping champagne for close to 15 minutes. Then they were approached by a stranger who took hold of Anna's gloved hand and pressed it to his lips with a charming smile.

"You must be Anna Weber, and this must be your fiancé, Max. I'm Greta's husband, Adam."

"I'm very pleased to make your acquaintance, Herr Kuckhoff," said Anna.

Max was disgusted to see her melting in the heat of Adam's smile.

Adam raised an eyebrow. "You know my family name?"

"Yes, of course. I have long admired your work. I loved your latest novel, *Scherry*."

"You're too kind. And what about you, Max? Have you read any of my work?"

"I'm sorry, no."

Adam signaled to Greta who hurried over and took Anna to meet one of the guests. "His name's Jürgen. You'll like him."

Adam steered Max into a quiet corner. "I've been told you helped Vigo deliver our broadsheet leaflets. Those are largely my work."

"In that case I have read something of your work."

"And what do you think of it?"

"To be honest, I thought the rallying cry was a little simplistic. People are unlikely to obstruct the Nazis, not if they want to stay out of the labor camps."

Adam chuckled. "Well said, young man. I'm sure you are right. But how do you feel about printing and distributing anti-Nazi material around the city?"

"I can understand why you do it, and I agree with the stand you're taking, but it's extremely dangerous."

"You agree with the morality of our position?"

"I agree with the morality of taking a stand against the Nazis, but I'm not a Communist."

"Neither am I. Some people in our group have Marxist leanings, but only a small number are members of the KPD." Max must have looked skeptical, as Adam assured him this was the truth. "Our objective is to undermine the Third Reich in any ways that we can. Ideology doesn't come into it."

"In that case, I'm with you."

Adam looked surprised by the obvious sincerity in this remark. It surprised Max just as much. Up to that point, he had been half-inclined to complete the task handed to him by Framzl, the Gestapo man. He realized that he was now fully committed to the cause of the Red Orchestra. Framzl would have to whistle for the information he wanted. Nervously, Max's tongue sought out the false tooth in his mouth and his fingers clutched the cigarette lighter in his pants pocket.

Anna returned looking pale and complaining of a headache. Max thanked the ambassador, and they left the party early.

#

As Arvid and Mildred Harnack were leaving the embassy, First Secretary Donald Heath handed Arvid a sealed envelope, marked 'Personal.' "Wait until you get home before reading it, Sport. Okay?"

Arvid knew it must be bad news. As soon as he got home, he tore it open.

My dear friend,

This is to inform you that, as a consequence of the actions of November 9, the State Department in Washington has decided to reduce its embassy staff in Berlin to a minimum. I am to be sent to Latin America, the location to be decided shortly.

Sincere apologies for this letter. I would have much preferred to give you the news in person, but I fear I would not have been up to the task.

I wish you well for the future of your endeavors and for your personal happiness.

Louise has asked me to convey her regrets to your beautiful wife, Mildred. I think our two wives have formed an association every bit as close as that between their husbands over the past 11 months.

I hope we will be able to keep in touch by correspondence and that we will meet again when the coming storm has passed and order in Europe restored.

Your good friend,

Donald.

Arvid read the letter again from the top, looking for a crumb of comfort, a hint of a possible reprieve. He found none. He was about to lose his most valuable contact, the only contact he had with a western power, and the one foreign contact that he trusted implicitly. Henceforth, the only remaining outlet for intelligence was Alexander Korotkov, his NKVD contact at the Soviet Embassy. Ideologically, he was in tune with Korotkov, but he never really trusted Joseph Stalin or his spymasters in the Kremlin.

Chapter 31

December 1938

𝐀 couple of weeks after the embassy party, on the second Saturday of December, Max received a call to attend a choir rehearsal at St. Angar's Church. He made the trip across the city by tram to the church at Klopstockstrasse. A turbulent overcast autumn had given way to a calm, cloudless winter. The sporadic warm and wet breezes of November had turned into blasts from the Arctic, and all over the city icy tram rails sparkled in the weak sunshine. Only the bravest souls ventured out on bicycles.

The church was busy with parishioners coming and going in and out of the two confessional boxes in continuous streams. Max took a seat in a pew at the back of the church and waited. He was not Catholic and had no time for the notion of sharing one's sins and peccadillos with a pastor, but he was impressed by the apparent change in demeanor of the people as they went through the ritual. Each penitent seemed to go into the box with furrowed brow, weighed down by their troubles and each emerged in noticeably brighter spirits. Perhaps it was his imagination.

As the crowd thinned, someone took a seat on the bench beside Max. He glanced at the new arrival—a tall, gaunt man of about 40 years, wearing a bulky overcoat like Vigo's and heavy horn-rimmed glasses on an elf-like nose.

As the last stragglers emerged from the confessionals to kneel in prayer before leaving the church, the stranger handed Max an identity card carrying the name Gunther Schlurr, occupation: Pastor. He couldn't fault the document. It looked genuine. He whispered, "Is this your work? It's very good."

"Yes, Comrade. I'm glad you like it," the man whispered back. His accent was difficult to place, difficult to understand. "I'll have the rest of your papers ready in time for your trip."

"What trip?"

"Vigo will tell you all about it later."

Max thanked the thin man. "What should I call you?"

"You could use my name. Everyone calls me Peter Riese."

Vigo stepped from the box and headed for the vestry. Riese and Max followed him. Inside the vestry, Riese took off his overcoat. It was equipped with deep pockets just like Vigo's, and the pockets were full of leaflets. Vigo and Riese set about removing these, placing them in a neat pile on a counter top.

Riese was as thin as a pencil. The 3-piece suit that he was wearing bore all the signs of having been crudely extended from a smaller garment. The sleeves and the legs of the trousers were too short, the waistcoat, a loose fit showing signs of familiarity with an ample paunch. The ensemble was topped off with a blue and black tie held in place with a gold tiepin in the shape of a swastika.

Once his overcoat was relieved of its cargo, Riese put it back on. He bid them good day and left.

#

"Where is he from?" Max asked Vigo. "He didn't sound German."

"He's Swiss-German, from Zurich."

Vigo handed Max a list of 17 names and addresses. Then he spread a map of Berlin on the table and took Max through all 17 of his drops, starting and ending at the church. "You need to be sure that you have the right house and the right person at each stop. You understand how disastrous it would be to make a mistake?"

"I understand."

Vigo pulled a dark shirt, cassock and trousers from the wardrobe. "Put these on."

"You're not serious."

"Yes, I'm serious. It's a perfect disguise."

Carrying his fresh identity card, Pastor Gunther Schlurr set out on his delivery run. The priestly vestments weren't a bad fit, but the coarse material scratched his skin and the dog collar interfered with his Adam's apple when he swallowed.

After no more than a few meters, Max was sweating under the

weight of the cassock. Vigo's overcoat with its deep internal pockets added to his distress.

All 17 drops went like clockwork. At the end of the route, he stumbled into the vestry, threw off the coat, the cassock and the dog collar and let his skin breathe for a few moments before getting back into his own clothes.

Vigo gave him a glass of cold water. Max gulped it down.

Max stood. Slipping a hand in his pocket, he wrapped his fingers around his father's cigarette lighter. He was eager to get home and switch back to his real identity. Every minute masquerading as Pastor Gunther Schlurr made him anxious.

"Before you go," said Vigo, "I've been asked to take a message to our friends in exile in Brussels for transmission to Moscow. And they want me to take you with me."

The trip that Riese had mentioned.

"How soon? My boss is not happy about the number of days I've taken recently from my annual leave entitlement, and I have to save up as much leave as I can for my wedding. It could be difficult to take any more time off."

"This will be a weekend trip. We travel out on Saturday and return on Sunday. You won't lose any work time."

Anna's not going to like that, thought Max. "Which Saturday are we talking about?"

"The first Saturday in January."

#

He told Anna that his boss, Herr Schnerpf, was sending him on a trip to Brussels early in January. He hated telling her a lie, but to tell her the truth would place her in danger from the Gestapo.

Anna was less than enthusiastic about the prospect of spending an entire weekend alone.

"I'll make it up to you," he said. "I'll buy you a gift in Belgium."

Finding a hiding place for the identity card presented a challenge. After some thought, he put it on top of the wardrobe under *Das Kapital*. Anna was scared of the book. She'd be unlikely to move it.

Chapter 32

December 1938

$\mathfrak{T}$wo months to the day after his first visit to the food court, Jürgen returned. He sat at the same table as before—alone, this time—and Anna took his order. She did her best to moderate her beaming smile, but without much success. It was such an integral part of her routine.

As she placed his food on the table, he returned her smile. "What time do you leave work?"

She avoided his deep blue eyes. "Can I get you anything else, sir?"

"Call me by my name. I'm Jürgen, remember."

She looked up and his eyes captured hers. "We are not allowed to fraternize with the customers, sir."

She asked Ebba to attend to him when it was time for Jürgen to pay his bill.

"You find him attractive, this Jürgen?"

"No, he's creepy, but have you seen his eyes? They're magnetic, and so difficult to avoid."

Ebba smiled. "I noticed his eyes."

They left the building together. Ebba said goodnight to Anna and went left, Anna turned right, rounded a corner, and found Jürgen leaning against a wall, waiting for her. He fell into step beside her. "I'll walk you home. Where do you live?"

A shiver of fear ran up her spine. She didn't want this Jürgen to know where she lived.

She gave him a weak smile. "There's no need. I'm not going home. I'm meeting someone at a Brauhaus."

"Who? Your boyfriend, Max-Christian?"

Another, more serious shiver of fear ran through her whole body. "How do you know my boyfriend's name?"

He cupped her elbow. "I'll walk with you to the Brauhaus. I'll explain along the way."

Jürgen seemed to know where they were going, and as he steered her along she realized he was heading to Max's favorite Brauhaus in Paulusstrasse.

He reached into a jacket pocket and flashed a bronze disc. "I'm with the Gestapo investigation department. We know that your boyfriend is mixed up with the Communists." She shook her head and would have objected but he said, "The Communists have been printing anti-German literature. We are aware of that and of Max's involvement. We are also aware of other subversive activities, much more serious, that Max may have been involved with. You will help me to uncover these activities. You will keep your eyes and ears open and let me know when you hear anything that may be of interest to me." He pressed a card into her hand. "This telephone number is attended day and night. As soon as you have anything of interest, no matter how small, ring this number."

"I'm sorry, Herr Jürgen. I know nothing of these matters."

"Let me be clear. There are men in Gestapo headquarters who would use other methods to obtain this information, men who are trained to beat the information from your boyfriend with ax handles. If you are unwilling to help me then I will not be able to keep Max from those men. Do you understand?"

#

Max made his scheduled trip to his mother's house on Saturday December 24. Christmas Eve. She opened the door and let him in to a cold, dark house completely lacking any seasonal decorations—no tree, no *Adventskranz* candles, no lights, no color of any kind. He was alarmed. He had never known a Christmas that his mother had failed to celebrate in some way.

On his way in to the parlor, he tripped over a pair of boots. He recognized his father's boots, covered in fresh mud.

"Are you all right, Mother? You do know it's Christmas?"

He got no answer. His mother sat on the sofa, looking unusually downcast. Her demeanor, her clothes and general appearance suggested she was going through one of the infrequent bouts of depression that punctuated her life.

He offered her a couple of gifts—a headscarf and some bath salts that Anna had picked out for her. She flapped her hands impatiently. He put the gifts on top of the piano beside the picture of his father, taking a moment to peer at the picture, a faded sepia image of a stern-looking soldier in uniform.

He took his seat on the piano stool. "What have you been reading, Mother?" While waiting for a reply, Max was struck by a feeling of guilt. Could she be lonely? She'd never shown signs of loneliness before. "You should come to Berlin and spend some time with Anna and me in our apartment. We can make up a bed for you."

"You don't have to keep visiting, you know." His mother spoke quietly, as if suppressing an urge to scream.

"I like visiting, Mother, and it is Christmas."

"You have your own lives to lead. I don't want to be a burden to you."

"You're not a burden, Mother. I just wish you'd get a telephone so that I can talk to you more often."

On the way home on the autobus he reran the conversation in his head looking for clues to his mother's impenetrable mental state. Then his mind turned to the muddy boots in the hall. Had she taken to wearing his father's boots? In the garden, perhaps?

Chapter 33

December 1938

The Joint Forces Contingency Committee was in session on the third floor of the War Office. Seven men sat around the table. All seven were smoking, and the air was thick with smoke. Six of the seven were in uniform. The seventh wore an understated pinstripe.

At the head of the table, Air Commodore Frank Scott spoke in a sonorous tone. "A few of you have read the Assistant Director's report on the Soviet Question, but I will ask him to take us through the main points. Briefly."

The Assistant Director of Military Intelligence, Sidney Blenkinsop-Smythe, or B-S as he was universally known, got to his feet. "Thank you, Air Commodore. Since the last meeting I have had a team working on an evaluation of the various possibilities with regard to the likely disposition of the Soviet Union in the event of a war with Germany. My report analyses each possible outcome and assigns a statistical probability to each. However, please be aware that this is far from an exact science. In the final analysis, the actual outcome will be decided by the actions of Hitler to the West and the Japanese to the East. But the most significant factor, the one that we cannot measure with any degree of certainty, is the mind of Joseph Stalin. Stalin's is an erratic, mercurial personality, an impossible man to predict at the best of times. All we can do is weigh up the plusses and minuses of each possible outcome, viewed through the prism of military strategy and see what emerges."

The air commodore glanced at his watch.

"First, we must consider how Germany and the Soviet Union will interact. Here we are faced with not one, but two unpredictable personalities, for Hitler has proven just as imponderable as Stalin.

From Hitler's speeches and the tone of his book, *Mein Kampf*, we know that he is intractably opposed to what he terms 'Bolshevism.' He hates Communism and has vowed to eliminate these two evils—as he sees them—from the face of the earth. We may assume that Stalin is just as antagonistic towards Fascism. However, the notion that either will attack the other is unthinkable. Each would have too much to lose. If Hitler starts a war in Europe, which, as we all know, is more than likely, we may expect the Soviets to remain neutral, at least until the final outcome has been decided. At that stage, we expect the Soviets to make land grabs in some of the smaller countries in Eastern Europe.

The air commodore caught B-S's eye and tapped his watch.

"We must consider the position of the Japanese. It seems likely that they would invade Russian territory from the east at the earliest opportunity after the commencement of a European war. This would keep the Soviets busy for a protracted period and keep them out of our hair, so to speak."

"If you could wind up..." said the air commodore.

"So there you have it. A Japanese invasion of the Soviet Union is the most likely outcome with a probability of 85 percent. The invasion of Germany by the Soviets is unlikely, say 10 percent, and an invasion of Soviet territory by Germany has a probability of less than 2 percent."

One of the committee members raised his hand. "Have you analyzed what might happen if the Japanese don't invade from the East?"

"Yes. In that case we can expect the Soviets to invade Germany soon after the start of the war, probably through Finland and/or the Baltic States, with an 80 percent probability. They may react immediately to the expected invasion of Poland by a repulsing move to drive the Germans back out of Poland. My analysts have given that a 75 percent probability. Remember that Stalin regards Poland as an integral part of the Communist bloc."

"Thank you, Director. You will circulate the report among the members here?"

"As you wish, Air Commodore. I would ask everyone to treat it as top secret."

Chapter 34

January 1939

On the Wednesday before his trip to Belgium Max received a telephone call at work. A voice he didn't recognize told him he should call in to the dentist's surgery after work.

The tram journey passed in a daze as his trepidation took hold.

Dr. Himpel was waiting for him, and so was Peter Riese, the stick insect from Zurich in the ill-fitting 3-piece suit. Riese handed Max a packet containing a set of papers—passport, Party membership and travel permit all in the name Gunther Schlurr.

Max flicked through them. They were impeccable forgeries, dog-eared, worn, and grubby as if they'd been in use for years. He thanked the forger, and Riese left the surgery, leaving Max to the tender mercies of the dentist.

"Hop up on the chair. I have something for you."

Max sat in the chair.

"Open wide." Dr. Himpel checked the cavity he'd previously created. "How does it feel?"

"Sore."

"It will be tender for a few week more, but it's healing nicely. Now open wide again. This won't take a moment."

He inserted a strange object into the cavity. Max explored it with his tongue. It was softer than a tooth and rocked slightly when he pushed it.

"How does it feel?" said Himpel.

"Painful. And it's loose."

"Open up. Let me take a look." Himpel poked at the object. "You need a little flexibility. I'm not unhappy with that."

You don't have to carry it around in your mouth, thought Max. "It feels soft. What is it?"

"I told you, it's a cyanide capsule. It's designed to withstand normal everyday use. It will only break if you pop it out and bite down on it. Try it."

"What?"

"Try popping it out. Don't bite down on it, obviously. You should be able to pop it out with your tongue and slot it back into the cavity using your tongue and your cheek."

The capsule resisted Max's first efforts, but he soon discovered where to press and it popped out.

Putting it back was more tricky. Dr. Himpel had to help. "You may have to use your fingers to start with, but keep practicing with your tongue. Use your cheek to hold it in place and press it down. You'll soon get the hang of it. How does it feel now?"

"It's back in the cavity, but it's quite sore."

"Yes, I would have preferred to let it heal for another few weeks, but we had to get on with it. I'll give you some painkillers."

#

Anna frowned at him as he came through the door. "It's late. Where have you been?"

"I had to go back to the dentist."

Her frown deepened. "I met Odelette, the dentist's assistant in the grocery shop the other day. She said she hasn't seen you since last summer."

"I went to a different dentist."

"Why?"

"The pain was intense. Someone at work recommended a dentist close to the office."

"Well, your supper is ruined. I'll have to heat it up again."

"Thank you, Anna. Sorry I couldn't get word to you."

In the bedroom he pulled a chair over to the wardrobe, stood on the chair and placed the rest of Herr Schlurr's papers under the book.

Chapter 35

January 1939

Max and Vigo met at the Lehrter Bahnhof. Max suppressed a laugh when he saw Vigo. Dressed in a tweed jacket and corduroy trousers, the priest looked like a British tourist. They took an empty smoking compartment on the 7:05 a.m. express from Berlin to Cologne and sat face to face by the window.

They spent the early part of the trip exchanging personal histories. Vigo was the youngest of five children, his mother German, his father Italian. He was fluent in both languages. Having studied and been ordained in a seminary in the Vatican, he had an abiding love for Rome, but his heart was in a small village in northern Italy.

Max asked Vigo who was minding the church while he was away. "Don't you have to say mass on Sunday?"

Vigo laughed. "The parish priest, Father Zauffer will look after that. I'm not indispensable."

Max told Vigo about Anna and their plans to marry. Vigo asked whether Anna was Roman Catholic. He offered to marry them in St. Angar's church.

"I'll have to ask Anna. She may have other plans."

A couple of hours into the journey they were joined in the compartment by a woman and her son. That killed their conversation. Max amused himself by counting sheep in the fields and then trying to work out how fast the train was traveling by measuring the time between telegraphic poles. He estimated an astonishing 90-100 kph. He was asleep within minutes.

By 3:00 p.m. the train rolled into the main station in Cologne, right beside the cathedral. They had an hour to wait before their connecting train. Vigo insisted that Max use the time to visit Cologne Cathedral, Germany's biggest and most impressive.

"Isn't it magnificent? The foundation stone was laid in 1248, but the building wasn't completed until 1880."

The second part of their train journey took them from Cologne to the border where the train stopped and several teams of Schupo uniformed police came on board. They worked their way through the train checking the papers of every passenger.

As Max handed his false identity card to a couple of officers, his knees began to tremble. He forced them together in an effort to disguise the shake.

"Good day, Herr Pastor Schlurr. From what church?"

Max gave the name of the Lutheran church in Wittenberg that he'd attended as a child.

"You're a long way from home." The policeman handed the identity card back. "The purpose of your journey today?"

"I am visiting a sick relative in Brussels."

And the policemen moved on.

Max planted his hands on his knees, horrified at the level of trepidation he'd felt during such a simple exchange.

The Schupo completed their checks and left the train. The driver gave two hoots on his whistle and the train lurched forward. Max stepped from the compartment and signaled to the priest to join him in the corridor.

Max waited until they had the corridor to themselves. Then he whispered, 'That was terrifying, Vigo. My legs were shaking."

Vigo laughed. "That was nothing. Surely you've had your papers inspected before?"

"Of course I have, but never with a false identity card. I don't think I'm suited to the life of a communist spy."

"You'll get used to it."

They stopped again at Welkenraedt where two disinterested Belgian policemen checked their papers. The last part of the journey took a meandering course through a series of rural valleys to the Belgian capital.

When they alighted from the train Vigo made straight for a shady-looking beer cellar in a back street close to the railway station. They took seats at the bar. Vigo ordered two beers.

A heavy-set man wearing a leather flat cap took the stool to Vigo's right. He shook hands with Vigo, and Vigo introduced him to Max as 'Gilbert.'

"Pleased to meet you, Comrade Gunther," said the big man. He spoke German with a guttural accent.

Vigo placed the cigarette pack containing the secret message on the bar. Gilbert placed an identical pack beside it. After a few minutes conversation with Vigo, Gilbert picked up Vigo's cigarette pack, shook hands again and he was gone. Vigo pocketed Gilbert's cigarettes.

Max expected more drama than an exchange of cigarette packs after a 17-hour train journey. "Was that it?"

"The job is done," said Vigo. "Tomorrow we go home."

Max thought Belgian beer a passable substitute for the real thing. It was certainly far superior to any of the mass-produced German beers. He persuaded Vigo to buy a second round and left the Brauhaus with a broad smile on his face.

They spent the night in a travelers' hotel, sharing a room.

Chapter 36

January 1939

Max slept like a stone. Vigo woke him early in the morning. They grabbed a quick breakfast and made their way back to the railway station to catch the early train back to Berlin.

When they arrived on the platform, Vigo hailed a young lady in a bucket hat. They kissed on both cheeks in the French style. Vigo introduced Gunther Schlurr and they shook hands.

Her name was Delma. A demure young lady with a pale complexion, wearing no makeup, she looked fragile.

They all boarded the train together. Delma and Vigo sat close together like intimates. Max was as broad-minded as the next man, but he thought the way Vigo acted toward Delma was not what one might expect from a celibate priest. For her part, Delma seemed totally enraptured by Vigo.

Delma slept, tucked under Vigo's arm. Later, when Vigo fell asleep, Delma slipped out from under his arm, and Max spoke to her.

She told Max her story. She was born of Armenian parents in the Ottoman Empire. The Armenians were treated like vermin by the Turks. Her family fled and settled in Romania to escape the dreadful pogrom of 1915. In 1928, at the age of 14, Delma moved to Austria to take a position in service with a rich family. Then in 1930 both her parents disappeared under suspicious circumstances. She gave up her position to go back to Romania to search for them. She found no trace of her parents, and was brutally attacked by a gang of Hungarians before making her escape and crossing into Germany.

"And that was when you met Vigo?"

She looked at the sleeping priest and smiled. "Father Vigo gave me shelter and support in my grief. He looked after me until I was old enough to look after myself."

"And was he the reason why you joined the Orchestra?"

"I hate the Turks with a passion. They are evil. I wanted to go back there and strike a blow against them. But what could one girl do against so many? Father Vigo showed me a better way. He taught me to control my hatred, to nurture it like a plant, and to find ways of fighting injustice from within. He directed my passion against the Nazis. The Nazis are every bit as evil as the Turks."

She asked Max his story. He told her a little of his own childhood. How his father died in the War in 1916 leaving him alone with his unstable mother in the house in Wittenberg. And he told her about Anna and their plans to marry.

#

As they approached the German border, Vigo insisted that the trio should break up. He sent Max toward the back of the train to find a seat. He set off toward the front.

The train was boarded by a team of four Schupo, German uniform police. They worked their way through the train checking the papers of every passenger.

As Max handed his false identity card to a couple of officers, his knees began to tremble again. He held his breath. The policeman glanced at his identity card and handed it back without comment. Max exhaled. And the policemen moved on.

Max went in search of Vigo and Delma. They had a compartment to themselves near the back of the train. Delma was sleeping on the seats on one side of the compartment. Max sat beside Vigo on the other side.

"I've been meaning to ask you what you told your girlfriend about this trip," said Vigo.

"I told her it was to do with work."

Vigo looked at him through hooded eyes. "Nothing good ever comes of telling lies, and once you start it will be impossible to stop. Lies breed like rabbits, and pretty soon you won't be able to remember what lies you've told and you'll start to contradict yourself."

"What are you saying?"

"You should tell her the truth."

"All of it?"

"As much as you can. Don't tell her anything secret or anything that might hurt her. But you should be honest about what you've been doing."

For a moment Max thought Vigo was hinting that he knew of Max's pact with the Gestapo. But how could he?

"You really think I should tell her about the Orchestra?"

"I do. If she has any spirit of humanity she will applaud you for striking a blow against the Nazis."

Chapter 37

January 1939

Max opened the door to the apartment, removed his shoes and crept inside. With any luck Anna would be in bed asleep.

He found Anna asleep on the sofa, two candles sputtering on the table laid for a meal for two. He squeezed her shoulder to wake her.

She rubbed her eyes. "What time is it?"

"It's after midnight. I'm going to bed. I'm exhausted."

"I thought you'd be home much earlier. What kept you? I made you a special meal, but it's probably ruined by now."

"Never mind, Anna. I had a meal on the train."

She went into the bathroom to freshen up. When she re-emerged he gave her a box of Belgian chocolates that he'd bought for her. She opened the box and selected one. Max helped himself to a couple.

They sat together on the sofa. Anna tucked herself under his arm. "Tell me about Belgium. Was it nice?"

"I suppose it was. Plenty of rolling countryside. Brussels has a lot of old buildings…"

"Do you think it's somewhere you'd like to live? What are the people like?"

"The people seemed normal. There's nothing remarkable about them."

"No Brownshirts, I bet."

"True. They looked like a peaceful lot."

She snuggled closer. "Maybe we could live there after we're married. Madam Krauss said we would travel by train. Did you see any snow-capped mountains?"

"I saw no mountains of any kind."

#

Anna stood by the stove making the coffee. The morning sun streaming through the window caught her hair like a halo. She looked radiant—and happy. It would be a pity to disturb her mood. He sliced the top off his egg. Perhaps he would tell her the truth in the evening after work.

She bent over him. He lifted his face to her and she gave him a kiss on the lips. As she straightened her back she smiled sweetly at him and handed him his passport. "I found this in the wardrobe after you'd gone. Perhaps you could explain to me how you traveled to Brussels without it."

Ah! Time to come clean.

"I need to tell you something, Anna."

"Go on."

"That trip to Brussels had nothing to do with my work."

The coffee pot froze over his cup. "What do you mean?"

"You know how I hate the Nazis, how we both hate them? Well I've decided to do something about that. I've joined the Red Orchestra."

The coffee pot trembled in her hand. "What do you mean, you've joined an orchestra? Don't be crazy! You don't play an instrument and you can't sing."

"It's not a real orchestra. The Red Orchestra is the name the Gestapo has given to the Communist anti-Nazi movement run by friends of Frau Greta's called Libertas and Harro."

Her hand shot to her mouth. "You're a Communist?"

"No, I'm not a Communist, but I've agreed to help them. The trip to Brussels was a courier run. I had to pass a coded intelligence message to the Communists in exile."

"What was in this coded message?"

"I have no idea. My job was to pass it to a contact in Brussels."

She pointed the coffee pot at him like a weapon. "You didn't think to talk to me before joining this orchestra? Didn't you think I would have an opinion about the matter?"

"I'm sorry, Anna. It just seemed like the right thing to do. You know how I hate the Nazis…"

"And aren't we a couple? Shouldn't we talk to one another before making important decisions? How can I trust you if you're going to do things like this behind my back?"

She slammed the coffee pot on the stove, turned to face him, and expanded on the subject of trust. Max held his peace while she delivered a well-deserved tongue-lashing. The color in her cheeks rose. As she vented her feelings he thought she came close to breaking their engagement. That was the last thing he wanted, but if she called off the wedding he would no longer be under the thumb of the Gestapo! But of course that would make no difference to Framzl who would still expect him to complete the task. There was no escaping the Gestapo once they had their claws in you.

Eventually, her words dried up and she became calm. "So tell me how you crossed the border into Belgium without your passport and identity card?"

He showed her his false papers. She went through them slowly, wide-eyed. "I see you're a pastor now!" She snorted. "Couldn't you dream up a better name than Gunther Schlurr?"

"It wasn't my choice, Anna."

She crossed her arms and glared at him. "So suddenly you're a Communist spy, going on missions to foreign countries."

He ignored the sarcasm. "I traveled with an experienced courier."

"A Communist?"

"No, a sympathizer, like me, a Roman Catholic priest called Vigo. He offered to marry us in his church."

"I've already spoken to my own priest, Father Untermair."

"He's an old man, Anna. Vigo's young. You'll like him."

Breakfast passed in silence. They were both going to be late for work.

On the way out the door, she said, "Tell me about this priest."

"Father Vigo. He's good fun."

"Where's his church?"

"St. Angar's Church on Klopstockstrasse. It's not too far from here."

She hesitated. "Well, all right, talk to him. I thought maybe Saturday March 11 would be a good date for our wedding."

"You don't think a later date would be better?"

"Why later? We agreed March, and Saturday is the best day for a wedding. Talk to your priest friend." She opened her bag and pulled out their Reich Marriage Authorization. "Take this with you. He'll need that before he can read the banns."

They reached his tram stop. A tram drew up. As he stepped on board, she called out to him, "Isn't it time you selected your witness?"

Chapter 38

January 1939

Ðe dropped from the moving tram as it turned the corner at Halensee. A black car drew up beside him. A voice said, "Get in."

Sitting in the back of the car, Framzl the Gestapo man, held the door open. Max climbed in. They drove as far as Hohenzollerndamm Bahnhof where they turned right and accelerated south.

"Herr Framzl…"

Framzl put a finger to his lips. Max was grateful for the chance to gather his thoughts. What could he say to this man? He hadn't found the source of the leaflets, but he had met a few members of the Red Orchestra, Frau Greta, Madam Krauss, Vigo, Himpel the dentist, Bruno and Riese, the Communists, and Delma, but he couldn't give any of those away. He would have to stonewall Framzl, play for time.

The car sped past a line of trees, flashing through bright sunlight. On and on they went, further and further from the city center. At last they turned right, and came to a halt in the Grunewald Forest. The driver switched off the engine.

Framzl removed his cap and wiped his forehead, revealing his widow's peak. "Now we can talk. What do you have for me?"

"I'm sorry, Herr Framzl, I haven't discovered where the subversive leaflets are being printed."

"But you have joined the Red Orchestra?"

"Yes, sir. I am a trusted member of the group. I expect to discover the printer location soon."

"You have the names of other members?"

"Only the actress, Libertas."

Framzl frowned. "You were seen boarding a train with a man dressed in tweed."

"That was Frobisher, a distant cousin from London. I promised to show him the city of Cologne."

"You showed him the cathedral?"

"Yes, he was most impressed. They have nothing like it in England."

"I believe the building started in the thirteenth century. Do you recall when it was completed?"

"The foundation stone was laid in 1248, but the building wasn't completed until 1880."

Framzl grunted. "Where is this Englishman now?"

"He's moved on. I believe his next stop was in Belgium and then Holland before returning to England on a ferry."

They drove him back to Halensee where they'd picked him up. Before they released him, Framzl gave Max a telephone number. "Ring me at this number the minute you discover where the printer is located."

#

Max blamed the autobus for his extreme tardiness at work. The autobus was often unreliable, unlike the trams. The trams ran like clockwork.

He unfolded the Reich Marriage Approval and glanced at it. Could the missing stamp and Framzl's signature have been added magically by elves during the night like in one of the Grimm Brothers' stories? No such luck! He hid the form in a drawer of his desk.

As he worked his way through his daily chores he marveled at how light the Gestapo questioning had been, and how easily they swallowed the story about Cousin Frobisher. Anna could teach the Gestapo a thing or two about their interrogation methods!

Working steadily through his pile of requisitions, he rang the railway company to arrange the transport of workers. As he worked an idea began to take shape in his head. Each requisition had been approved, stamped and signed by his boss. The RAD stamp looked identical to the stamp used by the Gestapo. He took out his identity card and compared them. There was no difference. Schnerpf guarded his stamp, keeping it under lock and key in his office—it was the one thing that elevated him above the workers in his department—but if Max could get his hands on it, he could stamp his incomplete marriage approval.

Framzl's signature was another matter. He would worry about that later.

#

During his lunch break, he took a tram to the Standesamt, the main registry office, in Schönstedtstrasse in the north Mitte, and booked a slot for 11:00 a.m. on March 25.

The registrar made an entry in his book. "You have your marriage authorization?"

"It's at home."

"Well, don't forget to bring it with you on the day."

Next, Max took a tram to St. Angar's Church. He found Vigo in the vestry doing a stock take of his candle supplies.

"You know that I'm engaged to be married?"

"To Anna Weber, yes, you mentioned that on the train."

"We've decided it's time to get married. Could I book the church for our wedding on the last Saturday in March?"

Vigo checked the calendar on the wall. "That should be all right."

"And can I ask you to conduct the ceremony?"

Vigo beamed. "I would be honored, my friend. Do you have your marriage authorization?"

"Not with me."

"You'll need to give it to me by Saturday March 4 at the latest. The banns must be read three Sundays in a row before the ceremony."

#

When he got home in the evening he told Anna that he'd reserved a slot at the registry office for the last Saturday in March, and spoken with Father Vigo.

"Why so late?"

"All the earlier Saturdays in March are unavailable..." A lie.

Anna was not pleased, but she accepted the date. "You gave him the authorization?"

"Yes, he has it." Another lie.

"Talk to him again. Make sure he has us in his calendar for that date. Tell him he'll have to start reading the banns on..." she consulted her wall calendar, "... Sunday March 5 at the latest. I don't want anything to spoil our day."

Chapter 39

February 1939

Saturday February 4, Max was in the vestry in St. Angar's Church getting dressed for his second solo delivery run. A young woman came into the church and called Father Vigo's name. She seemed in distress.

Vigo unlocked the file cabinet. "I have to attend to this parishioner. It shouldn't take more than a few minutes. Help yourself to the leaflets."

Max opened the drawers of the file cabinet searching for the parish records. He was hoping to find a folder containing green marriage authorization documents, but they weren't there. He gave up the search. By the time Vigo returned he had the shirt and trousers on, and he was struggling with the clerical collar.

Vigo laughed. He batted Max's hands down. "It's really not that difficult. Let me help you. Hold still."

While Vigo worked on the collar, Max said, "Where do you keep the parish records, the register, the marriage authorizations and so on?"

"We keep them safely under lock and key in the parish house. Why do you ask?"

"I just wondered why you don't keep them here in the file cabinet."

"Those are precious documents. They wouldn't be safe in the vestry. We take the parish register out for weddings and baptisms, and put them back under lock and key immediately afterwards."

The delivery run took just over an hour, leaving Max bathed in sweat. He had dropped the last of the leaflets and was approaching the church when a gray-haired Schupo, municipal policemen, approached him.

118

"Good morning, Father," said the old Schupo. "Where are you going?"

Max hadn't enough breath to reply. He pointed to the church and placed his identity card in the Schupo's open palm.

"Pastor Gunther Schlurr." He rolled the R's. "We haven't seen you here before. You must be new."

"Yes, I'm fresh from the seminary."

"Where from?"

"Wittenberg."

"I didn't know there was a seminary in Wittenberg. And isn't that Lutherstadt Wittenberg now?"

"I still call it Wittenberg. I was born there."

The Schupo handed the identity card back. "Welcome to the district, Father. Father Zauffer will be pleased. I expect we'll be seeing a lot of each other."

Vigo laughed when he heard about the encounter. "That's Gretzke. He's a fixture in the area. Nothing moves around here that he doesn't know about."

"Isn't that going to cause problems? Won't he expect to see me from time to time?"

"Don't worry about Gretzke. He's as thick as a docker's lunch."

#

Every day for the next three weeks, Max stayed late at the office. Waiting until all the other workers had gone home, he took the signature on the receipt that Framzl had signed and tried to copy it using various pens. The signature was elaborate, and made with a calligrapher's pen. He cursed his luck.

He was hoping for a chance to use Schnerpf's stamp, too, but no opportunity presented itself. Schnerpf was always most careful to lock the door whenever he left his office, even for trips to the bathroom.

Each night, before leaving the office and going home, he destroyed all the scraps of paper containing his failed attempts at the elusive signature.

#

Preparations for the wedding occupied all of Anna's spare time. The reception had to be booked, not to mention the flowers, the cake, the invitations, the photographer. She converted the gown she'd worn at the embassy party into a wedding dress by the addition of some lace across the neck.

She continually reminded Max of his responsibilities. "I hope you've ordered the rings. And have you chosen your witness yet? And have you decided what you're going to wear?"

"Not yet."

"Well, get on with it. There's less than five weeks to go."

Lying in bed that night, listening to Anna's rhythmical breathing, Max stared at the ceiling. Anna's wedding preparations were moving forward with the momentum of a juggernaut, and God help anyone who got in the way. Desperately he searched for a way out of his dilemma. Maybe they could leave the country, get married in Belgium. Or he could go to Belgium on his own, simply disappear from Germany. Would anyone find him in Belgium? Probably. The Gestapo's reach was long. He could break off the engagement, but he really wanted to marry Anna. Breaking it off so close to their wedding day would break her heart. He wanted to make her happy. He wanted to look after her as a loving husband and live with her into their old age. But how was that ever going to happen without official approval?

Anna lay beside Max, her eyes closed, breathing rhythmically, feigning sleep. Why has he not chosen a witness? Could he be having second thoughts? Maybe he doesn't want to marry me. Why has he been acting strangely towards me for at least three weeks and why has he been coming home late from work every single evening? Could there be someone else in his life? Doesn't he love me anymore?

Two months have passed since my meeting with Jürgen, the Gestapo man, and I have given him nothing. How long will he wait before handing Max over to those men with the ax handles?

Chapter 40

February 1939

On Tuesday February 28, Max finally gave up on finding the ideal opportunity to get his hands on Schnerpf's rubber stamp. He would have to get the marriage authorization to Father Vigo by the end of the week or there wouldn't be a wedding on March 25. He was going to have to make something happen, and fast!

He waited until mid-afternoon when everyone in the building would be dozing at their desks, then he climbed the stairs to the top floor and pressed the red fire alarm button in the corridor. The fire claxon sounded. He hurried back to his own floor and ran up and down the corridor shouting "Fire!"

The corridor filled with people. Everyone ran for the stairs. Schnerpf waddled past, his moustache twitching, shouting to his staff to leave the building in an orderly fashion. Max hid in the washroom. Once everyone was on the staircase on the way to the ground floor, he emerged and tried Schnerpf's door. It was locked. He took a heavy ashtray from the desk of a colleague and used it to smash open Schnerpf's office door. There was a fire in the building, after all. There could be someone trapped inside. Once inside, he searched for the precious stamp. It was not visible. He tried the drawers of Schnerpf's desk. No sign of the stamp, but one desk drawer was locked. Using the heavy ashtray he bludgeoned the drawer until it opened and there he found the stamp sitting neatly on top of its inkpad.

Quickly, he pulled the marriage approval form from his jacket, placed it on Schnerpf's blotter and applied the Third Reich stamp to both white and green copies. Having accomplished his mission, he put the stamp back in the drawer. Then he placed Schnerpf's wastebasket under his desk, stuffed it with papers, and used his father's lighter to start a fire. Finally, he ran for the staircase and joined his colleagues out in the street.

The fire brigade dealt with the emergency quickly. Schnerpf's desk was badly singed and had to be replaced. Luckily, his precious rubber stamp survived.

The following evening when all his colleagues had left the office, Max made a few more attempts at Framzl's signature. It was hopeless. Neither his pen nor his penmanship was up to the task. If only he could ask Peter Riese, the professional forger, to do the work for him. Then he had a thought. He opened his wallet and pulled out the receipt that the first Gestapo official had given him when he first submitted his marriage application. It wasn't going to be easy to copy, but at least this official had used a normal fountain pen. He practiced the new signature for an hour before taking a deep breath, placing a sheet of carbon paper between the white and green copies, and adding the signature to the document.

He took a tram from the office to St. Angar's Church and handed the green copy of the completed document to Vigo. Vigo ran his eye over it and locked it in his file cabinet.

"You won't forget to read the banns, Father?"

"I won't forget. The first reading will be on Sunday, after ten o'clock mass. I hope you've ordered the rings. They're quite difficult to come by these days."

Max spent the next two lunch hours searching for wedding rings. He had no success until one jeweler suggested he try the antique dealers. None of the antique shops had anything remotely usable. Finally, he bought two old rings from a pawnbroker.

When he showed them to Anna, she turned up her nose at them. "I was hoping for a matching pair, maybe even engraved. These are totally mismatched. One is thick and tarnished. Are you sure it's even gold? The other one is thin as a wire. It looks very old. Where did you get them?"

He made a miserable face and told her how difficult it was to find wedding rings in Berlin.

She threw her arms around his neck. "Never mind, lover. I'd marry you even if all you could find me was a brass curtain ring."

Chapter 41

March 1939

Ten days before the wedding, Max still hadn't found a witness. There was no one at work that he could ask, and his friends had all disappeared two years earlier when they learned that his live-in lover was a *Mischling*. He didn't blame them. No one wanted to be associated with criminal behavior. Max's liaison with Anna was borderline *Blutschande*—blood defilement—an indictable offence for which he could be sent to prison or one of the concentration camps.

He asked Vigo what he should do and Vigo suggested asking Greta if she could think of someone. He wrote Greta's telephone number on a piece of paper and handed it to Max.

Max rang the number. When he explained why he was calling, she answered with a froggy voice. "Come and see me, Max." She gave him her address.

#

Greta looked ill. Wrapped in a blanket, her nose and eyes streaming, she led him into the kitchen. "I'm sure Adam would be happy to be your witness. He's not here. I'll ask him for you when I see him this evening."

"Thank you, Frau Greta. Perhaps I should leave you in peace. You're obviously not well enough for visitors."

"I'd like you to do me a favor," she croaked. "There's a family that I visit every week. David and Matilde Rosen and their daughter, Sophie. They are confined to their apartment. I bring them food and newspapers. I haven't been able to visit them for a week. I'd like you to go in my place."

"Of course, Frau Greta. But why are they confined to their apartment?"

"They are Jews. David has an antique shop—or he had. The Brownshirts have targeted him. They burned out his business on Kristallnacht. They attacked him and broke his arm. I've made up a parcel of food for them. Take it with you. And perhaps you could pick up a newspaper for them, too."

She gave Max the Rosens' address and he left with the parcel.

#

Anna spotted the parcel as soon as he stepped through the apartment door. "What have you got there?"

"It's a food parcel. Frau Greta asked me to deliver it to a housebound family."

"Housebound?"

"They are Jews who've been attacked by the Brownshirts. I thought we might go round there together after our supper. They live on Alvensleberstrasse. It's not far."

Chapter 42

March 1939

Max knocked on the door.

"Who's there?"

"My name is Max Noack."

"And I'm Anna Weber. We have a parcel of food for you."

"And some newspapers."

"Go away. Leave us alone."

Max looked at Anna for ideas to break the impasse.

Anna knocked on the door again. "Frau Greta sent us."

They heard three bolts being drawn. The door opened slowly. Then it was fully opened. "Come in. Quickly."

They stepped inside and Matilde closed and bolted the door.

"I'm sorry," she said. "We can't be too careful. The Brownshirts are making our lives impossible. Come in to the kitchen. I'm Matilde. You are Anna?"

Anna held out her hand, and Matilde shook it. "This is my fiancé, Max."

"Welcome to our home."

Anna handed over the parcel. Matilde was prematurely gray. Her clothes were stained, her hair in need of the attentions of a hairdresser. Her shoes were down at the heel, her stockings laddered. She wore no makeup, not that makeup would have made much of an impression. She might have been able to disguise the wrinkles in her skin, but no amount of face cream could have hidden the bags under her eyes, and the downturn of her mouth looked permanent.

She swept a stray gray hair from her face and opened the parcel. There was meat and vegetables and fruit, and under the food a second small parcel containing a children's reading book. "All this is from Greta, yes?"

Max handed her two newspapers. "Yes. She said to apologize for not visiting last week. She has been sick. She asked us to deliver the parcel."

Matilde looked alarmed. Anna stepped forward. "It's not serious. I'd say it's no more than a heavy cold. I expect she'll see you again next week."

A small face appeared at the kitchen door. Matilde waved and a young girl ran to her mother's side. Anna thought she might be six or seven.

"This is Max and Anna. This is my daughter, Sophie. Sophie, say Hello to Max and Anna."

Sophie hid behind her mother's apron. Anna picked up the book. She found a chair and sat down. "Come and take a look at the book we brought for you, Sophie."

Sophie retreated further behind her mama.

Anna opened the book, holding it up in front of her face. "Oh, no, I think this book is too advanced for someone of your age."

Sophie ran over, sat up on Anna's knee and began to read. She was a good reader for her age. It took her about five minutes to reach the end of the book.

Anna gave her a broad smile. "Well, that was amazing, wasn't it, Max? I would have thought this book was too hard for someone of your age. Either that or you must be older than you look."

"I'm seven."

"That's astonishing, isn't it Max? Who would have thought a 7-year-old girl could read a book like that?"

"I have more books upstairs. Would you like to see them?"

Matilde intervened. "I'm sure Max and Anna will want to go to their own homes…"

Max smiled at Sophie. "We'd love to see what books you have."

Sophie ran upstairs to fetch her books and Max said to Matilde, "Frau Greta tells me you've had trouble with the Brownshirts."

A shadow passed over Matilde's face. "They've destroyed my husband's business. They burned his shop. They beat him and broke his arm."

"Have you thought about leaving Germany?"

"We have applied for permission to travel to France, but the whole process is taking too long."

Sophie came bounding down the stairs, a bunch of books in one hand, a large lifelike doll in the other.

Anna reached out and took the doll. "Who's this?"

"Aschenputtel."

"Well hello, Aschenputtel," said Anna. "My name is Anna." She put the doll to her ear. "Aschenputtel says 'Hello, Anna.'"

Sophie chuckled.

Anna admired Aschenputtel's clothes, her hair, and her neat, flat shoes. Then Sophie jumped up on Anna's knee, and they went through Sophie's books, one by one.

"Can you really read all these?" said Anna.

"Yes, I can," said Sophie. And she read them all.

#

Anna was bubbling after the time she'd spent with young Sophie. "Wasn't she gorgeous! I hope we have a child like that. What do you think, Max? Will we have a little girl like Sophie some day?"

"I'm sure we will, Anna. With your looks and my brains, how could we fail?"

#

The wedding preparations accelerated. Anna sent out invitations to her friends at work and asked one of them—Ebba—to be her witness. Max included Libertas and Harro Schulze-Boysen on his guest list. He explained to Anna that Libertas was the 'L' on the note who had made it all possible. And Libertas had agreed to host their wedding reception in her house in Pankow in the north of Berlin.

Anna was familiar with the affluent area. "What sort of house is it?"

"It's a mansion. Wait 'til you see it!"

Anna checked both lists. "Who else are you inviting?"

"Frau Greta and Ule?"

"They're on my list. What about the Rosens and Madam Krauss?"

"Send them invitations. Madam Krauss might come, but I doubt that the Rosens will venture out."

Max sent an invitation to his mother.

Chapter 43

March 1939

Two days before the wedding, Max called in to Greta Kuckhoff's apartment to meet with Adam. Max thanked him for agreeing to be his witness. Kuckhoff gave him his most charming smile and said he was honored to be asked.

They discussed a few details about the ceremony. Max handed over his two mismatched rings.

Adam slipped them into his waistcoat pocket. "Who have you invited to the ceremony?"

"Just you and Greta and Ule, of course. Anna's parents will be there. Anna's witness is someone from her work. I've invited my mother, but I'm not sure she will attend. She's a bit ... odd."

"What about Libertas and her husband, Harro?"

"They've been invited, and so has Delma."

Bouncing the massive Ule on her knee, Greta said, "That's quite a crowd, isn't it, Ule?"

Ule slid to the floor and crawled about on the carpet, and then stood against the furniture. He looked about ready to take his first steps.

"Speaking of Delma," said Adam, "we have an important piece of intelligence that must be delivered to the Soviets tomorrow. I've asked Delma to drop it in to our contact at the Embassy. I'd like you to pass it to Delma. Do you think you could do that?"

Suddenly there was a lump in Max's sternum. "Isn't there someone else you could ask?"

"It's a simple procedure. You take a cigarette pack to a café, sit beside Delma and let her pick up the pack. That's all you have to do."

"I can't see the need. Why not give the packet to Delma? Why involve a second person?"

"Trust me, there are good reasons for doing it this way. Will you do it?"

"Do I have a choice?"

#

When Max woke and got dressed in the morning, he searched his pockets for the cigarette pack.

"Anna, I had something in my pocket. Did you see it?"

"Something? You mean this?" She placed the cigarette pack on the kitchen table.

Max reached for it, but she picked it up and stepped away. "When did you start smoking?"

"I didn't. I don't. The pack contains a message I have to deliver this afternoon. Give it to me."

"A message from your Communist friends? Who's the message for?"

"You don't need to know that, Anna. Now give it to me." He strode across, grabbed her wrist and took the pack.

#

The café was in a crowded area close to a Friday fish market. Max took a seat at an outside table and ordered coffee. Ten minutes later, Delma came over and sat at his table. She ordered tea.

"Hello Delma." She looked even paler than the last time he'd seen her and she had a nasty raking cough.

"Hello Max. I'm hoping to make it to your wedding tomorrow."

"My last day as a single man, and here I am having a secret liaison with another woman. I don't know what Anna would say if she knew."

"I'm looking forward to meeting your lovely Anna. How long have you known her?"

"We've been together for two years. I knew her for a couple of years before that. How about you? Are you married or do you have a boyfriend?"

"Nothing like that, I'm afraid. I have a nasty disease in my lungs that forbids close intimate contact." Max gave her a quizzical look and she added, "It's called Tuberculosis."

She reached under the table. He did the same and handed the cigarette packet to her. She finished her coffee and left.

The whole process was surreal.

He watched her disappear into the crowd. But as he watched, he noticed three men, all dressed alike in beige coats, maneuvering around her.

Gestapo!

He jumped from the table and ran after her to warn her. If he got to her in time, she could get rid of the evidence.

He was too late. The three men closed in and grabbed her. A black car drove up. They bundled Delma in and drove away.

Chapter 44

March 1939

Taking a tortuous route to throw off any possible followers, Max hurried back to Greta and Adam's apartment. Adam opened the door.

Max was out of breath. "Delma was taken by the Gestapo."

"You saw this? Did she have time to deliver the packet?"

"Not unless the drop was in the square in front of the café."

"It was in the fish market."

"She never made it that far. There were three of them. They seemed to know who she was."

Adam swore. He bit his lip hard enough to draw a drop of blood.

"You could send the message again. Let me deliver it."

"I'm not worried about the message, Max. To hell with the message. Delma is too fragile to withstand interrogation."

"You think she might talk?"

"I'm afraid she might die in their hands. The only names she knows in Berlin are yours and Vigo's."

Max remembered how close Delma and Vigo had been on the train. "I can tell you she won't give them Vigo's name."

Greta came in to the room wiping her hands on a towel. "Is everything all right?"

Adam said, "Delma's been picked up by the Gestapo."

"The message was encrypted. Without the code, there's no way they can read it. Delma doesn't know the code, and she can't identify any of us."

"Apart from Max here and Father Vigo."

"She won't give them Vigo," said Greta. "Have you seen the two of them together?"

"So Max is the only one at risk."

Max stood. "Delma's at risk. You said so yourself, Adam. We'll have to cancel the wedding. We can't have all those members of the Orchestra together in one place. It's too risky."

Greta smiled grimly. "What makes you think Anna will let you cancel?"

Adam stood up. "We mustn't cancel. To do so would cast suspicion on us all. No, we must carry on as if nothing has happened and hope that Delma holds her nerve. I'll ring Libertas and Harro and let them know what's happened."

Three minutes later, Adam replaced the telephone. "Harro says they'll come."

Greta said, "How does Libertas feel about the reception?"

"She's happy for that to go ahead."

#

Max woke in the morning after about two hours sleep and with a searing headache.

Anna laughed at him. "I can see you had a bad night. I didn't sleep too well myself. But never mind, you'll be able to catch up on your sleep tonight." She winked at him.

She really had no idea. He'd lain awake long into the night worrying about Delma and about what was to come the next day. Would the marriage be legal if it was based on a forged signature? If not then all their children would be illegitimate—if they ever managed to have any. The Gestapo might even prevent the wedding from taking place. The reading of the banns would have alerted them. They must surely know what he'd done. He was facing the prospect of a disastrous wedding ceremony. Anna would be horrified if the Gestapo broke it up and prevented the marriage.

Dressed in his best suit, Max made his way on foot to the Kuckhoffs' apartment. Greta and Adam had agreed that he could use their apartment as his bachelor base prior to the ceremony.

Adam was dressed in a neat 3-piece suit, the wedding rings safely tucked away in his waistcoat pocket. Dressed in a housecoat, Greta was attending to her large offspring. "How are you feeling, Max?" The outfit she'd selected for the ceremony—a light knee-length dress with a red floral pattern—hung on a hook behind the bathroom door where Ule couldn't put his grubby hands on it.

"Just a bit nervous."

Adam slapped him on the back. "That's normal."

#

Libertas hugged Anna like a long lost sister when they met. She had offered her house to Anna and her witness, Ebba, as their base of operations. Anna asked her hostess if she could borrow some foundation cream.

Libertas laughed. "I can do better than that, child. Come with me." She took Anna and Ebba to her private rooms and sat Anna down at an actor's makeup station. Anna had never seen so many different creams, eyeliners, and lipsticks. There were unlabeled jars of mysterious creams whose purpose she could only guess at. Libertas opened a few and showed her how to use them.

When all three women were content with Anna's makeup, Ebba helped Anna to put her wedding dress on.

"Isn't that what you wore to the embassy ball?" said Libertas, rather tactlessly, Anna thought.

"Yes, I've adjusted it slightly. Do you like it?"

"I love it," said Libertas.

While she waited for Adam to arrive, Anna showed Ebba her wedding presents: a cuckoo clock from Ebba, a complete set of bed linen from her own parents, an antique vase from Libertas, the latest model electric kettle from the Kuckhoffs, and a set of pots and pans from Frau Noack.

#

Adam picked up Max from his apartment and drove him in his battered green Horch to the Schulze-Boysen's house. The house was no more than a stone's throw from the registry office. Anna's witness, Ebba, was wearing a blue dress with a heart-shaped neckline. Anna was wearing bright red lipstick and rather more make-up than Max was used to. She looked stunning, dressed in a long, fine wool dress in cream, decorated with gold thread and lace that looked vaguely familiar. She wore matching gold sandals.

Anna introduced Ebba to Adam. Adam shook her hand warmly, flashing his charming smile.

From there, Adam drove them the short distance to the city registry office. The office was busy. Hordes of people stood around in the corridors and outside on Schönstedtstrasse with anxious looks on their faces, waiting their turn to get married.

Anna threw her arms in the air. "My God, Max. Look at the crowds. We're going to be here for hours."

Max was secretly pleased. Perhaps a registrar under pressure wouldn't scrutinize a Gestapo signature too closely. "We have an appointment for eleven o'clock. I don't expect they'll delay us too long."

"It's already past eleven!"

By 11:30 the crowd had thinned slightly. A clerk called their names and they hurried into the registrar's office.

"Sorry to keep you waiting," said the registrar. "You have your Authorization?"

Max handed over the document and the registrar glanced at it.

"These are your witnesses? What are your names?"

Adam and Ebba gave their names, and the registrar took them through the ceremony at the speed of lightning. Once they had exchanged rings, everyone signed the register, the next couple and their witnesses hurrying in as they left.

"What just happened?" said Anna.

Max laughed. "I think we got married."

She threw her arms around his neck and kissed him on the lips.

Adam put a hand on Max's shoulder and pulled them apart. "You can do that later, you two. Give me the rings." Anna and Max slipped the rings off their fingers and handed them to Adam. They would be needed again in the church. "Now get in the car."

Chapter 45

March 1939

Adam drove to the Schulze-Boysen mansion where he dropped Anna off and picked up Max's mother. Then he drove Max and his mother to the church. Libertas and Harro had made their sleek Daimler-Benz saloon car available for the bride and her father.

Max was pleased to see his mother there, looking herself again, not happy, exactly, but he could tell her melancholia had lifted. She wore an outlandish outfit in canary yellow that she must have bought for the occasion.

On the stroke of noon, Max and Adam took their places side by side at the top of the aisle. A warm breeze wafted through the open door of the church. Max couldn't have felt any worse if he'd been waiting to face a firing squad. Getting through the civil ceremony had been a minor miracle, but he had a premonition that his luck had run out and a disaster was about to befall him. A bead of sweat ran down his back.

Adam said, "Take it easy, Max. I'm sure she'll be here in a minute or two." He gripped Max's arm. "Are you all right? You look a bit queasy."

Max waved a hand. He was having difficulty breathing.

"Sit down for a minute. Catch your breath."

Max sat on the pew. He wiped his brow.

Adam babbled on. "It's just nerves. I was the same when I married my first wife. I was a bit calmer the second time around, and Greta was a breeze. Mind you, Greta was four months pregnant at the time. Take a few deep breaths. You'll be fine."

Sitting directly behind Adam, Max's mother touched him on the shoulder. "Did I hear you say you're divorced?"

"Yes, that's true."

Sitting beside her with Ule squirming on her knee, Greta smiled. "I'm Adam's third wife, Frau Noack."

Frau Noack tutted. "Divorced people cannot be witnesses in a Christian marriage. You'll have to find someone else, Max."

Adam hurried into the vestry. "The bridegroom's mother says a witness can't be divorced. Is that true?"

Vigo was half dressed in his priestly garments. "Yes, that's true. Who is Max's witness?"

"I am."

"You'll have to find him someone else."

Adam went back to his place. "It's true. I can't be your witness." He looked around the church. "The only other males here are the photographer and the usher. You could ask one of them. Or you could wait and ask Harro. I'll have a word with him when he gets here."

On the bride's side of the church sat Anna's mother corralled amongst a murmuring gaggle of Anna's workmates, wearing bright colors and strange hats. Amongst the guests, red seemed to be the predominant color. Greta wore a red floral dress and red hat, two of Anna's workmates wore red, Adam Kuckhoff and the bridegroom wore matching red ties. The exceptions were the bride's mother, who wore beige, Ebba in blue, and Max's mother in her bright yellow suit and matching hat.

Near the door at the back of the church, the photographer fiddled with his camera. Then the smooth purr of the Schulze-Boysens' car signaled the arrival of the bride. A murmur ran through the assembled guests. The organist, who had been playing something unrecognizable, launched into the wedding march with gusto. Father Vigo emerged from the vestry carrying a book. Max snuck a glance over his shoulder and saw Anna walking down the aisle on her father's arm. Everyone stood up. The photographer took a few pictures as the bride and her escort strode down the aisle, followed by Ebba.

Max's knees turned to rubber. Adam grabbed his arm and held him up.

Libertas and Harro slipped into the church and joined the congregation on Max's side in the pew behind Greta. Adam went back to explain the situation and hand over the rings to Harro. Looking very smart in his Luftwaffe uniform, Harro joined Max in the first pew.

The bride and her father arrived at the altar. She was wearing the same dress, but had added a white veil. She knelt on the kneeler to the left. Max knelt beside her. She smiled at him through the veil. He did his best to smile back.

The organ music died away, the usher closed the church doors, and Vigo began the ceremony. "Dearly beloved, we are gathered here in the sight of God to witness the joining together..."

Max tuned out, praying silently that nothing would go wrong, that Vigo would hurry and complete the ceremony.

"...if anyone here knows any reason why these two people may not marry, let him speak now or forever hold his peace."

Vigo paused. Max held his breath. No one spoke. Max exhaled. And Vigo continued. "Please stand."

Max and Anna stood.

"Do you, Max-Christian Noack, take this woman, Anna Weber..."

They repeated the words of the wedding vows. They exchanged rings. Vigo smiled and raised his voice. "I now pronounce—"

The doors at the back of the church flew open with a loud crash. Four men in jackboots and gray uniforms charged down the aisle.

One of them shouted, "There he is."

Vigo held up a hand like King Canute trying to turn back the tide. "This is the house of God."

The Gestapo men charged toward Max. Max braced himself, but they pushed him aside and seized Harro Schulze-Boysen. Libertas shouted and beat the nearest man with her fists. The young women on the bride's side of the church all screamed. Anna's witness fainted. Anna went to her aid.

The Gestapo hauled Harro down the aisle and out to a waiting Kübelwagen while Libertas screeched like a banshee caught in a bear tap. Max grabbed Vigo's arm. "For God's sake, man, finish the ceremony."

Part 3

Chapter 46

March 1939

"I now pronounce you man and wife," said Vigo.

Anna tossed her bouquet over her head. No one caught it. Then the couple and Ebba rushed into the vestry to sign the church register. Anna wondered fleetingly if it mattered that they had only one witness signature. Then she remembered that they had two signatures on the official register in the registry office in Schönstedtstrasse. They were definitely married.

When they emerged from the church, the photographer took a few pictures. He seemed as shocked as everyone else. Anna thought all her wedding photographs would probably be blurred. While Adam and Anna's mother did their best to console Libertas, Max's mother gravitated toward Anna's father, who took her arm.

Anna clung to Max. "Your mother looks pale, and I don't like that distant look in her eyes."

Max said, "Don't worry about Mother. That yellow outfit she's wearing makes her look paler that usual, and her eyes always look like that."

Adam asked Libertas if they should make alternative arrangements for the reception. Libertas was furious. She insisted that the reception would go ahead as planned. Everything was ready. She wasn't going to let the Gestapo ruin the young people's wedding day.

The Schulze-Boysen's car was unavailable. The key was in Harro's pocket. Libertas took the front passenger seat in Adam's car.

Max, Anna and Greta all squashed together like sardines in the back with Ule on Greta's knee.

Adam started the car. He checked his back seat passengers before moving off. "Everyone all right back there?"

Libertas replied, a snarl in her deep voice, "They're fine, Adam. Just get us home as quickly as you can."

Ule formed an instant attachment to Anna, crawling onto her knee from Greta's. Anna held onto the infant to stop him from falling off. "What happened? Why did the police arrest Max's witness?"

Libertas whispered, "*That witness* was Harro, my husband."

"I'll explain later," said Max.

The maid was waiting for them at the front door, her eyes red from crying. Libertas swept past her into the house before the girl could say anything.

Anna and Max heard Libertas's howl before they reached the door. They stepped inside.

The mansion had been ransacked. Everything that could be moved had been thrown on the floor in every room. Only three books remained on the bookshelves that covered three of the four walls in the study. The rest were piled high in a mountain on the carpet. White boot marks littered the carpets in the hall and on the staircase. Following them back to their source, Anna came to the kitchen where the floor looked like a giant cake in the making with ingredients tossed in a heap and stamped into the ground by heavy boots.

Max called Anna to the front parlor. The food for their reception lay scattered on the floor. Something stirred in Anna's stomach. She righted one of the chairs and sat down.

Max hunkered down beside her. "Anna? Are you all right? Should I fetch a glass of water?"

"Go outside and send the guests away. I don't want them to see this."

"What should I tell them?"

"I don't know. Think of something. Tell them the reception has been called off."

"What about Ebba?"

"All of them. Just send them all home."

More howls from Libertas in the upstairs rooms.

Adam climbed the stairs after Libertas. Greta took one quick look around and went into the garden with Ule.

Anna found the maid, Pauletta. "Who did this?"

The maid whimpered. "Three men in gray uniforms. They had a piece of paper. They said it gave them the right to search the house."

Anna was distracted by the thought that just three men could cause so much mess in—what—an hour? Through the front window she saw Max standing at the gate. When the wedding guests arrived in two taxis, he gave them her message. Ebba took some persuading, but both taxis drove away. Anna's parents arrived in their car and hurried into the mansion. Anna rushed into her father's arms.

"I warned you," said Anna's mother. "Didn't I warn you not to marry him?"

Anna left her parents in disgust and went looking for Max.

Libertas came back down the stairs accompanied by Adam Kuckhoff.

Greta stood by the front door keeping a firm grip on her wriggling, whining offspring. "I'd like to get home as soon as we can, Adam. I can't let Ule loose in the house. He'd spread the mess around even further."

Libertas waved an arm at Adam. "Greta's right. You need to get home."

Adam nodded. "I'll drop in to Arvid's house and warn him. We should ring the Communists and Dr. Himpel." He picked up the telephone on the hallstand.

"Leave that to me, Adam. That telephone is not safe." Libertas looked distracted. "I'm going to need help cleaning up all this mess."

"We can help," Anna said.

"Nonsense." Libertas ran a hand across her face, leaving a streak of baking soda on her cheek. "There are people who do that sort of work for a living. You've already suffered enough on your wedding day."

Adam offered to take Max and Anna home, but Libertas had other ideas. "Take Greta and the boy home, Adam. I'll look after these two."

Chapter 47

March 1939

Adam drove away with Greta and Ule. Libertas led Anna into the back parlor. Max followed.

Anna perched on a chaise Longue. "I wanted to thank you for helping us with our marriage application, Frau. We would never have got permission to marry without your help."

Libertas hunted around and came up with an unbroken bottle of schnapps. She poured some into a glass and handed it to Anna. "You look a bit pale, my dear. Drink this. It will make you feel better."

Anna was a little lightheaded. She took a sip. The schnapps started its long journey down her gullet to her stomach.

Libertas went off to make a telephone call. Max found a glass and poured himself a glass of schnapps. He sat beside Anna. They held hands.

Anna looked into Max's eyes. "What happened? You said you would explain."

"I will, my love, but not now."

Libertas returned. She said, "I need to speak with your husband alone for a moment."

My husband!

Anna waved consent with her glass. Max followed Libertas out the door.

Anna took a mouthful. It chased after the first one. For a woman who'd just had her home destroyed by a Gestapo demolition crew, Libertas was strangely calm, although her eyes seemed unusually bright.

Libertas and Max returned within a few moments. His glass was empty. Libertas refilled it, poured a glassful for herself and drank half of it. "Max tells me he has spoken to you about what Harro and I do."

Anna took a third sip. "You're an actress and Harro works in the Air Ministry for the Luftwaffe."

"That's right, but that's not all we do."

"Oh, you mean all that other stuff with the Communists."

"We are not Communists, but we don't like the Nazis. We do what we can to disrupt them. We resist."

"And Max helps with that. Yes, he told me." Anna swallowed some more schnapps and closed her eyes. She was tired.

"Anna, open your eyes. Look at me, Anna."

Anna opened her eyes. Libertas was blocking her view. She couldn't see Max.

"Listen to me Anna. I'm going to ask you some questions. You need to answer them truthfully. Do you understand?"

What did this actress woman want?

"Tell me you understand. You must tell me the truth."

"I'm not a child. Ask your questions."

"Very well. Did you tell anyone about the Red Orchestra?"

"No."

"Maybe someone at work?"

"No. Nobody."

"Did you mention my name to anyone—anyone at all? Think carefully before you reply."

"I told Ebba that you were hosting the reception."

"You told her my name?"

"I think so. Yes, I'm sure I did."

"What else did you tell her about me?"

"Nothing. I told her nothing."

"You're certain?"

"I may have said you're an actress." She closed her eyes again. It had been a long, long day. She just wanted it to end.

Libertas gathered her petticoats and strode to the door. "Wait for me here. I have a visitor coming, and I'd like you to meet her. Her name's Emmy."

"Who is she, this Emmy?"

"She's an actress like me. She's the one who arranged your marriage authorization."

"I thought that was you, Frau Libertas."

Libertas patted Anna's hand. "I passed on your request, dear. Emmy was the one who arranged it."

Libertas left the room, and Max sat beside Anna again.

Anna rolled her eyes. "Madam Krauss passed our marriage application to Frau Greta, Frau Greta passed it to Libertas, Libertas passed it to her friend Emmy. Perhaps Emmy passed it to the German football team."

Emmy was a pretty, slightly plump woman with wisps of gray in her hair. She spent a few minutes talking to Libertas in private before Libertas presented her to Anna.

Anna did a passable curtsey while holding on to the furniture. "I want to thank you, Frau Emmy, for arranging our marriage authorization."

Emmy smiled at her. "You're welcome, child. How could any force or device of man stand against the power of young love? And besides, it wasn't I that made the arrangements. That was my husband, Hermann."

"Well, please thank Herr Hermann from us," said Max.

"I will," said Emmy.

By the time Emmy had gone, Harro's car had been returned to the house. Libertas offered to drive the newlyweds to their apartment.

"We can take the S-Bahn," said Max.

Anna struggled to her feet. "Thank you, Frau Libertas. That's very kind."

Chapter 48

March 1939

Max and Anna took the autobus to Lutherstadt Wittenberg the next day. Max's mother had agreed to let them spend the first two weeks of their married life in her home. Anna was enjoying the ride. Since the wedding ceremonies—especially the one in the church—she felt utterly changed. She had always wanted to be a married woman. And Max was the only man she had ever wanted to marry. She held his hand tight while looking out the window watching hedgerows, fields and small towns roll by.

"You do realize who that was?" said Max. "That was Emmy Göring, the wife of Minister Hermann Göring."

"So our request to Madam Krauss passed through three pairs of hands before reaching someone who could do something about it, and that someone was Hermann Göring?"

"The second most powerful man in the Fatherland." He squeezed her hand. "That's how important you are to me."

"Which of them gave you... that book... to read?" she whispered. Apart from one old woman sitting right at the front, there was no one else on the bus, but Anna was being careful.

"Libertas. Did you see the number of books she had in the study?"

"A mountain of them. And bookcases to go with them. What do you think the Gestapo were searching for?"

"Heaven knows. Evidence against Harro, I suppose."

"I thought they might be looking for the printer that was used to print this." She pulled a sheet of paper from her handbag, unfolded it and placed it in Max's lap.

Max leapt in the seat as if he'd seen a rattlesnake. "Put that away. Where did you get it?"

"I found it behind the cushion on the chaise longue."

"Put it away. If anyone sees you with that you could be arrested."

She folded the leaflet and put it back in her bag. "You were going to explain what happened in the church."

Max took her hand. "The Schulze-Boysens, Harro and Libertas, are leading members of the Orchestra…"

"I understand that much."

"Someone must have told the Gestapo that they would be at the wedding together. The Gestapo took the opportunity to arrest Harro and conduct a search of their home."

"That was why Libertas asked me if I'd mentioned their names to anyone at work? She thought I was the one who alerted the Gestapo."

"Unwittingly, yes."

"But I didn't."

"I know, but there were very few people who knew they would be there."

"Greta and Adam knew. You knew."

"Yes, and Father Vigo."

#

Anna was enchanted by Max's family home. "Look at those eaves, the dormer windows, the leaded panes."

"It's an old building."

"It's not just old, it's beautiful, Max. Where's your soul?"

Max grunted. "You wouldn't think it was so lovely if you'd spent your childhood in there."

Anna remembered some of the tales that Max told her about his childhood. His father had gone to war when he was three and never came back. His mother had been far from easy to live with. "That all happened a long time ago. I'm sure our time here will be full of joy and happiness."

Max knocked on the door. Anna hung from his arm while they waited. No one came.

"Use your key."

Max opened the door.

Chapter 49

March 1939

The dark hallway was just what she expected. She had been in old buildings even darker than this. Her father had explained that natural light was not considered important by architects in earlier centuries, even though they had only candles in those days. The temperature was a surprise. Outside it was like summer, inside the house was winter.

She slipped her hand into Max's. He took her into the front parlor. This room was just as cold and nearly as dark as the hall. Anna took an instant dislike to the period furniture, the dark red carpet, and the heavy curtains. She loved the room in spite of the lack of light. It had a high ceiling, maybe close to three meters. One look at the windows was enough to make her heart flutter. If the house were hers—if ever she inherited it—she would toss out all the furniture and replace the curtains and carpet with something bright, but not too modern.

The kitchen was brighter than the rest of the house, but only because it had black and white tiles in a checkerboard pattern on the floor. It had the same high ceiling as the parlor. The range was black, the heavy porcelain sink with one tap, like something from the dark ages! The shelving on the walls looked like they'd been there since the house was built. This was not what a kitchen should look like. Those tiles would have to go. The old range would be removed and a modern cooker put in its place. The shelves could stay, but they would have to be painted in a bright color, white or yellow, maybe.

"Wait here. I'll go and see if I can find her."

While Max was upstairs, Anna had a closer look at the kitchen.

The skirting boards were filthy and showed definite signs of rodent activity. Higher up the walls there were cobwebs gathering dust. A long brush would sort those out in a trice.

Max returned with his mother.

"You've found the kitchen, I see. The range is lit. Why not put the kettle on and make your mother-in-law a cup of tea."

Anna lifted the kettle from the range. She put it in the sink, removed the lid and turned on the tap. The water pipe rattled and banged against the wall.

"You need to hold the pipe and turn the tap on slowly. Here let me show you." Frau Noack turned off the tap. Then she placed a hand on the water pipe where it was bracketed to the wall. She turned the tap on slowly. The rattling started but then died. The water from the tap was dark brown.

"You can't drink that!" said Anna.

"It won't do you any harm, girl. I've been drinking it for fifty years and it's never done me any harm."

#

Anna lay in Max's arms wearing her new nightdress. This was not how she'd imagined her wedding night. The bed was a 4-poster without a canopy. It was freezing. Max's feet were like ice blocks. And dark shapes were moving in the dusty cobwebs above their heads. She'd insisted on leaving the light on.

She tried to remain quiet and let Max sleep, but after an hour and a half he was still awake. "Why did your mother put us in this room?"

"It used to be my room."

"I hate it."

"It is a bit cold. Come closer. I'll try to warm you."

She couldn't come any closer without coming into contact with his icy feet.

"It's not the cold I'm worried about, Max. It's those things over our heads."

"When I slept here, there was a canopy."

148

"That would have been better."

"Not really. I could hear the spiders scuttling about on there."

She shivered. "How could you sleep?"

"You get used to it."

"I never would. You'll have to do something about it in the morning."

Chapter 50

March 1939

In the morning, when Anna attempted to make breakfast for Max, Frau Noack pushed her away from the stove. "I'll do that. Go and sit down."

Anna sat at the table and Frau Noack served a breakfast of oatmeal and tomatoes in olive oil with thin slices of cheese.

"This looks lovely, Frau Noack, but Max and I usually have eggs in the morning."

"You can have what you like in your own apartment, my girl. You're in my house now. Here, we have oatmeal, cheese, and tomatoes in olive oil. It's healthy food. Tell her, Max-Christian."

Max stuffed his mouth with oatmeal.

After breakfast, Anna asked Frau Noack if she had a long broom.

"Whatever for?"

"I want to clear the cobwebs in the bedroom. I don't like spiders."

"Spiders will do you no harm. And they keep the flies down. Tell her, Max-Christian."

"I'm sorry, Frau, but I can't sleep with spiders over my head. I had to leave the light on all night."

"You did what? Max-Christian, tell me you didn't leave the light on all night."

"Yes, Mama, I'm afraid we did."

"Well, that is most inconsiderate of you, girl. I hope you won't do that again."

"Not if you let me clear away the cobwebs with a long broom."

Later, Anna was in the bathroom. Frau Noack knocked on the door. "Whatever are you doing in there, girl? Other people need to use the bathroom, you know."

Anna found a broom. She wrapped a scarf around her head, stood on a chair and swept the cobwebs in the high ceiling of the bedroom. Spiders fell and scuttled about. Max stamped on them. When she'd finished, she attempted to open the window to allow the dust to escape. The hinges on the window were rusted and stiff. She asked Max to help.

He gave her his doe-eyed look. "I don't think Mama will be happy."

"I don't care. I've raised a lot of dust. We need to open the window."

He forced the window open a fraction. "That's all I can manage."

#

They went for a walk before lunch.

"Your mother doesn't like me."

"Of course she likes you, Anna. Everybody does."

Anna snorted.

"Pay no attention to her. She's harmless. Really. And she's delighted to have us stay with her."

"Well, she doesn't show it."

Max laughed. "She does have her strange ways. Whatever you do, never cut your fingernails in the kitchen."

#

Anna insisted on being allowed to use the stove to make a midday meal for Max. "We're married now. It's my job to make his meals."

Frau Noack conceded the kitchen stove to her, reluctantly. She watched everything Anna did, offering unwanted suggestions every few minutes. After the meal, Anna and Max washed up. They replaced the crockery in the presses and on the shelves. Frau Noack allowed them to do all this and then she pounced. Anna had put everything in the wrong places and look at the untidy state of the kitchen!

Anna threw her dishcloth onto a chair and stomped out of the kitchen.

#

They went for another walk arm-in-arm around the town in the afternoon.

"I'm not sure I can live with your mother for two whole weeks, Max. She's a witch."

"She's been living alone for so many years she's not used to having another woman in the house. She'll come around eventually."

"I may strangle her first."

"You may strangle me first. There's something I have to tell you. I made up my mind to tell you weeks ago, but I thought I'd wait until we were married."

Anna's stomach did a somersault. She let go of his arm. "What is it? Tell me."

"You're not going to like it."

Her mind went into a spin. He was going to tell her something horrible. Was he going to admit there was another woman in his life? "Max—"

"Remember I told you that I joined the Red Orchestra to strike a blow against the Nazis?"

"Yes."

"That's not exactly why I joined. I joined because the Gestapo forced me to."

Not another woman!

"How could they force you to? I don't understand."

"That day when I collected our marriage authorization from Herr Framzl, he said he would only complete the authorization if I joined the Orchestra and spied on them for him."

"But he completed the authorization. How else could we have got married?"

Max shook his head. "He withheld his signature and the official stamp. I used a stamp from the office and I... I forged the signature on the Authorization."

"You what? You forged a signature! What are you saying? Are you saying we're not properly married?"

"No, we are married. The church wedding is valid..."

"But not the official one in the registry office?"

"That could be contested if the registrar ever finds out." He held up his palms. "But I'm sure he won't find out."

Anna stared at him. What had she married? "Oh, Max, how could you? How could you spoil our wedding day? You're a... a monster."

"You had your heart set on a March wedding. What else could I do?"

"You could have discussed it with me first."

"Yes, I'm sorry. I didn't want you to be disappointed. I was trying to make everything right for you."

"You're an idiot, Max-Christian Noack. My mother warned me not to marry you. I should have listened to her."

"I'm sorry."

Anna took a deep breath. "Tell me the whole story from the beginning."

When he'd finished, she took his arm again. "I suppose you had no choice. That Gestapo man is a bastard. We should complain to Libertas, get her to tell Frau Emmy Göring what he did."

"We can't do that, Anna. I'd have to admit that I was a Gestapo informer. They'd probably shoot me."

"Oh, you're right. So how do you really feel about Libertas and Harro and Frau Greta and the others in the Red Orchestra?"

"I'm with them all the way. They're all friends, and I believe in what they're doing. I would die before I'd betray any of them now."

Frau Noack was waiting for them. "Who opened the window in the bedroom?"

"I did, Mama."

"You know how I feel about open windows, Max-Christian."

"I asked him to," said Anna. "We needed to let in some fresh air."

"You should have asked for my permission first."

"Would you have allowed it?" said Max.

"Yes, if you'd explained your reasons."

Anna snorted.

Chapter 51

April 1939

The Tuesday after Anna's wedding, Vigo was in his church when a black car drew up outside. A tall man with a crew-cut wearing a full-length leather coat came into the church and flashed a Gestapo identity disc. "You are Father Vigo?"

"Yes."

"You married a young couple last Saturday. Am I right?"

"Anna and Max-Christian Noack, yes."

"Show me the Authorization form."

Vigo went to the parish house and found the green form. He handed it over.

The Gestapo man ran his eyes over the document. "Come with me."

They drove him to Gestapo headquarters, took him to the basement and threw him into a cell.

Vigo was mystified. He wouldn't have been surprised if they arrested him for subversive activities, for aiding and abetting enemies of the State, for distributing Communist literature, but how could they object to a wedding ceremony?

The place was cold and lacked a window. There was a persistent smell that he tried hard not to identify. Everything about the place spoke to Vigo of the hundreds of unfortunates that had passed his way. He blessed himself and prayed for the souls of those departed.

They let him stew in the cell for two hours. Then they took him to a room with 'Department B Race and Ethnic Affairs' painted on the glass. He was made to stand in front of a desk. Behind the desk sat a tall man in uniform wearing the death's head insignia of the SS on his cap. On the wall behind him, a picture of the Führer and two swastika standards.

"This authorization..." He held the green form at arm's length between finger and thumb. "Where did you get it?"

"The bridegroom obtained it from this department."

"It's a forgery. Didn't you check the signature?" He waved the form at Vigo. The priest stepped forward and took it.

Vigo examined the signature. It consisted of a series of loops and reverse lines as illegible as any signature he'd ever seen. "I can't read it. Was it not signed by one of your men?"

"It's a forgery, and a crude one at that."

"I assumed the registrar would have checked the authorization before their civil marriage in the registry office."

The Gestapo man removed his cap, wiped his forehead and put his cap back on. "That is not your concern. You are obliged to check with this office before performing religious marriage ceremonies."

Vigo recalled an ancient rambling letter from the authorities along those lines, but he knew of no priest that double-checked the green forms. He spread his hands in a gesture of appeasement. "I'm sorry, but I didn't think it was necessary. Every priest that I know takes the green form as an official sanction."

The Gestapo man waved for Vigo to hand it back. Vigo did so, and it disappeared into a desk drawer.

Two men in leather coats came in. They took Father Vigo by the arms and took him back to his cell. Once inside the cell, they closed the door and beat him, taking it in turns. Most of the blows were to his body, but some were to his face. The beating was like a performance, carefully choreographed, designed to impart some brutal message. It took no more than 10 minutes.

The original interrogator reappeared. He waved the other two away. "Release him."

Vigo fell to his knees. He was bleeding from the nose and eyes.

"Let that be a lesson to you. Be sure to follow correct procedures in future. Now get out of my sight."

#

Vigo went directly to the hospital where a nurse bathed his facial wounds with a damp cloth. She told him that he would be left with some scarring. The Gestapo certainly knew how to make a lasting impression!

He took a tram to the office of the registrar in Schönstedtstrasse. The registrar confirmed that he had been summoned by Kurt Framzl of the Department of Race and Ethnic Affairs and similarly berated. He had made the same mistake, but when his staff checked the form against others on file they were able to satisfy themselves that the signature was indeed a forgery.

"A very unusual case," said the registrar. "I understand that the couple was attempting to frustrate the Nuremburg Laws in respect of racial protection of the German bloodstock."

Next, Vigo took a tram to Greta Kuckhoff's apartment. She was shocked by his appearance. "You should see a doctor."

"I've come from the hospital, Greta. I'll be fine. The Gestapo beat me because I performed Anna and Max's wedding ceremony. They said the couple's marriage authorization was a forgery."

"That makes no sense, Father. Max and Anna's union was sanctioned at the highest level. This Gestapo officer must be playing games with you."

"To what end?"

"I can't imagine. Perhaps he suspects something about your leaflet delivery route and wanted to give you a fright."

Vigo shook his head and grimaced. "That makes no sense. I've spoken to the registrar and he confirms that the document really is a forgery."

Chapter 52

April 1939

𝕬 week after the wedding, Libertas, whose hearing was on permanent alert, picked up the sound of an engine as it approached the gate. "It's Harro."

The maid opened the door and Harro fell into Libertas's arms.

"Pay the taxi driver. I have no money. I promised him double fare if he drove me home."

Libertas paid the driver before joining her husband in the study. The room had been tidied, the books all returned to their shelves. They embraced like labor camp survivors. He was dressed in the uniform he'd been wearing when he was arrested. His body odor was overwhelming.

"Tell me what happened. Did they beat you?"

"No beatings. They wouldn't dare. They have no concrete evidence. I was interrogated endlessly. They allowed me very little sleep."

"What did you tell them?"

"I told them nothing."

Libertas ran a finger over his face, tracing some new lines around his mouth. "They searched the house while we were at the church, made a frightful mess. Poor Pauletta nearly had a heart attack. They found nothing. Do you know why they let you go?"

"I assume the Air Ministry demanded my release. Or perhaps they simply gave up when I refused to talk."

"I asked Emmy to help. Hermann may have had words with Heinrich Himmler. I asked her to put a word in for Delma as well. Did you see Delma in there?"

"I saw no one but my interrogators. I heard nothing but questions.

Tell me no one else was taken. Did Max and Anna complete their wedding?"

"Vigo completed the wedding ceremony. But you may have to go back to the church and sign the parish register. They've gone to Wittenberg on their honeymoon."

Harro was starving. He'd had had very little to eat during his ordeal. Pauletta prepared a meal while Harro had a hot bath.

Libertas was shocked by his appearance once he'd scrubbed himself clean and put on fresh clothes. She smiled at him. "Good to see you back to your old self."

Thin as a greyhound, he looked stooped and shorter than he had been, his hair showing unfamiliar streaks of gray around the temples.

While he ate Harro waved his knife about. "The Gestapo is obviously watching us. It could only be a matter of time before they find the Hectograph. We'll have to move it."

Libertas sat down at the table and touched his arm. "Moving it could be the worst idea. It could be just what they want us to do."

"I know. It's a bit of a conundrum."

She topped up his coffee. "What does Delma know? What could she tell them?"

"She knows Gilbert in Brussels, and Vigo, and she's met Max. She knows Arvid, of course. She has carried messages to the Soviet Embassy for him from time to time, so she knows his contact there by sight. She made a few leaflet deliveries in the early days, so I suppose she could compromise parts of the distribution network…"

"Can we trust her?"

"I think so. As long as Arvid, Vigo and Max are at liberty, we can assume she's given them nothing. I'll get the men to check the distribution network next week. Gilbert is out of reach in a foreign country, and Arvid's Soviet attaché is untouchable."

"I'm really worried about Delma's health. The last time I saw her she looked like death's younger sister."

Harro nodded. "What did Emmy say when you asked her to help?"

"She said she'd try, but there's a limit to Hermann's influence. It would be easier to get her out if she worked for one of the ministries."

Chapter 53

April 1939

Arvid Harnack was having breakfast when there was a knock on his apartment door. He opened it and found an envelope on the floor with his name on it. He checked the stairs and caught sight of a schoolboy disappearing below.

He tore open the envelope. It contained a single line note:

'The Dom at noon, AK'

Arvid recognized the handwriting of his contact at the Soviet Embassy, the NKVD agent, Alexander Korotkov. The summons was more than unusual. Arvid hadn't spoken to Korotkov since their first meeting, two years earlier.

Arvid went to work at the Economics Ministry, keeping his eyes and ears open for anything unusual that might explain Korotkov's unprecedented summons. Nothing emerged.

He took an early lunch and traveled by U-Bahn to the cathedral in the center of the city. Arvid, a committed Marxist, hated everything about the Dom cathedral, a massive 3-domed concrete monstrosity, a permanent testament to an earlier age, the age of the Prussian Emperors that ended with the abdication of the insufferable Kaiser Wilhelm II.

He arrived just before noon. Korotkov appeared at 12:05. They knelt together in a side altar.

"I've had word from a trusted source that the Gestapo will raid your print station first thing tomorrow."

Arvid was skeptical. "Who is this source?"

"I can't tell you that, but the information is cast iron. Your printer location is under surveillance as we speak. They will raid it before 3:00 a.m. Don't attempt to save your printer. If you send someone, they will be captured and tortured."

Arvid was speechless. He could count on the fingers of both hands all the people who knew the secret location where they kept the Hectograph. Who could have betrayed them?

"There's something else," said Korotkov. "I'm sorry to tell you, Comrade, that I've been recalled to Moscow."

"Permanently?"

"Looks like it. Uncle Joe has decided to withdraw all his intelligence agents in Germany. God knows why. My personal future is uncertain. Many agents recalled in the past have been arrested, tried on trumped up charges, and sent to the gulags. Some have been executed."

"I'm sorry to hear that, Alexander."

Korotkov shrugged. "I have one chance. Stalin's head of intelligence, a man called Beria, knows me. We trained together many years ago. He may stand by me. He may not."

The two old friends knelt side by side in silence for a several moments. Arvid was a German, Korotkov a Georgian, but they had worked together successfully for two years. Arvid remembered their first contact and some of the most important intelligence reports he'd passed to the attaché. The loss was going to hit the Red Orchestra badly.

"Can you put me in touch with someone at the embassy, someone reliable?"

"There's nobody, I'm sorry." Korotkov got up to leave. Arvid stood and they shook hands. "Goodbye my friend."

"Goodbye, Alexander, I hope it works out for you."

On the way back to his apartment, Arvid went over his options. He had a second reserve Hectograph. He would have to find a new location for the print operation.

The loss of Alexander Korotkov was a more intractable problem. The Russian had been passing Arvid's intelligence to the Soviets for two years. The US Embassy had been in hibernation for nearly six months, his collaboration with Donald Heath no more than a fond memory. As a committed Marxist, his preference was to find someone from the Soviet Embassy to replace Korotkov, but if that was not possible, he would be happy to pass his intelligence to any of the forces standing in opposition to the Third Reich. His personal political affiliation was subordinate to the need to bring down the Nazis.

He could try the British again. He'd approached them a year earlier, but they had rejected his overtures. They had their own well-established intelligence network and weren't prepared to trust any other sources.

The only way he could communicate intelligence to anyone now was by passing it to Harro Schulze-Boysen and asking him to send it to the Soviets through his contact in Belgium. There were many problems with that, not the least of which were his distrust of Schulze-Boysen, who was obviously under Gestapo scrutiny, and the amount of time the intelligence would take to reach Moscow by that roundabout route.

Chapter 54

April 1939

At 2:00 a.m. the Gestapo raided the most secret location of the Communist Resistance, a derelict house in a highly populated easterly quarter of the city. They seized a hectograph, a supply of inks and several reams of paper. The raiding party waited and watched the house for a week, but no member of the Red Orchestra appeared. Obviously, they had been tipped off.

#

As soon as Max and Anna returned from Wittenberg, Max rang Greta. "Tell me Harro has been released."

"Yes, they kept him for a week. The Air Ministry intervened and they had to let him go. They had no evidence against him."

"How is he? Is he all right?"

"He's fine."

"And Delma?"

"We've heard nothing about Delma. She may be under interrogation still or they may have moved her to a camp somewhere. We just don't know."

Max swore.

Greta said, "Can you meet me tomorrow evening at Vigo's church?"

"Why? What's happening?"

"I'll explain when I see you. Shall we say six o'clock?"

The S-Bahn was crowded with workers on their way home from their offices, the women dressed in late season spring outfits.

Everyone was in high spirits. Max did his best to reflect the general mood, but his mind was working overtime on the meeting to come. If they wanted him to go the Brussels again, he would refuse. After their miserable honeymoon, Anna needed him in Berlin.

Vigo and Greta were deep in discussion when Max arrived at the church. Greta patted the pew. Vigo stood to allow Max past. He sat between the two of them.

Vigo's dark stubble seemed heavier than usual. He scratched it with his fingers. "How was your holiday? Did Anna have a good time?"

"Some of it was all right. I don't think Anna enjoyed it much. My mother is not the ideal hostess."

Vigo said, "But your mother must have been happy to spend time with you."

"If she was she didn't show it. Now what did you want to talk to me about?"

Greta said, "We suffered a significant setback while you were away. Someone betrayed the location of one of our Hectographs to the Gestapo. The house was raided. We lost all our paper, all our ink, and the hectograph."

"That's terrible news. Did they catch any members of the Orchestra?"

"No. We were warned beforehand. They captured no one. But that location can never be used again, and we've lost a vital piece of equipment."

Max's mouth was dry. His tongue rocked the cyanide capsule in his mouth. "Who betrayed us?"

Vigo glanced at Greta. She looked away. Vigo said, "We don't know that. There was something else we wanted to talk to you about. I had a visit from the Gestapo while you were away. They took me to Prinz-Albrecht-Strasse. They claimed that your marriage authorization is a forgery."

Max came to a quick decision to tell a version of the truth. "It's true. I forged the signature. The Gestapo man, Framzl, wouldn't sign it."

"Why not?"

And Max lied. "He demanded money."

Greta looked shocked.

Vigo said, "How much?"

"500 Reichsmarks. I couldn't raise that sort of money. Anna had set her heart on a spring wedding."

Greta looked down at her hands. "So you forged a signature?"

"What else could I do?"

Vigo placed a hand on Max's shoulder. "Your civil marriage may not be recognized by the State. The registrar may issue an annulment. But whether that happens or not you will still be married in the eyes of the Roman Catholic Church. You can tell Anna that."

Max shook his head. "I'd rather not say anything about this to Anna. There's no point worrying her unnecessarily."

"If the annulment is issued, she'll have to know."

"Yes, but you said yourself that might not happen. I'd rather say nothing to her until I have to."

#

On her way home, Greta tossed Max's story around in her mind. She knew Max was not the one who betrayed the location of the Hectograph. They had been careful to keep that from him. As for the forgery, the SS were strict when it came to excising corruption from their own ranks. She had heard of several SS officers who had been tried and expelled on charges of corruption. Some had been shot. 500 Reichsmarks was a lot of money, perhaps half a year's wages for someone like Max. But would this Framzl really risk his neck for such a sum? It seemed unlikely, but what other explanation could there be for Max's actions?

Chapter 55

April 1939

𝐀nna was preparing their evening meal when the telephone rang.

It was Max. "I'm going to have to stay at work for a couple of hours, Anna. A mountain of work has accumulated while we were in Wittenberg. I'll find something to eat here. You go ahead and eat without me."

Anna was not happy. "I've already started cooking our supper. Could you not have contacted me sooner?"

"Sorry, my love. I'll try to get home before dark."

Anna stirred the pot on the stove. She had a thick vegetable soup and a beef pie with pastry and potatoes. More than enough for two.

When the food was ready she sat down and ate half of it. Loathe to throw the other half away, she came up with an idea.

She poured the soup into an empty jam jar and wrapped the beef pie and potatoes in a tight parcel. Then she put the food into a basket and set off on foot toward the Rosens' apartment in Alvensleberstrasse.

Matilde let her in. Anna handed her the basket of food. "Max is working late. He couldn't make it home, so I had some food left over. I thought…"

"That's really kind of you, Anna. Come in. I'll call Sophie."

Sophie was more subdued that usual. She read a few pages from her book, but her shoulders were hunched. She looked miserable.

"Where's Aschenputtel today?"

Sophie shook her head.

"What's the matter, Sophie?"

"Mama wouldn't let me visit my friend on my birthday. And Papa spends all day in bed."

"When was your birthday?"

"A week ago. I'm eight." She brightened a little. "Would you like to see what Mama and Papa gave me?"

"Yes, please, Sophie."

Sophie ran back to her room.

Anna asked Matilde why Sophie couldn't visit her friend.

Matilde shook her head. "The streets are not safe for us, now. And some of our neighbors have been harassing us. I've had to keep Sophie indoors. I think David has lost the will to live since he lost the shop. That shop was his whole life."

Sophie reappeared carrying her doll, Aschenputtel. She showed Anna a miniature silver brooch pinned to the doll's chest. "This is what Mama and Papa gave Aschenputtel for her birthday."

Anna examined the brooch. It was an exquisite piece containing a tiny cameo of a woman in profile.

"It was Aschenputtel's birthday?"

"Yes, and mine, too."

"What a beautiful gift," said Anna. "I hope Aschenputtel said thank you."

#

The misery of the Rosen family clung to Anna like a cloud all the way home. The injustice of their circumstances struck a chord deep within her. What had they done to deserve such harsh treatment? What sort of country would condemn an innocent 8-year-old to a life of penury? It was no more than an accident of birth that Anna herself had been brought up a Roman Catholic. With two Jewish grandparents, she could so easily have been brought up a Jew and suffered a similar fate.

#

Arvid asked Greta to take a message to Harro, inviting him to a meeting in the same warehouse near Tempelhof where they'd met before. Harro was to take precautions to ensure that no one followed him.

Arvid took his usual care, hopping from autobuses to trams to the subway. He arrived 30 minutes late.

An iron panel had slipped on the roof. Pools of water covered large parts of the floor and ten thousand dust particles danced in a beam of sunlight streaming from above. The pervasive smell of rust was gone, in its place the musty reek of mold.

Harro sympathized with Arvid on the loss of his Hectograph. He sounded sincere, but the turn of his lip suggested amusement, perhaps even a touch of *Schadenfreude*. Whatever it was, it disappeared from Harro's face when Arvid pointed out that he had a spare Hectograph.

Arvid explained that he had lost his contact in the Soviet Embassy. He had no outlet for his intelligence. Harro's Belgian radio operator was now the only conduit for his intelligence reports to Moscow.

"What are you suggesting?" said Harro.

"I'm suggesting that we merge our two operations. I could make more regular use of your courier runs to Belgium, and we could amalgamate our two distribution networks for broadsheet leaflets and flyers."

"I was never happy with your broadsheets," Harro replied. "Our leaflets are smaller, easier to hide and we get the point across in fewer words."

Arvid bristled at the implied editorial criticism. "That's not a problem, Harro. I suggest we should use just one Hectograph. We should use yours. It's newer and bigger than ours."

"Agreed. And I'll be happy to concede editorial control to Adam Kuckhoff."

"That's very generous of you. We should examine our two distribution networks and see how best we might combine them."

"That's Libertas's domain. I'll mention it to her."

Arvid prepared to wrap up the meeting. He was eager to put as much distance as possible between himself and Harro. "We must keep physical contact to a minimum. The Gestapo has shown their interest in you. They are not yet aware of my involvement and I'd like to keep it that way."

"We'll need to set up the Hectograph at some new location. Do you have any ideas where?"

"I'll give that some thought," said Arvid.

Chapter 56

May 1939

Anna packed a basket of food and went back to visit the Rosens again early in May. Early summer. All over the city, window boxes overflowed with color. Citizens on bicycles filled the streets.

When she arrived at Alvensleberstrasse, she found the apartment door wide open, and no one inside. Fighting a growing panic, she searched the apartment for clues.

All the furniture was in place. There was no food in the larder. Matilde and David's clothes had been removed, and Sophie's books and toys were all gone. It was a puzzle, but Anna's conclusion was that the family had moved out. She said a silent prayer that they were safe.

When Max got home from work she told him what she'd found.

He held her, trembling in his arms. "Perhaps they've left Germany, my love. Hopefully they are already beyond the reach of the Nazis."

"I need to know where they are, Max. I feel guilty that I didn't visit them more often. I haven't brought them any food since last month."

He held her tighter. "Frau Greta visits them twice every week. I'm sure they weren't depending on you, Anna."

"Talk to Frau Greta. Find out what happened to them. I need to know."

Max rang Greta on the telephone and asked her to meet him. She agreed to a meeting in Max's favorite Brauhaus in Paulusstrasse roughly halfway between the two apartments.

#

Max had started his second beer by the time Greta arrived. He offered to buy her a drink, but she declined. "I don't have time for drink. What do you have for me?"

"Anna went around to the Rosens' apartment today. They've gone. She wants to know where they are."

Greta hesitated. "You can tell Anna the family is safe. The Gestapo has started transporting Jewish families to the camps. They were surrounded by hostile neighbors, so they moved."

"Where are they? Anna would like to carry on visiting them, bringing them food."

Greta made no reply.

Max asked another question. "I admire what you're doing for the family, Frau Greta, but I wondered why?"

"What do you mean? They need help. I give it to them. Is that so difficult to understand?"

"I mean why this particular family? Berlin must be full of families like the Rosens."

"I would help any family in difficulty if I could. But you're right—I do have a special bond with the Rosens. They were early members of the Orchestra."

"So, are you going to tell me where they are?"

"I can't. Just tell Anna they are safe. And they don't need food. If the situation changes, I'll let you know."

Chapter 57

May 1939

Greta received a telephone call from an excited Libertas. "Delma has been released."

"How do you know?"

"She's here with me, now."

"How is she?"

"Her spirits are high, but her health has deteriorated. I've called my doctor. He'll be here within the hour. Why don't you come around tomorrow at lunch time. I've invited Mildred. We have a lot to talk about."

#

Delma looked like death. She'd lost a lot of weight and she was coughing up blood.

Greta embraced her. "You saw Libertas's doctor? What did he say?"

"He said I should travel to a warmer climate. He recommended the Alps where the air is pure. My lungs are infected. It's pretty serious."

Greta asked, "Do you know anyone in Switzerland?"

Delma shook her head and burst into a protracted coughing fit.

"Maybe I can arrange something," said Libertas quietly when the coughing subsided.

Libertas took Delma up the stairs and found her a bed. When she returned to the study she said, "The poor girl. Doesn't she look dreadful? I'll look after her for a few days. Pauletta can keep an eye on her when I'm not here."

When Mildred Harnack arrived the three women discussed the merging of the two operations.

Libertas was delighted. "It's something I've been dreaming about for at least two years. It's so obvious that we should be working as a single unit. It'll make all our work more efficient, don't you agree?" Mildred and Greta both murmured agreement. "I can't understand why they couldn't have done it ages ago. There's just no accounting for the way men's minds work."

Mildred explained Arvid's reluctance. His thinking had always been that smaller cells distanced from one another were more secure than a single large cell. "He got the idea from studying the organization of the Republican rebels in Ireland before they won their independence in 1920."

They discussed combining the two distribution runs. Greta's had 200 subscribers, Libertas's close to 400. Combining the networks would require bigger print runs. They'd need more paper and more ink. Mildred agreed to organize that. She worked in the Department of Propaganda and Public Enlightenment. She also had an artist friend who had a legitimate reason for buying lots of stationery supplies.

#

Mildred left, and Greta and Libertas got down to the basics of how to combine their two distribution networks. Libertas spread a map of the city out on the dining room table, and they went over it, armed with a box of thumbtacks.

When Libertas was happy with that, she put the map away. She offered Greta a glass of white wine. It was her way of inviting Greta to leave.

Greta declined the offer. "Before I go, there's one other matter I'd like to talk to you about."

Libertas poured herself a glass of hock. "Go ahead, I'm listening."

"I thought you should know that Max and Anna's official marriage authorization was a forgery. The Gestapo took Vigo to task over it. I asked Max about it, and he admitted that he forged the signature."

Libertas came close to spilling her wine. She put her glass down on the table. "I don't understand. Emmy set that up for them. She assured me everything was arranged. She even gave me the name of the Gestapo man that was looking after the case."

"Kurt Framzl."

"Was that the name? I can't remember. Anyway there should have been no problem. Why did he have to forge a signature?"

"According to Max, Framzl demanded a bribe that Max couldn't afford to pay."

"Do you believe that? There are severe penalties for bribery and corruption among SS men."

"I don't know, but clearly whatever Herr Göring did wasn't enough."

"I'll talk to Emmy."

#

When Arvid heard that Delma had been released and that Libertas was looking after her, he was livid. "That's Libertas all over. I should have been informed immediately. Doesn't she realize Delma will have to be debriefed very carefully? We need to know what questions she was asked and what answers she gave the Gestapo. I need to know if any of my team is compromised."

Greta waved a finger at him. "Forget that, Arvid. She's seriously unwell, and she assured Libertas that she told them nothing. You have nothing to fear from Delma."

"And you believe every word she said? She could easily be a plant, primed to report our every move back to the Gestapo. We can't use her ever again, and she needs to be put into immediate information quarantine."

Mildred put her foot down. "That's nonsense, Arvid. Delma's too ill to work for us, and she's certainly too ill to report anything to anyone. Believe me, I've seen her. Libertas thinks she won't survive another seven days. She has sent for Father Vigo."

Chapter 58

June 1939

Adam paid a visit to the dentist. When the last patient had gone, Dr. Himpel's assistant made a fresh pot of coffee. She kissed the dentist and left for the night. Dr. Himpel locked the front door behind her. He invited Adam into his surgery, opened a hidden panel in one of his cabinets and pulled out a Hectograph.

It was bigger than the one the Gestapo had seized from Arvid and looked more modern. Adam measured the plate. If he was careful, he should be able to lay out the text so that each turn through the machine would print a sheet containing two copies of the leaflet.

Dr. Himpel put the Hectograph back in its secret compartment and Adam got to work preparing the text. He worked for an hour. Then he showed his editorial piece to the dentist. It was a warning to the people of Berlin that the Soviets may be planning an invasion.

Dr. Himpel scratched his head. "Isn't that a little far-fetched?"

"Of course it is," said Adam, "but the news needs a little spice to make it more interesting than the pap dished out by the Nazis in their newspapers."

By 10:00 p.m. the master was ready. Adam applied the gelatin and ink to the plate, Dr. Himpel provided a bundle of paper and Adam began to churn the leaflet out. Adam replenished the ink after each 50 turns of the handle, and Dr. Himpel separated the copies using a large scissors. After 150 turns of the handle—300 copies—Adam had to rest. Dr. Himpel took over on the handle.

By 11:30 they had 750 copies of the leaflet, printed, dried and separated, ready for delivery. Adam thanked the dentist for his help and took a late tram home.

#

On Saturday, June 10, Max was sent to help Vigo with a delivery run. The priest was somber and distracted following his visit to Delma's bedside.

Max asked about Delma's health.

Vigo shook his head. "She's been seen by Libertas's doctor. He's prescribed infusions, but I'm not convinced that they'll make any difference. Her health has been declining ever since I first met her and spending seven weeks in a Gestapo cell can't have helped."

"That was my fault. I saw the danger that day in the fish market but I was too late to warn her."

"That was not your fault, Max. You mustn't blame yourself."

Vigo gave Max an overcoat similar to his own so that they could make the deliveries together.

"Do I have to wear that, Vigo? It's high summer."

"Not if you can come up with a different way of carrying your bundle of leaflets."

The new leaflet looked more professional than the previous ones, and it was smaller. Max read the headline:

'Is Moscow Planning an Invasion of the Fatherland?'

"No one's going to believe this headline."

Vigo ran his eyes over it. "You're probably right, but we still have to send them out. Come on, get your coat on."

Vigo's delivery run had been expanded. It was now three times what it had been with 100 drops. The run took the best part of the day, but when they'd finished, the two of them gasping for breath from the heat of the day, a bundle of leaflets remained.

"What are those for?" said an exhausted Max.

"Those are for delivery tomorrow."

#

They started again after early Sunday Mass. This time they spread out around the city dropping leaflets in railway and bus stations, on U-Bahn platforms, in the Tempelhof air terminal as well as in autobuses, U-Bahn and mainline trains, on the S-Bahn and in trams and buses.

Vigo was back in the church in time to offer 10 o'clock mass. Max had completed his part of the delivery run by 11:30 a.m. He shed the overcoat, the clerical shirt and collar, the cassock and trousers, and sat in the vestry in his underwear, gasping like a fish out of water.

Vigo laughed at him. "Now you know a little about how it feels to be a priest."

"The overcoat is a killer. Don't you have a summer uniform, Vigo?"

"What, like a knee-length cassock and black shorts?"

"Why not?"

"I'll write to Rome and suggest it."

#

Max skipped his midday meal. Instead, he took the autobus to Lutherstadt Wittenberg for his scheduled visit to his mother. She took a few moments to answer the door, and when she did her hair was tied up in a headscarf.

She looked surprised to see him. "What are you doing here?"

"It's time for my June visit."

"Well, you'd better come in, so. I'm busy cleaning the house. Wait for me in the parlor. Try not to touch anything."

Max took a seat in the parlor and waited. After 30 minutes, he went looking for her. He found her in the kitchen reading a newspaper and smoking a cigarette. She was a voracious reader of novels, a member of the public library, but he'd never seen her reading any newspaper, and certainly not the Nazi paper, *Völkischer Beobachter*. He'd never seen her smoking.

He sat beside her at the kitchen table. "You've taken to reading the news, I see, Mother."

"Why not? Don't you read the news?"

"I do, but I thought you never bothered with it. That rag is nothing but Nazi propaganda. And when did you start smoking?"

"I used to smoke before you were born. I decided to take it up again a couple of weeks ago." She handed him a pack. "Take one."

"I don't smoke, Mother. Don't you remember how you always told me it was a filthy dirty habit?"

"Yes, and quite right too." She wiped the table where his hands had been resting. "I hope you didn't touch anything in the parlor. I cleaned in there this morning. Tell me why you're here again?"

"I don't think I touched anything. I just dropped in to see how you were."

"Well, there's no need. You're a married man now. You shouldn't have to keep calling to see your old mother."

"I'd be happy to telephone you from time to time, but you haven't got a telephone yet, have you?"

His head was spinning on the return autobus journey. Apart from forgetting he was there and leaving him waiting for 30 minutes in the parlor, she seemed a different person. They had completed a conversation about reading and smoking, entirely without tangents or deviations. Her obsessive cleaning was a worry, though.

She had acknowledged that he was a married man, but she hadn't said a word about Anna, good, bad or indifferent.

Chapter 59

June 1939

The Gestapo picked up Max again on his way to work on Monday morning. They drove him to headquarters, frog-marched him to Framzl's office, and dumped him in a seat.

The man standing behind Framzl's desk was not Framzl. He wore the same gray uniform, the same death's head on his cap, but he was younger, taller, with small, steely blue eyes and almost white blond hair. He slammed a copy of the new leaflet on the desk. "What the hell is this?"

Max shook his head.

"Concerned citizens have been handing this filth into police stations all over the city. Every day since the weekend. They have been found all over the city, in bus stations, U-Bahn carriages, and even in the terminal at Tempelhof. Read what it says."

Max picked up the leaflet and read the main headline: 'Is Moscow Planning an Invasion of the Fatherland?' The byline read 'Grock.'

The Gestapo man's voice rose half an octave. "It's utter nonsense, obvious Communist propaganda designed to stir up unrest, to unsettle the good people of Germany."

"The Communists ought to be arrested."

"Who is this 'Grock'?"

"I don't know."

"You don't know. How long have you been working with the Communist Resistance?"

"Six months?"

"So you admit membership of the subversive organization."

"Yes, of course. Herr Framzl forced me to join."

The Gestapo man blinked. "I would advise you to weigh your words carefully. This is not a game. You have admitted membership of the Red Orchestra."

The left hand of the Gestapo didn't know what was in its right hand!

"Yes, but as I said, I joined at the express direction of Herr Framzl. Check with him. He will confirm my story."

"That is not possible. Framzl is no longer with this office, and he won't be returning."

Max felt the ground shift under his feet. "I spoke with him six months ago. He promised to approve my marriage application, but only if I joined the Red Orchestra."

"Go on."

The glint in the Gestapo man's eyes suggested this was an invitation to Max to dig himself deeper into the hole he was already in. He touched his false tooth with his tongue.

"Framzl wanted me to bring him the location of the subversives' printer. He said if I gave him this information he would approve my application."

"I see, and you agreed?"

"Naturally. I had no other option."

"And have you located the printer?"

"No."

"You say you've been with the Communists for six months and you expect me to believe you still don't know where their print operation is?"

"It's a closely guarded secret, but I'm getting close. To tell you the truth, I believe I was on the brink of discovering it when…"

"When what?

"You arrested Harro Schulze-Boysen."

The Gestapo man blinked again. "The arrest of Schulze-Boysen was entirely justified and legal."

"Maybe so, but since then, the Red Orchestra has locked everything up."

The Gestapo man left the room for several minutes, leaving Max under the watchful gaze of the picture of Adolf Hitler. His tongue rocked the cyanide capsule in his mouth. When the Gestapo man returned, he was carrying a folder. "Your marriage authorization has been identified as a forgery. It was never approved by this office."

Max said nothing.

"Tell me why you found it necessary to forge your Authorization."

"I told you. I couldn't find the subversives' printer but my fiancée wanted to get married. She fixed the date. What else could I do?"

"Forgery is a most serious crime. Tell me why I shouldn't throw you in a cell right now and let two of my men exercise their ax handles on your bones."

A tremor ran up Max's spine. He said nothing.

"Our records show that SS-Sturmbannführer Framzl also attempted to extort money from you for his signature. Is that correct?"

Max shook his head, intending to tell the truth, but then he thought, if Framzl has been shipped off to a camp for corruption, why not leave him there?

"Yes, that's right."

The Gestapo man checked the folder again. "The report we received was traced back to a Salvatore Vigo, Roman Catholic pastor. Do you know this man?"

"He was the one who married us."

"What about Pastor Gunther Schlurr, a colleague of Pastor Vigo's, do you know him?"

Max shook his head. "I don't know him."

He snapped the folder closed. "This whole episode stinks like rotten fish. Your story makes little sense. However, the activities of the Red Orchestra must be brought to a halt at all costs. From now on you will report to me. Is that clear?"

"Yes, Herr..."

"Traut. SS-Sturmführer Jürgen Traut. Remember the name. And remember if you fail to give me what I need, your young bride will quickly find herself drawing a widow's pension."

Chapter 60

June 1939

Harro Schulze-Boysen called an emergency meeting of the two newly merged networks of the Red Orchestra. They met in the Schulze-Boysen mansion in Pankow under cover of a social event. Max knew just a few of those present. Frau Greta was there with Adam, and he recognized Bruno, the Communist. Libertas seemed especially close to an American woman called Mildred and her husband whose name was Arvid. Max looked around for Vigo, but couldn't find him.

Pauletta, the maid, ensured that everyone had a drink in hand before Libertas opened proceedings. "Thank you all for coming, tonight. Harro and I want all members of our network to know that we are grateful to every one of you for your support and help in the past. We look forward to working much more closely together with Arvid and his network. I am sure you will all agree that merging our two networks was the right thing to do at this time. Like combining the strings and the bass in a real orchestra, I'm sure the Red Orchestra will make more and better music in the future."

This was greeted by polite applause.

"Now Harro has something to tell us. Harro?"

"Thank you, my darling. I'm sure everyone will agree that our efforts in the past would never have been as successful without Libertas's diligent work."

More applause, more boisterous this time.

"Last week I was called into the office of the Secretary General of the Air Ministry. I really had no idea what to expect. I thought maybe they had wind of our little printing enterprise. But that wasn't it."

He paused. Everyone held their breath.

"He informed me that the Air Ministry has promoted me. I am to be moved from head office to the office of Luftwaffe Command."

Immediately, the room was humming as each person realized the implications of what Harro had said. He had been the jewel in the intelligence gathering activities of the Orchestra from the beginning. The intelligence that he had collected within the Air Ministry had been of the highest quality. A move to the Luftwaffe would see him even better placed to collect military intelligence.

"That's not the full story." Silence descended on the group. "I am to be placed in the Intelligence Office within the Luftwaffe."

The room erupted. There was a round of cheers. Glasses were heard chinking together.

Adam shook Harro vigorously by the hand. "Wonderful news. Wonderful."

Arvid clapped him on the back. "Many congratulations, my friend."

Harro held up a hand for silence. "It's good news, yes, but it comes at the worst possible time. Arvid's contacts in the Soviet and U.S. Embassies would have been invaluable for rapid communication of information to those interested beyond our borders, but without those contacts, we are forced to rely solely on our couriers to carry the intelligence to our friends in Belgium and France for transmission to Moscow. I'm sure you know that our overtures to the KPD in exile in Prague and Paris have been rebuffed. As an intelligence network, we are adrift. We will try to improve on that situation. In the meantime, we must accelerate our printed output and expand our distribution networks wherever possible. I would ask all of you to think about new outlets for our leaflets."

Arvid left early, but the party continued well into the night. As the guests were leaving—one by one or in pairs—Harro asked Dr. Himpel to remain. When all the guests had gone, he invited the dentist into his study. Libertas asked the maid, Pauletta, to rustle up coffee.

Harro waited until Pauletta had left the room and closed the door. "I've been informed about a major Wehrmacht strategic plan for the possible invasion of the Soviet Union. The plan is called Operation Fritz. We need to alert Moscow as soon as possible. I've spoken to Arvid and Adam about this, and they have agreed that we should reach out to our Marxist comrades in exile for help. The KPD is holding a weekend conference in Zurich early next month. We'd like you, Dr. Himpel, to go to the conference and establish contact with any of the KPD in exile who can help us. You know them. They will listen to you. Pass on the information about Operation Fritz. Explain our difficulty and ask them to exert whatever influence they have with Moscow to let us have our own shortwave radio transmitter here, in Berlin."

Dr. Himpel nodded. "Leave it to me."

"Take Peter Riese with you. He should be a great help. He is a member of the Communist Party and he's Swiss-German. I want you to take Delma with you as well. Our doctor has advised her to seek out the clean Alpine air of Switzerland."

Chapter 61

July 1939

On the Wednesday evening of the first week of July, there was an urgent hammering on Max's apartment door. He opened it and Bruno the Communist stepped inside.

He was out of breath. "Can you travel on Saturday?"

"Travel? Where to? Belgium?"

"Switzerland. Dr. Himpel and Delma are taking the train to Zurich. Peter Riese was supposed to go with them, but he's unavailable. Herr Schulze-Boysen has asked me to give you this." He thrust a travel permit at him. It was made out in the name Gunther Schlurr.

"Unavailable? What does that mean?"

"I'm not sure." He put the permit in Max's hand. "I have to go."

#

Friday night at 9:00 p.m., Max and Dr. Himpel boarded an overnight express train to Zurich. They had a compartment to themselves. The flickering lights in the ceiling cast shadows over the dentist's deep-set eyes and under his nose, giving him the look of an evil madman.

"Where's Delma?"

"She's in a sleeping compartment."

The movement of his mouth did nothing to humanize Dr. Himpel. Elizabeth Browning's monster sprang to Max's mind. "So tell me what the trip is about and what will be expected of me."

"The KPD is holding a major conference with delegations from all over Germany and other countries in Europe. We are hoping to strengthen our links with the Communist Party in exile. The group in Zurich is particularly strong, and they have solid contacts in the Kremlin. Our principal objective is to get them to persuade Moscow to let us operate our own shortwave radio transmitter in Berlin."

"And my role?"

He lifted a shoulder. "We are the official delegation from Berlin. One man wouldn't constitute a delegation."

Himpel closed his eyes, terminating any further discussion.

The train rattled on through the night. At midnight, the compartment lights were extinguished. The sky was partially overcast, and there was a strong wind blowing. A half moon played hide and seek above the clouds. Dr. Himpel began to snore.

Max closed his eyes and reviewed his situation. He was a married man, although the Berlin registrar might issue an annulment at any time. Anna would be devastated if that happened. Her mother, even more so.

His tongue toyed with the false tooth in his mouth, and his father's lighter turned and turned in his hand. The members of the Red Orchestra were now all good friends. Max would rather die than betray them. He smiled. That was certainly not what Framzl had intended when he introduced him to the group.

Kurt Framzl may have gone, but Max was still under the thumb of the Gestapo. This new man, Jürgen Traut, seemed even nastier than Framzl. He was going to find it difficult to keep fobbing off the man with excuses.

Anna had been disgusted when he told her he was going away again and she would have to spend another weekend alone. He would make it up to her somehow.

#

In the middle of the night Dr. Himpel got up to find the washroom and tripped over Max's feet at the door. "Sorry, Max."

"What time is it?"

"Three-thirty. Sorry I woke you."

Max stretched and moved to correct a crick in his neck. He tried various positions selecting the least uncomfortable, his head wedged in the corner of the head rest. When the dentist returned, he asked him, "What happened to Peter Riese? Bruno said he was 'unavailable' for this trip. What did he mean?"

"They couldn't find him in time. I expect he was busy with party affairs. He's a leading figure amongst the Communists in Berlin."

Himpel was soon snoring again. Max closed his eyes.

#

The train crossed the border as dawn broke. The Swiss border guards were even more lackadaisical and disinterested than the Belgians. Max got his first view of the Alps, jagged and majestic, bathed in gold by the rising sun. He searched and found distant peaks still capped with snow. In July! The sight almost convinced him that Madam Krauss's prediction would come true.

When a steward came around announcing breakfast in the dining car, Himpel went off toward the front of the train to rouse Delma. He came back 15 minutes later with a long face that made Max laugh. "What's the matter, Doctor?" Then he realized that something was seriously wrong. "It's Delma, isn't it? She's not well?"

"She's dead, Max. She passed away during the night."

The idea of the young woman alone in a train berth coughing her life away turned Max's stomach. Then he thought about how Vigo was going to react to the news. He made a dash for the washroom.

The train was delayed while the Swiss authorities removed Delma's body and sorted out the paperwork. Acting as her immediate guardian, Dr. Himpel signed the papers to have her interred in Switzerland. There was little point in returning her body to Berlin. She was a refugee from Romania with no kin in Germany. Apart from Vigo.

#

Delma's passing threw a blanket of gloom over Max and the dentist. Max did his best to respond to the conference delegates who all called him—and each other—'Comrade.'

185

The conference consisted of a series of lectures with strange titles such as: 'The Proletarian Dream - Toward a Distant Utopia' and 'The Enemy Within - Fascism in Modern Europe.'

The real business of the day was conducted outside the lecture rooms where Dr. Himpel peddled the wares of the Red Orchestra. Now a united group with valuable contacts in a broad selection of German ministries, the range and depth of the intelligence on offer was priceless and should have been enough to make any Communist salivate, or so Max thought. But one by one the delegates from each country, the Swedes, the French, the Dutch, the Spanish, and those from the Baltic States turned them down. Moscow would not be interested in their intelligence information, not even where that information had a direct bearing on Soviet interests.

"It's hopeless," said Himpel. "We're wasting our time here. I'm sure they think of us as bourgeois reactionaries."

Max said, "We're not Communists. Perhaps that's the problem. If Peter Riese was here, we might have had a better response."

Dr. Himpel curled a lip. "That wouldn't have made any difference. They still wouldn't help us."

They took an early train back to Berlin.

Chapter 62

July 1939

Anna answered a knock on the apartment door. Max! She hadn't expected him that early. He must have forgotten his key. She ran to the door and flung it open. Confronted by the blond figure of Jürgen, wearing a gray SS uniform, she reeled backwards.

Jürgen stepped across the threshold and closed the door. "It's good to see you again, Anna."

"How… How did you find me?"

"I've been posted to the East. I wanted to see you one more time before I leave. I have an hour."

"Jürgen, I'm a married woman, now…"

"Yes, but I know you like me. I'm not asking for a long-term commitment, just an hour of your time." He grasped her arms above the elbows and pulled her to him.

She pushed at his chest. "I don't love you, Jürgen. I could never be unfaithful to my husband. Please leave."

She could feel his mounting sexual frustration. She could smell it.

He put a hand on the back of her head and pulled her to him. He kissed her roughly. She bit his lip—hard—drawing blood.

He pushed her from him. "You whore. I'm bleeding!"

"I told you, I don't want this. Just leave."

"Get me something for the blood."

She went to the kitchen and ran some water over a dishcloth. She handed it to him and he dabbed at his lip. "You shouldn't have done that. What's the matter with you, woman? We could have had a pleasant hour together."

"I don't want that. I love my husband. I don't even like you."

Quick as a snake strikes, he struck her across the face. "How could you turn me down? You know that the Fatherland will soon be at war. I could easily be killed."

Hopefully.

She took a step backwards. "Just leave."

#

Max arrived back in the apartment early on Sunday evening.

Anna hadn't expected to see him that early. "Have you eaten?"

"No, and I'm hungry."

"I gave all your food away to the Rosens."

"You found out where they're living?"

She shook her head. "I gave the food to Frau Greta to pass on."

"She had news of the family?"

"They are all well. She keeps them supplied with food. They've applied for visas for Britain. Apparently there's an official in the passport office of the British Embassy sympathetic to the plight of German Jews."

Anna made him an omelet from vegetable scraps. While she stood at the stove, he told her about the conference. Finally, when Anna had extracted as much fun as she could from his descriptions of the delegates, the lecturers and their lectures, he told her about Delma.

"We were escorting an agent to Switzerland."

"A Communist?"

"I don't know. I think she might have been."

"*She?* How old is she? What does she look like?"

"She was very sick, Anna. She passed away on the train."

"Oh, how sad. What was the matter with her?"

"She had consumption."

Max's gloom returned. Delma had been too young to die in such a miserable way.

While he ate, Anna fantasized about escaping to Switzerland.

She said, "It would have to be the German part of Switzerland."

Max agreed. "Yes, Anna, but the German they speak there is very different. It's difficult to understand."

"I expect we'll get used to it in time. Tell me what the houses are like."

"Much the same as here."

She poured him a cup of coffee. "How old was she, this agent who died?"

"Her name was Delma. She was about your age."

"What did she look like?"

"She was very sick, very pale."

"Tell me about your sleeping arrangements on the train."

"Doctor Himpel and I shared a compartment. Delma slept in a berth."

She gave him a weak smile. "Tell me about the Alps. Did you see any snow-capped mountains?"

"Yes Anna, I saw a few as we crossed the border."

Chapter 63

August 1939

Every scrap of intelligence collected by the combined Resistance group during August pointed to an imminent military action to the east. Harro and Arvid were convinced that the Wehrmacht was planning to put Operation Fritz—the invasion of the USSR—into action. An invasion of Poland would be a prerequisite for this. They chronicled a massive build up of troops and equipment on the German border with Poland. Reports from Madam Krauss confirmed their worst fears. Senior figures in the Wehrmacht were getting jumpy about being sent to war in the east, which was now regarded as a racing certainty in military circles.

Sketchy reports in the newspapers suggested frenzied diplomatic activity between the German and Polish Foreign Ministries. The British and French had signed agreements of mutual support, both countries insisting that diplomatic discussions must continue between Germany and Poland.

On August 21, Germany's Foreign Minister set off on a trip to Moscow. Speculation had it that Stalin would take the opportunity to issue a stern warning to Hitler not to consider moving his troops any further east than Germany's existing border with Poland. Meanwhile, diplomatic sources confirmed that an Anglo-French peace mission to Moscow had broken up without agreement, the Soviets insisting that Polish territory and rights of passage must be conceded.

On August 22, Harro was invited to the home of Adolf Hitler, the Berghof on the Obersalzberg in Bavaria. Everybody who was anybody was there, from Hitler's deputy, Rudolf Hess, through the senior members of the government, the OKW and all three branches of the Wehrmacht. German wine was served with delicate canapés. It reminded Harro of one of Libertas's cocktail parties, but without the women.

As several clocks chimed 4:00 p.m., the Führer made a dramatic entrance dressed in an elaborate uniform modeled on the Wehrmacht style. The guests all hushed. Hitler stood on a low platform and made a long, rasping speech that left no doubts about his intentions toward Poland and the Polish people; he intended to exterminate the people of Poland and colonize their land with Germans. Harro was shaken by the experience. He arrived back in Berlin in time to hear the triumphal announcement that the Soviet Foreign Minister Vyacheslav Molotov and the German Foreign Minister Joachim von Ribbentrop had signed a non-aggression pact between the two countries. Under the terms of the pact, Germany and the Soviet Union agreed not to initiate hostile action against each other and to remain neutral if either were to be attacked by a third party.

Harro and Arvid held a secret meeting to discuss the pact. They agreed that the implications for their Resistance group were as serious as they could be. The lead story in their latest broadsheet had suggested a possible invasion by the Soviets. This non-aggression pact had holed that theory below the waterline. What was much more important, their relationship with Soviet Intelligence had been blown out of the water. Given the amount of material they had been sending to Moscow pointing to a planned invasion of the Soviet Union by Germany, any meager credibility they had with Stalin would now surely be in tatters.

Chapter 64

August 1939

In Whitehall, the Joint Forces Contingency Committee was in emergency session. Assistant Director of Military Intelligence, Sidney Blenkinsop-Smythe, was on his feet, but no one was listening to him. The room was in uproar.

Air Commodore Frank Scott rapped the table with the bowl of his pipe for silence. "Gentlemen, a bit of decorum, please."

The hubbub subsided. The members of the committee resumed their seats. Blenkinsop-Smythe picked up where he'd left off. "The situation is critical. We are days away from war with Germany. I don't need to tell you what a cataclysmic prospect faces us now that Hitler and Stalin have become allies."

The air commodore waved Blenkinsop-Smythe into his seat. "Thank you, Assistant Director. Our task today is to consider how His Majesty's armed forces should respond to this new and immediate threat." Five voices all began to speak at once. The air commodore held up a hand. "I suggest we go around the table. That way all three armed services will have an opportunity to speak. Group Captain Pinkley, perhaps you'd care to start."

Group Captain Cameron Pinkley of the RAF got to his feet. "Thank you, Air Commodore. As the only other representative from the RAF around this table, I'd like to say that Great Britain and her allies would have no realistic prospect of victory in a ground war against such insuperable odds. Our best course of action, in the opinion of Air Command, is to pump all the resources we have into our air defenses. We need more aircraft and we need more pilots to fly them. We need anti-aircraft artillery to defend our cities against enemy aircraft. And we must give the highest priority to the design and development of new aircraft to keep us ahead of our enemies. Surely, the lessons of the last War have shown us the destructive effectiveness of a well-directed bomb thrown from an aircraft."

"Thank you, Group Captain. Perhaps we could have a response from the Royal Navy next…"

The more senior of the two RN officers rose to his feet. "Air Commodore, gentlemen, I'm sure I don't need to remind everyone here of His Majesty's Royal Navy's enviable reputation all around the world. Since the time of Sir Francis Drake, we have been masters of the sea in all four corners of the globe."

"This is no Spanish Armada we are facing, Rear Admiral," someone muttered.

"I don't need to be told by anyone here that modern naval warfare is more sophisticated than it has ever been. You should recognize that many, if not all, recent technical advances worldwide are Royal Navy developments. There is not a single fleet at sea that can compete with us on strength, on reach, or on technical capabilities. Let them try." He brought a fist down on the table. "We are ready for them."

"Thank you, Rear Admiral."

A major general of the Army sprang from his chair. "I must disagree with my two colleagues on several grounds. Firstly, there has never been a military engagement in history that was fought entirely in the air. Such a proposition is preposterous. I accept that our Royal Air Force will have a role in bombing inaccessible places that can't be reached by our artillery, but sooner or later every battle boils down to boots on the ground, well-trained men with well-oiled rifles and trusty bayonets. As for the Royal Navy, they have always provided valuable support to our boys in onshore engagements, but let's face it, they have limited use in inland battles. What we are facing is the prospect of land engagements on several fronts against overwhelming odds. The Nazis and the Red Army may have a combined force in excess of 15 million men, outnumbering our combined force by five to one. It must be obvious to even the most myopic observer that we will need to build our numbers and pour whatever resources we have into equipment and ordnance for the land struggle to come."

The air commodore waved the major general back to his seat. "Gentlemen, we all know this is not 1914. The craft of warfare has moved on. This coming war will be unlike any that has preceded it. It will be fought with advanced machines and technologies that have yet to be devised. The days when armies of men faced each from trenches and charged into deadly machinegun fire across wasteland—those days are behind us. We must adapt to the new realities or perish."

Chapter 65

August 1939

In the fortune teller's house in Kurfürstenstrasse, Greta pushed the door open and parked the pram in the hallway.

Madam Krauss came bustling out from her lair. "Oh, it's you. I wasn't expecting anyone. I meant to lock the front door."

"How are they?"

"They seem fine. Sophie's a little unhappy about the enforced confinement, and Matilde and David are tired of the cramped conditions, but they seem healthy enough."

Madam Krauss looked into the pram. Ule was sleeping. "I'll watch him for you if you like."

Greta reached down, lifted the infant from the pram and placed him on her shoulder. "Thank you Frau, but Sophie likes to see him."

Carrying her basket in one hand and with the baby on her shoulder, she climbed the stairs. The stairs took her to the attic floor under the high, pitched roof. Against one wall there stood a heavy wooden closet. She opened the doors and knocked three times on the back wall. It swung open to reveal a secret room built into the attic of the adjoining house. Matilde smiled at her, leant out and took the basket. She set that to one side and took the baby. Greta ducked her head and stepped into the secret room. Matilde handed back the baby and closed the secret door carefully.

The room was no more than four meters by five, with no windows. In one corner, David Rosen sat hunched in an old armchair reading a newspaper in the light from a hurricane lamp. Sophie lay sleeping on a makeshift bed set against one wall.

Matilde unfolded a fold-away table and set out three places.

Obviously the food supplied by Greta was sorely needed. She made a mental note to visit more often.

"How've you been, Matilde?"

"Bearing up," said Matilde. "We keep hoping to hear something from the British about our visas. I can't imagine what could be taking so long. And it's so frustrating that we can't go round there and ask them."

"When did you apply?"

"Not long before we moved here.

"When was that? About four months ago?"

David Rosen cleared his throat noisily. "It's been eighteen weeks and two days. April 6 is when we applied."

"What address did you put on the application?"

Matilde replied, "Care of Madam Krauss at this address."

"I'll go around there tomorrow and make an enquiry on your behalf."

"Thank you," said Matilde.

She laid out the food and woke Sophie.

Sophie rubbed her eyes. Her face lit up when she saw Ule. Ule held up his arms to Sophie and she picked him up. Greta marveled at Sophie's strength. Ule was not light.

#

Greta paid a visit to the British embassy the next day, August 30. The place was in chaos. The reception desk was unattended. Greta wandered from room to room unhindered, and everywhere she went she found embassy staff packing tea chests.

"What's going on?" she asked one man.

"We've been told to prepare for evacuation. Can I help you?"

"I'm here on behalf of some friends who've applied for visas."

The man shook his head. "The visa office closed last week. Apologize to your friends, but tell them the embassy won't be issuing any more visas in the foreseeable future."

When Greta conveyed the bad news to David Rosen, he was not surprised. He thanked her. He shrugged. "We're on the brink of war. I thought it was unlikely that we would get out before it started."

Chapter 66

September 1939

On the first day of September 1939, Radio Berlin announced that a group of Polish soldiers had carried out an attack on a German radio station in Upper Silesia, seizing the station and broadcasting an anti-German message. In response to this unprovoked hostile action, German troops had crossed the border into Poland.

On the third day, Neville Chamberlain, the British prime minister, spoke from London. His message was clear, even to those who spoke no English. "This morning the British Ambassador in Berlin handed the German Government a final note stating that, unless we heard from them by 11 o'clock that they were prepared at once to withdraw their troops from Poland, a state of war would exist between us. I have to tell you now that no such undertaking has been received, and that consequently, this country is at war with Germany."

The French declaration of war soon followed.

For the next month the population of Berlin sat by the radio listening for every morsel of news from the east.

#

The German war machine moved through Poland's defenses like a hot knife through butter, pushing the Polish Army into a small defensive position to the southeast.

In their apartment in Kolonnenstrasse, Anna sat close to Max on the sofa. "Oh, Max, why did we have to invade Poland and start a war? It's horrible."

"The Poles started it. They refused to give us back the city of

Danzig. That's all we wanted from them, but they refused to negotiate. Then they attacked our radio station."

She poked him in the ribs. "You don't believe any of that, do you?"

"No. Hitler wanted a war, so he started one."

"It doesn't feel right, Max. I don't feel German anymore. Do you know what I mean?"

"I think so, Anna. I feel the same way. We should think about leaving."

"We'd have to give up our jobs. We could go to Dresden, maybe. We could live with my parents until we found new jobs."

"I meant we should leave the country."

She sat up and looked at him. "And go where?"

"Somewhere. Anywhere."

"It would have to be somewhere the people speak German. Austria's no good. Switzerland's neutral. Zurich, maybe."

"Do you know anyone in Zurich or anywhere in Switzerland?"

She shook her head.

"Me neither. I've seen Belgium. It's nice and peaceful."

"But they speak Flemish there, don't they?"

"Yes, and French and German in some parts of the country."

"We'd have to go where they speak German. I wouldn't want my children growing up speaking a foreign language."

The mention of children sent the conversation in a whole new direction.

Chapter 67

September 1939

Max was on the autobus en route to Wittenberg. Anna was shopping with Ebba and her work friends. He had listened to an anodyne domestic drama on the radio with Anna before leaving the apartment. He regretted it now. Some of the ridiculous dialog was rattling around in his head.

"Oh Heini, how can you leave me here alone with little baby, Adolfina?"

"You know I love you and the baby, Agnetta, but my Führer needs me."

He shuddered.

A stray theory had been worming its way through his subconscious for weeks, and it finally surfaced. The theory rested on two solid bricks.

The first brick concerned his father's cigarette lighter. He took it out of his pocket, flipped it open and turned the wheel. It sparked but produced no flame. He tried four more times without success. He turned it over and opened the fuel compartment. The material in there was dry. He'd had it almost a year. Assuming it was full of butane when his mother gave it to him, it had taken about a year to evaporate. The last time his father had touched the thing had been in 1916, 23 years earlier. Would his mother have refilled it? She could have, but was that the sort of thing she would do, and why would she? Max had no answers to those questions. His mother was an imponderable enigma. Always had been.

The second brick of his theory was those muddy boots. They were far too big for his mother, but someone had been wearing them just before his last visit.

"But Heini, what if you never return?"

"Never fear, Agnetta, my Führer will protect me."

Maybe his theory was correct. Suppose his father had not died in the War. Suppose he had come back but couldn't return to the family for some reason. He might have been severely wounded or suffering from shell shock.

The butane in the lighter should have evaporated long before his mother gave it to him, but as the lighter was working when he got it, it must have been refilled within the past two years.

Could his father be alive and visiting the family home from time to time, perhaps doing repairs in the muddy garden?

#

His mother was as scatterbrained as ever. She offered to make tea and then forgot.

There were no traces of cigarettes or ashtrays anywhere.

"Have you given up the cigarettes again, Mother?"

"I hope you haven't taken up smoking those things. You know how I feel about that. It's a dirty filthy habit."

"The last time I saw you, you were reading a newspaper and smoking, don't you remember, Mother?"

"Try not to leave finger marks on the furniture, dear."

He pulled the cigarette lighter from his pocket. "I wanted to ask you about Father's lighter. Do you have any fuel for it?"

"That was your father's. Where did you get it?"

"You gave it to me a year ago, don't you remember? Where do you keep the lighter fuel?"

Her eyes glazed over. "We were a handsome couple, Wilhelm and I. I wore a full-length white gown. He was very good looking in those days."

"The butane, Mother? Is it in the kitchen somewhere?"

She shook her head and smiled. "Not so good-looking now, though. You'd like some tea." She stood.

"I'll make it, Mother. You stay where you are."

She sat down again, a vacant expression on her face. Max went into the kitchen. Pressing his hand to the pipe on the wall the way she'd shown him as a child, he turned on the tap. The kettle filled with brown water, but the pipe never rattled. Someone had fixed it!

While he waited for the water to boil, he searched the kitchen for a bottle of butane lighter fuel. Then he ran upstairs and did a quick search of the bedrooms. Before he left, he searched the parlors, front and back. He found no lighter fuel anywhere in the house.

He had more to ponder on his journey back to Berlin. He probably should have asked her if she'd called a plumber to fix the rattling pipe in the kitchen, but everything about his mother was so fluid, so unreliable, her answer would probably have confused the picture even more. The repaired plumbing was a third brick supporting his theory, although the absence of lighter fuel was inconclusive. She could have refilled the lighter and thrown away the butane container.

Chapter 68

September 1939

On September 17, Poland was invaded from the east by the Red Army. Trapped between two huge forces, and with little or no help coming from the British or the French, the battle was lost. The bulk of the beleaguered Polish armed services escaped into Romania while the members of the Polish government made their way to London to set up a government in exile. Poland never officially surrendered.

Stalin turned his beady eyes toward Finland and the Baltic States.

#

On Saturday, September 23, Max took a tram to St. Angar's Church. He hadn't seen Vigo since their last delivery run in early June. He wanted to sympathize with the priest over the death of his charge and close friend, Delma.

Vigo was nowhere to be found in the church. Max knocked on the parish house door. The parish priest opened the door.

"I'm looking for Father Vigo," said Max.

Father Zauffer replied, "I haven't seen him for over a week."

"Oh, where is he? Is he away?"

Father Zauffer shrugged. "He sometimes disappears for a day or two. Never for a whole week, at least not without telling me where he's going."

Max was dismayed by the news. "Perhaps you should report his disappearance."

"I have reported it to the archbishop. I can't be expected to run the parish entirely on my own."

"Shouldn't you report it to the police?"

#

Air Commodore Frank Scott stared across his desk at the Frenchman. No doubt General Marchand was a high ranking member of the French military establishment—he had the appropriate height, bearing and gray hairs—but what he was suggesting was inconceivable—always assuming that nothing had been lost in translation.

"Ask the general if I've understood correctly. He seems to be suggesting an unprovoked first strike against the Soviet Union prior to any declaration of hostile intent either from them or from us."

The air commodore's aide translated the question in stuttering school French, and the French general replied with much manual gesticulation. The air commodore tried to interpret the Frenchman's reply through his body language, but without success.

"He confirmed what you said, sir. A first strike, a surprise attack. He is adamant that anything less surreptitious would be doomed to failure. He says facing the combined armies of the Germans and the Soviets places both Britain and France in an unsustainable position."

The French general shrugged. "*Oui, situation absolument impossible.*"

"Ask him if he has any concept of the rules of war. Ask him if he has read the Hague Convention on the conduct of war, which requires a declaration of intent before any hostile action. An attack of the kind that he is suggesting would be in breach of one of the fundamental tenets of that law. Ask him that."

The aide passed on the message, which the French general had understood perfectly well. The Frenchman shrugged again. He stubbed out his foul-smelling cigarette in the air commodore's ashtray and immediately lit another one.

His next outpouring translated as, "Anything less surreptitious would be a pointless act of suicide, an act of supreme madness."

The air commodore considered his next words carefully. The French general had a point. "Tell him... Tell him we are in basic agreement. Ask him to develop the idea. We'd like a written proposal for an action plan that we can discuss with the War Office."

The aide translated.

"Tell the general I'll set up a meeting of the entire Joint Forces Contingency Committee when he has something concrete to discuss."

Afterwards, the air commodore thought about what he'd said. Surely, any surprise attack on such an insuperable enemy would be doomed to failure. Their best course of action might be an immediate, unequivocal and abject surrender.

Chapter 69

October 1939

On a dark, stormy Sunday night in early October, Anna shook Max awake. "There's someone at the door."

"Who could it be at this hour? What time is it?"

"It's after midnight."

The wind and rain battered at the window. He sank lower under the covers. "Maybe they'll go away."

They hammered on the door again. Max slipped some clothes on. "Who is it?" he said through the closed door.

"Open the door, Max."

Max slid the bolt and opened the door. He found Bruno on the doorstep, looked more disheveled than usual. "How did you get into the building? The concierge must be asleep."

"Never mind that. I need your help. Put your shoes on and come with me."

"It's the middle of the night, Bruno, and it's stormy outside. Can't it wait until the morning, whatever it is?"

"No, it can't. Let's go."

He went into the bedroom to find his shoes.

A sleepy Anna said, "Who is it, Max?"

"I have to go out."

"Max…?"

"I won't be long. Go back to sleep."

Bruno had a red Volkswagen, the people's car. Holding the doors against the high wind, they ducked into the car. Max was aware of a second man huddled in the back seat. Bruno started the engine and set off through the storm. He drove east under a heavy blanket of cloud, toward a dim glow in the sky.

"What's this all about, Bruno?"

Bruno made no reply. They passed through the center of the city, deserted apart from one early coal dray on its way to load up for the day's deliveries. Some distance to the east of the city, Bruno stopped the car and switched off the engine.

"You know I trust you, Max. Can I rely on your absolute discretion?"

The rain hammered on the roof and butterflies stirred in Max's stomach. Without the car lights and the windscreen wipers, there was precious little light in the car, but Max could see Bruno's eyes reflecting light from somewhere. He glanced at the man in the back seat and got an impression of a big man with the muscles of a weightlifter. "What's this all about, Bruno?"

"There's a body in the trunk. I want you to help us dispose of it."

The butterflies in his stomach took flight. "Whose body is it? You've killed someone? Why, what did he do?"

"He was a traitor, a Gestapo informer. That's all you need to know."

"Shit, Bruno, why involve me?"

"I needed someone I can trust. Can I trust you, Comrade?"

"Don't call me that. I'm not a member of your party."

"Can I trust you?"

"I suppose you're going to have to, now that you've told me you have a body in the trunk."

Bruno and Max got out of the car. Bruno held the door open while the big man in the back climbed out. Then he opened the trunk and pulled out two shovels. He handed one to Max and the other to the muscleman and they stepped over a low stone wall into a church cemetery. Tombstones stood about silently in the rain, the newer ones erect, the older ones, weathered, made of gray stone, leaning at crazy angles. A sign at the entrance to the church read: Holy Cross Roman Catholic Church. It showed the times of the Sunday services and the name of the parish priest: Father Schmitt.

Bruno led the way to a recent grave. He threw the flowers to one side and retreated to shelter under the wall of the church. Max and Muscleman began to dig. The rain continued to pour down. The soil was heavy, saturated with water. Both men were soaked to the skin within a minute. Within 20, they were both caked in mud from head to toe. The hole was long and wide enough for a body.

Muscleman stopped digging and straightened his back. Bruno came over to inspect their work. "It needs to be deeper. Dig deeper."

The big man climbed out and Max continued digging on his own. As he worked, rivulets of rainwater ran down the sides, depositing wet soil back into the hole. It crossed his mind that he might be digging his own grave. He'd had no more than a quick glimpse inside the trunk. He hadn't seen a body, only what looked like a roll of carpet.

Max's shovel struck the lid of a coffin.

"That's it," said Bruno. "You can stop digging. Come on, give me a hand."

Bruno opened the trunk again. The roll of carpet clearly contained a body, a pair of black shoes protruding from one end.

Muscleman took the end with the head, Max the other.

"On three. One. Two. Three. Lift."

They lifted carpet and body out, carried it across to the grave and dropped it in. The rain pounding on the carpet made a pattering noise that seemed totally at odds with the environment and loud enough to attract attention. Max's end fell outside the hole. Muscleman climbed down and tugged at the carpet.

"Help Edmund, Max."

Max stood on the coffin lid beside muscleman, Edmund. He took a handful of carpet and they pulled the body into position in the grave. Max could see the top of the head. He recognized the tonsure of black hair. "It's Vigo! You've killed Father Vigo."

Part 4

Chapter 70

October 1939

Bruno hissed, "Keep your voice down. Now fill it in."

They climbed out and worked their shovels together to cover the body. Max was shaking with emotion, his heart racing, although he couldn't put a name to what he felt.

As they toiled, the rain eased and then stopped. The wind continued to howl around the tombstones.

All three got back in the car, Max in the back this time. They headed west, dawn light emerging from under the blanket of cloud in the sky behind them.

"Tell me why." Max struggled to keep his voice under control. "Tell me why you killed Father Vigo."

"He was a Gestapo informer. We have suspected him for some time. Yesterday, we put the final piece of the puzzle in place."

Sitting in the front passenger seat, Edmund grunted agreement.

"You tortured him?" Max's blood boiled. These Communists were no better than the Brownshirts!

"We didn't have to torture him. The evidence was clear."

"What evidence?"

Edmund answered in a surprisingly high-pitched voice, "We found a map in the parish house."

"You killed him because of a map?"

Both men clammed up again. Then Bruno said, "We had other evidence. Vigo was the worst kind of wolf, a wolf disguised as a sheep."

"I can't believe that." Max was shouting. "Vigo worked tirelessly for the Red Orchestra. He delivered hundreds of leaflets. He took countless risks. How could he have been a traitor?"

Bruno turned his head, taking his eyes from the road. "What do you think the Red Orchestra is? It's a Communist Resistance movement. And what do you think is the number one enemy of the Roman Catholic Church?" He spat the words out. "Every Roman Catholic priest is dedicated, from the day of his ordination, to the absolute destruction of Communism. This is their secret mission in life."

Max was silent after that. Could it be true? Could Vigo, his friend and companion, the man who stood by Delma when she arrived in a foreign land as an orphaned teenager—could this man have been working secretly to bring down the Communist Resistance all this time?

#

Anna was horrified when she saw the mud on his clothes. "Where were you? What were you doing all that time?"

Max stripped off his clothes. "We'll talk about it tonight after work."

"We'll talk about it now, Max. How could I get back to sleep not knowing what mischief you've gotten up to?"

He left his clothes out to dry and went to bed. She got in beside him. "Tell me, Max."

"I'm tired, Anna, just let me sleep. I'll tell you all about it in the morning, I promise."

She relented, and Max fell into a deep sleep.

She got up early and checked his muddy clothes. They were nearly dry. She used a stiff brush to scrub the dried mud from them. Then she put the clothes in a basin to soak, and cleaned his shoes.

Next, she prepared his breakfast. When the food was ready she woke him. Max leapt out of bed. He got dressed and sat at the table. She waited patiently while he devoured his food. When he'd finished, she said, "Now will you tell me what happened last night?"

Max hesitated. She locked her eyes onto his and waited for an answer.

"That was one of the Communists at the door. He needed my help."

"With what?"

He blinked and his eyes darted away. "The Communists killed a man, Anna. They said he was a traitor. I had to help them dispose of the body."

She couldn't believe her ears. "You went out in a storm in the middle of the night and... what? Buried a body!"

"I didn't have a choice. They said they needed my help. They didn't tell me why until it was too late. I couldn't refuse."

"Where was this? Look at me, Max."

He met her gaze again. "Holy Cross Church Cemetery. It's a long way from here."

She clenched her fists. "Didn't we agree that we would act together in future? That you wouldn't take any major decisions without discussing it with me first?"

He looked at his watch. "I have to get to work. We'll talk about it tonight." He kissed her on the cheek and was gone.

Anna left the apartment shortly after Max. She usually took the tram to work, but today she walked. She needed time to think.

What had she married?

I thought I knew Max, but first he admitted he was mixed up with Communist subversives. That was bad enough. But now he's gone out in the dead of night to bury someone!

Her head was reeling.

Mama was right. I should never have married him.

#

Max called Greta and they arranged to meet at the canal on his way home from work.

"Tell me why Vigo was killed."

"I'm sorry, Max, I know you liked him. I asked Bruno and his comrades to find out who betrayed the location of the hectograph to the Gestapo. They started with a list of three names. Vigo, Edmund and you."

Max opened his mouth to object, but Greta continued, "I told them you didn't know where the printer was located. That left two names. They investigated and decided Vigo was the culprit."

"Based on what evidence?"

"They broke into the parish house and found a map of the city. The map had a pinhole marking the location of the printer."

Max was silent for a few moments while he absorbed this information. "You're telling me they killed him because of a pinhole in a map? How do they know that Vigo put the pinhole there?"

"Who else could have put it there?"

"Edmund, maybe? Was he there when they found the map?"

Chapter 71

October 1939

At the police station on Storkowerstrasse, Kriminal Kommissar Erhart Neumann approached the booking desk. "Anything I should know about, Rainer?"

With two hours left on his shift, the desk sergeant had one eye on the clock. A week of wind and rain had been followed by two nights of extreme Brownshirt activity. The station was inundated with floods of complaining citizens. Neumann marveled at the calm way the desk sergeant dealt with the public, entering everything into the incident book with endless patience.

"Nothing, Erhart. It's been busy, but it's all trivial stuff."

There was a bond between the two men. They were of similar age, and both had joined the police force at roughly the same time, 20 years earlier. It was nothing but the vagaries of Fate that had propelled Neumann to a position as a high ranked detective while his friend languished in obscurity at the desk.

Neumann ran his eyes over the book. There were several beatings in the streets, two missing dogs, a spate of burglaries, and a report from a woman who claimed someone stole her dead grandfather.

"What about this one? Give me the sheet."

Neumann took the sheet to his desk and studied it. The woman's name was Frau Glueck. Her grandfather, Bismarck Rachwalski, had been buried two days earlier. She claimed that his grave had been interfered with during the night. She was convinced her grandfather's body had been spirited away by grave robbers.

Neumann showed it to his assistant. "What do you think of this, Fischer?"

Kriminal Oberassistent Fischer read the sheet. "It's probably nothing, Boss. Maybe some wild animal looking for an easy meal."

"I've never heard of anything like that before. I thought that's why they buried them deep and in wooden boxes."

Fischer shrugged. "You don't really think Herr Rachwalski has been dug up and taken away, do you?"

"No, but I think we should take a look. Grab your keys."

#

In the cemetery behind Holy Cross Church a light mist clung to the ground between the ancient gray slabs. The grave of Bismarck Rachwalski was easy to spot, freshly dug with no gravestone, a dirty bunch of flowers on the soil. All around the grave, traces of scattered soil in the grass and waterlogged footprints suggested recent activity.

Neumann scratched his square chin. "What do you think, Fischer?"

"It looks untidy, but shouldn't the mound be lower if the coffin has been removed?"

"We're going to have to take a look. Wait here. I'll talk to the pastor."

Fischer pulled his coat tighter around his chest. "I'll wait in the car, if you don't mind, Boss. Graveyards give me the creeps."

#

Neumann's boss, Oberst Vogel was not convinced. "What are you expecting to find?"

"I don't know, sir. Maybe nothing. I just have a strange feeling about the case."

"Don't you have a full caseload already?"

"Yes, sir, but my instinct tells me this one is special."

Vogel gave the go-ahead. "Do it by the book. I don't want any citizen's complaints landing on my desk."

The disinterment authority took a week to arrive. It took three days more to find two volunteers willing to dig up a fresh corpse.

They arrived at the cemetery early on a misty October morning. The two volunteers discarded their tunics, rolled up their sleeves and began to dig. Father Schmitt, the parish priest, stood nearby with Frau Glueck in case they were needed.

Fifteen minutes later they uncovered what looked like a rolled up carpet. They dug some more, uncovered the carpet and hauled it onto the grass. They unrolled it to reveal the body of a priest dressed in a cassock.

The parish priest crossed himself several times when he saw the body. "Saints preserve us!"

"One of yours, Father?" said Neumann.

"No, that's Vigo. Father Salvatore Vigo." He crossed himself again. "He's from St. Angar's Church on the far side of the city."

The coffin lid was visible beneath where the body in the carpet had been. The digging party continued until they could unscrew the coffin lid.

Neumann called Frau Glueck over and asked her to identify the body in the coffin. Covering her mouth with her hand she looked down and confirmed that the body in the coffin was that of her grandfather. They replaced the coffin lid. A sobbing Frau Glueck retired to the church with the parish priest.

Fischer used the parish house telephone to ring for a police ambulance. The ambulance arrived within 15 minutes and took the body and the carpet to the city morgue. Then Neumann, Fischer and the digging party began a careful search of the cemetery.

Thirty minutes later, Fischer gave a loud cry. "Over here, sir."

Neumann hurried across. "What have you found?"

Fischer pointed into the long grass close to the cemetery wall. "It looks like a cigarette lighter."

Chapter 72

October 1939

Kriminal Kommissar Neumann walked into Oberst Vogel's office.

Vogel was stuffing his pipe. "I hear you found a body in the cemetery."

Neumann didn't appreciate the obvious joke. "Yes, sir, the body of a priest from a parish on the other side of the city. He was rolled up in a carpet."

"Probably the Brownshirts," said Vogel. "You know how they feel about religious pastors."

"I don't think this was the Brownshirts, sir. They don't usually go to the trouble of burying their victims. No, this is something else. I'd like to open a murder file."

"Do you have any leads apart from the carpet?"

"Just one. We found a cigarette lighter with War markings on it."

"Let me see it."

"I've sent it to the laboratory for fingerprint investigation."

"Very well, but don't spend too much time on it. And keep me informed."

#

The police photographer took a picture of the dead priest.

Neumann and Fischer set out for St. Angar's Church. They found the parish priest, Father Zauffer, in the parish house. Concerned about how the old priest might react to the bad news, Neumann asked if they could all sit down before Fischer showed him the photograph.

As soon as Father Zauffer saw the picture, he covered his mouth and scuttled from the room. When he returned, he took the picture from Fischer. "That's Salvatore Vigo. What on earth happened to him?"

"He was one of your priests?"

"He was a priest of this parish, yes. He has been missing for several weeks."

"When did you last see him?"

Father Zauffer checked the calendar on the wall. "He conducted a Baptism on September 14. That was the last time I saw him. What happened to him?"

"He was killed and buried in a graveyard on the far side of the city. Holy Cross Church Cemetery, do you know it?"

"I know it, yes. That's Father Schmitt's parish."

Neumann signaled to Fischer to retrieve the photograph. It was buckling in Father Zauffer's fierce grip. Fischer eased the picture from the old priest's hand.

Neumann said, "Did you report his disappearance?"

"No, he leaves me from time to time. He has—had—interests outside parish affairs."

"What sort of interests?"

"I don't know. He never told me, and I didn't like to ask."

Fischer and Neumann exchanged a glance.

"Did he have any enemies?"

Father Zauffer had regained some of his composure. He shrugged. "No more than any other priest in the Third Reich."

"And why do you think he was at the Holy Cross Church?"

"I have no idea."

#

Neumann took the car keys from his assistant and got behind the wheel. Driving the powerful car gave him the sensation that he was taking charge and doing something to solve the case. "Why would anyone want to kill a priest?"

The question was rhetorical, but, like a good *Kriminal Oberassistent*, Fischer tried to answer it. "The Communists hate the

Romans, the Jews hate the Romans, the Nazis don't get on with anyone. And there's the Calvinists, the Lutherans..."

"Yes, yes, but we're talking about murder." Neumann chewed his lip. "We'll talk to Otto." Narrowly avoiding a group of schoolgirls on bicycles, he executed a crude U-turn and headed back toward the city center.

#

They found Doctor Otto Schranck, the Medical Examiner, in his laboratory, peering into a microscope.

"Take a seat, Kommissar. I'll be with you in a minute."

Kriminal Kommissar Neumann peered at Vigo's naked corpse laid out on a bench, his head at a strange angle to his body. The priest looked resigned to his fate.

Fischer said, "He looks peaceful."

"He does. He would have known what was coming. He would have prepared his soul to meet his God."

"Unless he was wearing a blindfold when they killed him." Doctor Schranck stood between and behind them. For one horrible moment, Neumann thought the Medical Examiner was going to put his arms around their shoulders, like pals at a football match.

Neumann stepped away. "Was he shot?"

"Not at all. His neck was snapped." He clicked his fingers. "Like a dry twig. Death would have been instantaneous. Was he wearing a blindfold at the time? Who can say?"

"When was he killed?"

"Ten days, maximum. It's difficult to be more precise than that."

Neumann thought that was remarkably precise. Herr Rachwalski had been buried on October 6. That gave them a 2-day period for the killing, October 7 - 8. "Was he killed in the cemetery or elsewhere?"

"He was almost certainly killed somewhere else. People don't usually keep carpets in cemeteries. Wherever the carpet came from, that's probably where he was killed."

"That's very helpful, Herr Doctor. Is there anything else you can tell us? Was he beaten or tortured in any way?"

"No, I don't believe he was, but there is evidence that he was subjected to a severe beating some months ago. I can't be sure when exactly, but I would guess four to six months before the shooting. The abrasions on his face are not recent."

#

Back at the police station on Storkowerstrasse, the desk sergeant told Neumann that the technical team had recovered a good set of fingerprints from the cigarette lighter. They had already started to search their criminal records.

Neumann drove a fist into his palm. "Well done, Rainer. Let me know the minute they find a match."

Chapter 73

November 1939

The Joint Forces Contingency Committee was preparing for a session in Whitehall, Air Commodore Frank Scott in the chair. The members were unusually subdued as they all eyed the two interlopers in their midst.

"Gentlemen, take your seats," said the air commodore. "I'd like to introduce General Marchand of the French Army. The general is here representing the combined armed forces of the Republic of France. You all know my aide. I have asked him to act as translator. I met with the general in September when he suggested a bold approach to the problems posed by the non-aggression treaty between Hitler and Stalin. I've discussed the basic idea of a pre-emptive strike with each of you privately, so we don't need to dwell on the ethics of the thing. Our allies in Paris have now taken the basic idea and added flesh to the bones. The general will now outline the detailed plan."

General Marchand got to his feet and delivered his proposal through his translator.

"The puzzle that we must solve, gentlemen, is how to strike a decisive blow against the enormous combined force of Germany and the Soviet Union. I have no wish to overstate the peril that we face, but the combined force of the Wehrmacht and the Red Army could easily amount to 20 million men. 100,000 tanks and 150,000 combat aircraft. If unleashed against us, a force that large would certainly obliterate both of our nations and could quickly sweep the world. Since my encounter in September with your air commodore, the best available minds in the joint armed forces of the Republic of France have been applied to find a solution to this puzzle, and they have determined that there is one weakness, one glaring vulnerability that both our enemies share. And that is?" He paused for effect. No one responded. "The oilfields in the Caucasian region of the USSR. This is the one vulnerable asset that both our adversaries depend on. The oil that is produced and refined there is used to power both the Red Army and Hitler's Wehrmacht. My plan, which we are calling 'Operation Folie,' is to execute an airstrike against these assets before it is too late."

The general paused. Ten seconds of silence followed, and then the room erupted. Air Commodore Scott applied the bowl of his pipe to the table. When he had restored a measure of order, he gave the floor to the Royal Navy's senior representative.

"That area is bordered by the Black Sea to the west and the Caspian Sea to the east. The Navy has no access to the Caspian Sea. Passage to the Black Sea is possible with the agreement of the Turkish government, but I doubt whether it would be either desirable or wise to position any navy vessels in such a restricted area. I can't see the Admiral of the Fleet sanctioning Royal Navy participation in such a plan."

A red-faced army major general stood up. "I cannot speak for the Field Marshal, but speaking for myself, I would have to say that this plan is nothing short of total madness. I would have thought such an unannounced sneak attack may well provoke the worst imaginable reaction, driving the Soviets and the Nazis into each other's arms and bring annihilation down on all our heads. If this plan is ever put into action, I predict Red Army tanks in the Mall and Nazi troops on the Champs-Élysées."

Group Captain Cameron Pinkley of the RAF spoke last. "As must be clear, the RAF Readiness team has been engaged in detailed discussions with our colleagues in Paris. We have examined the practicalities of the plan, and it is entirely feasible. Given the element of surprise, three attack vectors, from our bases in Iran, Syria and Turkey, and given the overwhelming destructive power of the ordnance we will bring to bear, we anticipate an entirely successful outcome. Indeed, it is difficult to see how these raids could fail to achieve their objective. Gentlemen, this joint Anglo-French enterprise carries a high probability of complete success. And let me say in conclusion that it remains our one and only chance of survival in the gathering storm."

#

The door to No. 10 Downing Street swung open and Air Commodore Scott was admitted to the office of the Prime Minister's personal private secretary. He handed over the French document, and outlined the thrust of its argument.

The secretary ran his eyes over the summary. "Obviously, our options are limited. I have to tell you this is the only proposal on the table at the moment. I shall pass it to the Prime Minister as soon as an opportunity presents. In the meantime, might I suggest you give it to the analysts in the War Office for a thorough evaluation."

Chapter 74

November 1939

On Thursday November 30 everyone was glued to their radios as news came through that the negotiations between the Finns and the Soviets had broken down and the Soviets had launched an all out attack against Finland. The Propaganda Ministry spokesman sounded close to hysteria, describing the incursion as a full-scale invasion by a world power of a small, neutral nation and calling on the League of Nations to condemn the action. The voice on the radio went on to pour scorn on the French and the British who had promised to protect the Finns, but did nothing to intervene.

#

That evening, Max went around the apartment searching for something, looking under the furniture and down the back of the sofa cushions.

Anna watched him. "What are you looking for?"

"My father's cigarette lighter. Have you seen it? Have you tidied it away somewhere?"

"I haven't seen it. I thought you carried it everywhere with you."

"It was in the pocket of my pants."

"When did you last have it?"

"I'm sure it was in the pocket of these pants," he pulled a pair of pants from the wardrobe, "but it's not there now."

"When was the last time you wore those?" Then she remembered. "Oh! Aren't those the pants you were wearing when you went out that night in the storm? That night…"

The blood drained from Max's face. "You must have found it when you washed the mud from my clothes."

"No, I didn't."

"You're sure you haven't forgotten."

"Certain. Check the floor at the bottom of the wardrobe."

Max got down on his hands and knees. He removed all the shoes and ran his hands over the floor.

"Any luck?"

He growled at her. "Nothing but a couple of startled spiders. You're sure you haven't put it somewhere?"

Anna searched through the shoes. He looked at her. She shook her head. Max checked the shoes himself. Then he went back to the wardrobe, pulled out all the clothes, item by item, running his hands over them and dropping them on the floor. Anna could see that he was in the grip of a raging panic.

"You brushed the mud off in the kitchen before you washed them. Maybe it fell out then."

"I don't think so, Max. I would have noticed."

She searched the kitchen floor.

"It must have fallen out when I was digging. I must have dropped it in the cemetery."

#

Two days later, Max caught an eastbound tram. He sat by the window with a clear image in his head of the Holy Cross Church. He jumped from the tram when he spotted it.

There was a funeral in progress, a small group of mourners gathered at a freshly dug grave. He cursed silently that he hadn't dressed for a funeral. He should have thought of that. The new grave was close to the one where he and the two Communists had placed Vigo in the carpet.

Max sidled up behind the funeral party. He cast his eyes over Vigo's last resting place. It looked surprisingly neat and tidy with fresh flowers on the grave. A shiny new gravestone declared that this was the grave of Bismarck Rachwalski, born October 1856, died

October 1939. He circled the grave, keeping his eyes on the ground. He saw nothing. He traced his path back from the grave to the cemetery wall, but found nothing.

His quest was hopeless. The lighter was probably under the soil with poor Father Vigo and Herr Rachwalski, his companion in death.

"Can I help you?"

Max turned to find a young priest standing uncomfortably close.

"No, thank you, Father. I was lost in thought."

"Ah yes, memories of your departed dearly beloved. What was his or her name?"

"Bismarck Rachwalski, my grandfather."

"I remember the funeral. It was well-attended. He was a remarkable man in his time. You must be related to Frau Glueck, so, his granddaughter."

"We are cousins. Thank you for your kind words, Father, I must leave now."

"Good to talk to you. Go in peace." Max took a couple of steps toward the entrance. "I'm sorry about that nasty business with the grave, but as you have seen it's all been set to rights now."

Max stopped in mid-stride. "What nasty business, Father?"

"The police, the disinterment, the extra body. Frau Glueck was most upset. Didn't she tell you about it?"

In hushed and scandalized tones the young priest told Max how the police had dug up the grave and discovered a second corpse wrapped in a carpet. Nothing like it had ever happened at Holy Cross Church before. The archbishop had paid them a visit, threatening to hold the parish priest personally responsible.

Anna dropped the last of her mother's willow pattern saucers when he told her. "If the police have found your lighter in the grave and they trace it back to you, you could be arrested for murder."

"I'm not worried about it, Anna. I don't see how they could possibly trace the lighter back to me." It was a lie, for himself as much as for her.

Chapter 75

December 1939

Oberassistent Fischer strode into his Boss's office. Kommissar Neumann was lighting one of his long Russian cigarettes. He offered the pack to Fischer.

Fischer declined. "I don't know how you can smoke those things, Boss. They're mostly air."

Neumann ignored the comment. No doubt he'd heard it before. "I've been thinking about our dead priest, Fischer. We should take a look into his life, find out what he's been up to recently and see what emerges."

"I was hoping the carpet would lead us somewhere, Boss. Have you spoken to Doctor Otto about that?"

"The state of the carpet and the grave gave him a probable date for the burial. It must have been during that storm on October 8. He got nothing else from the carpet. It's a cheap carpet. Any evidence it might have contained was covered in mud and washed away by the rain. No, I'm hoping the fingerprint search will identify our man. In the meantime, I'd like you to take a trip to the church. Talk to the old priest, see if you can find anything. Father Vigo must have made an enemy. He was Italian. Maybe he upset the Italian Mafia. Maybe he was having an affair with someone's wife. Find me something. Anything."

Fischer said, "I found a report of a burglary in the parish house about the time the priest went missing, Boss, and one of our Schupo colleagues came up with some information that might be relevant. Officer Gretzke pounds the beat near St. Angar's Church. He says a new priest started there in February." He consulted his notebook. "Name of Gunther Schlurr."

"That's all good. Talk to this Father Schlurr."

Fischer took the car to St. Angar's Church. He knocked on the parish house door and Father Zauffer, the parish priest, opened it.

The first question he asked produced a surprising response. "I'd like to speak with Father Schlurr."

"Who?"

"Father Gunther Schlurr. I was told he started in this parish recently."

"We haven't had a new priest here for years,"

Fischer set that aside for later consideration.

"You reported a burglary in September. Was anything stolen?"

"They broke the front door and threw my books around, but we have little enough to steal."

"So they stole nothing?"

"They stole a map."

"What sort of map?"

"A map of the city. It's difficult to be sure, but that's the only thing we're sure they took."

Fischer subjected the parish priest to a battery of questions about Father Vigo's private life. When they first interviewed him, Father Zauffer had said that Vigo had interests that took him away from the parish from time to time. Could he be having an affair? What about his friends and acquaintances? Father Zauffer's answers led nowhere. Finally, Fischer asked for a list of the work that Father Vigo had been involved in for the three months prior to his disappearance. Father Zauffer wrote out a list containing 7 Baptisms, 29 funerals and 10 weddings.

Fischer went to work. He spoke to 7 sets of happy parents and admired 7 newborn babies. He met with 29 grieving widows or relatives. Nothing surfaced that was remotely helpful. He asked Father Zauffer if he had any Italians in his congregation. Father Zauffer gave him the name of a family that ran a pizza and pasta restaurant in the parish. Fischer spoke to them and found a pleasant, hard-working family devastated by the loss of their beloved Italian priest.

Next, Fischer turned his attention to the weddings. He checked the parish register back to the start of the year and found one wedding that looked odd. Father Vigo had married Max-Christian Noack and Anna Weber on Saturday March 25. It was signed by the bride and bridegroom but by only one witness.

"Why only one witness?" Fischer asked.

Father Zauffer scratched his bald pate. "I'm not sure. The Gestapo interrupted that ceremony. Perhaps the witness forgot to sign in the confusion. I'm not sure, sorry."

"The Gestapo? What happened exactly?"

"I didn't see the incident, but I gather they barged into the church and arrested one of the guests."

Fischer asked to see the marriage authorization and the priest went into the parish house to fetch it. He returned with a bemused expression on his face. "It's not there. I looked through our records—twice. It's not there."

Fischer knew then that he had something. A lead. A trail to follow.

He drove to Schönstedtstrasse and interrupted the registrar in the middle of someone's wedding. "I need to see the Authorization for the marriage of Max-Christian Noack and Anna Weber on March 25 of this year."

"You'll have to wait. Can't you see I'm conducting a marriage ceremony?"

"It can't wait. I'm conducting a murder investigation."

The registrar objected again.

"Please find the document immediately." Fischer put his hand on the butt of his pistol.

The registrar searched his files for the Authorization. March 25 had been a particularly busy day. As he handed it over, he remembered the unpleasantness with the Gestapo.

"I had a visit from a member of the Gestapo not long after that wedding. He claimed that the Authorization was a fake. He said the signature was a forgery. He threatened to have me removed from office. He never came back, though."

"And is it a forgery?"

The registrar shrugged. "I've no way of knowing. The signature is illegible. It carries the official stamp."

"I'll hold onto this, thank you."

"You say you're investigating a murder? Surely there can't be any connection between a wedding and a murder?"

"One more question," said Fischer. "What was the name of the Gestapo man?"

"Franz, Franzl, no, Framzl. Kurt Framzl, that was his name."

Fischer sped back to the police station. The case was unfolding at last!

Kommissar Neumann hadn't moved from behind his desk where Fischer had left him. And he was still smoking one of his Russian coffin nails.

"Officer Gretzke's information proved faulty, Boss. The parish priest never heard of a Father Gunther Schlurr."

"Talk to Gretzke again. Anything else?"

Fischer placed the marriage authorization on Neumann's desk and told him what he'd discovered.

"And you say it's a forgery?"

"I can't say that. That's what the Gestapo man told the registrar. He might have been making some kind of mischief. You know what the Gestapo are like."

"Did you get the name of this Gestapo officer?"

"Kurt Framzl."

Kommissar Neumann picked up his telephone and dialed a number.

"This is Kriminal Kommissar Erhart Neumann. I'm ringing from Police District 6 on Storkowerstrasse. I need to talk to one of your men." He listened for a couple of moments. "Kurt Framzl. It's a murder enquiry. I believe Herr Framzl may have information—" Another pause. "I see. Where? Thank you." He replaced the telephone on its cradle.

Fischer looked at his boss. "What did they say?"

"That's a dead end, I'm afraid, Fischer. Kurt Framzl is no longer with the Gestapo. He has been stripped of his rank and sent to Sachsenhausen concentration camp."

Chapter 76

December 1939

On December 7, leaving Ule with his father, Greta Kuckhoff paid a visit to Madam Krauss in Kurfürstenstrasse. She came bearing gifts as well as her usual basket of food for the Rosen family. December 7 was the first day of Hanukkah, the Holiday of Lights.

The front door was open as usual. She called Madam Krauss's name. Getting no answer, she went into the back parlor. A scene of devastation greeted her. The room was in disarray, tables and chairs thrown about, Tarot cards scattered. No sign of Madam Krauss. Greta ran up the stairs to the attic. The closet door was open and inside the closet, the secret door had been kicked open, the place ransacked. The family was gone, leaving the few possessions they owned scattered on the floor.

Greta sank to the floor in disbelief. Someone must have informed on them. She gathered up some of Sophie's reading books. The thought of Sophie in the hands of such thugs gave her cramps in her stomach.

In hopes of finding a clue about where Madam Krauss and the Rosens had been taken, she searched every room upstairs before going back downstairs. She searched all the rooms downstairs, but found no clues. Perhaps Libertas could use her magic with Emmy Göring to find out where they had been taken, maybe even to get them released.

Greta was in the hall preparing to leave when she heard a slight sound. What was it? Where was it coming from? She listened and waited, but heard nothing more. She must have imagined it. She opened the front door. Then she heard it again. A whimper, like a dog in distress coming from somewhere on the ground floor.

"Hello? Is anybody there?"

Nothing.

She closed the front door and moved quietly toward the rooms at the back of the house, listening for the sound. In the kitchen she heard it again, a definite whimper, a child's cry, coming from one of the kitchen presses.

"Sophie?" She opened the press and found Sophie inside, knees tucked up to her face, her eyes tightly closed.

"Hey Sophie, it's me, Greta. Come out of there."

Sophie crawled out and threw herself into Greta's arms. She cried long and loud. Greta held her tightly.

When her cries became gulping sobs, Greta used a dishcloth to dry her eyes. "Tell me what happened, Sophie?"

This question was greeted with another flood of howling tears.

"Come on, girl, dry your eyes and tell me."

Between sobs, Sophie told Greta how men in gray uniforms had taken her parents. She was in the washroom in the house when they broke into the secret room. She managed to hide in the kitchen.

"It was my fault," she wailed.

"Don't be silly, child. How could it have been your fault?"

"It was. Frau Krauss had a visitor in a gray uniform. I saw him from the top of the stairs."

"When was that?"

"I don't know. A few days ago."

"And the man saw you?"

"No, no, I don't think so. But when Frau Krauss was talking to him, Mama said I should be extra quiet. I... I dropped a cup on the floor. It made a terrible noise."

"And the man came up the stairs to see what the noise was?"

"No. Frau Krauss said it was all right. She said she was trying to contact the man's father who was dead."

"A séance."

"She said the noise of the cup falling made the man think his father was there, listening."

"So Madam Krauss said the noise was a good thing, not a bad thing?"

She nodded. "Yes. But then the man sent his friends and they took Mama and Papa away." She howled again, dry-retching.

"It wasn't your fault, Sophie. You can't blame yourself for what bad men do. Now come with me. Look, I have some of your books. Is there anything else upstairs that you need to take with you?"

"Aschenputtel."

"Where is she? Is she upstairs? Come on, we'll go get her."

Dragging her heels, Sophie followed Greta up the stairs. She stopped halfway up.

"Wait here," said Greta. She ducked into the secret room and grabbed the doll.

Sophie took the doll and clung to it. Greta carried child and doll down the stairs.

#

Back at Greta's apartment, Greta and Adam spoke about this new turn of events while Sophie played with Ule in another room.

Adam said, "You did the right thing, Greta, but we can't keep her here. We should ask her aunt Pauletta to look after her."

"You think Libertas and Harro will be happy about that?"

"I'm sure they won't object."

Greta took Sophie to the car and Adam drove them to the Schulze-Boysen's house. When Pauletta opened the door, Sophie threw herself, sobbing, into her arms.

Pauletta picked her up. "Whatever's the matter, Sophie?"

Sophie was too upset to reply. Pauletta took her into the kitchen.

Greta followed her. "Matilde and David have been taken, Pauletta."

Sophie interrupted her sobs to say, "It was my... my fault."

Greta rubbed Sophie's shoulder. "Nonsense, Sophie. You mustn't blame yourself."

Pauletta drew a sharp breath. "Do we know where they've been taken?"

Greta shook her head. "We thought we should bring Sophie here."

Libertas appeared at the kitchen door. Pauletta began to explain. "Sophie needs my help..."

Libertas stopped her with a wave of her hand. "Adam has told me. You can make up the small bedroom for her." She hunkered down to talk to Sophie. "Sophie can stay with us for a while. Now, tell me what your beautiful doll is called."

#

Max answered a knock at the door. Anna was reading a book. She heard a whispered conversation and then Frau Greta appeared at the kitchen door wearing a serious frown.

Anna knew something was seriously wrong. "Is it Sophie? Has something happened to her?"

Frau Greta shook her head. "The child is fine. She is safe, but her mama and papa have been taken."

Anna slumped onto a kitchen chair. "Oh no! Where is she?"

"I've left her with her aunt. She'll be safe there until we can arrange to get her out of the country."

Max said, "What happened?"

"I'm not sure. They were hiding with Madam Krauss. The Gestapo found them. Sophie hid under the kitchen sink. The poor child blames herself for what happened."

Anna was having trouble focusing. She wiped her eyes. "How can Sophie blame herself? What about Madam Krauss?"

"She was taken too."

"Where were they taken?"

"We don't know."

Anna's heart ached for the Rosens and for the child, orphaned in the most cruel way imaginable. "Is there any hope for them?"

Frau Greta shook her head. "Libertas will ask Emmy to intercede for them, but there's a limit to what even Hermann Göring can do."

As Frau Greta was leaving, Anna hugged her and handed her two children's books that she'd bought for Sophie. It was all she could do.

Chapter 77

December 1939

On Christmas Eve, Max knocked on the door of his mother's house in Wittenberg. She opened the door without a word, turned on her heels and left him standing on the doorstep. He stepped inside and closed the front door.

Once again the house was dark, with no tree, no lights, and no candles. Christmas had been cancelled in this small corner of the universe.

In the hallway, he saw a new hallstand and on the stand a shiny new black telephone.

He followed her into the front parlor. She stood in the far corner of the room in a self-hugging pose facing the window. This was odd, even for her.

"Mother, how have you been?"

She moved her head in an ambiguous gesture.

"Are you all right, Mother? You do know it's Christmas Eve?"

No answer.

"I've brought you a gift. It's from Anna and me." He strode across the room, holding out a small parcel wrapped in Christmas paper.

She ignored him.

"I'll leave it here. You can look at it later." He placed it on top of the upright piano beside the picture of his father in his uniform. He got no word of thanks, and not even a flicker of curiosity as to the contents of the parcel.

"I see you have a telephone at last, Mother. Why didn't you ring me and let me know? How long have you had it?"

She turned her head and snapped, "You should have called me."

"I would have if I had your number. Give it to me now."

"What are you doing here?"

"It's Christmas Eve, Mother. I always visit on Christmas Eve. I've brought you a gift."

"Well, you shouldn't have."

"Don't you like me visiting you?"

"There's no need. You can ring me on the telephone in future." She turned her body to face him. "You can see yourself out, can't you?"

That was a short visit! All of seven minutes.

Max went out to the hall. He found his mother's telephone number written on a pad on the hallstand: 58515. He turned to the second page to write his own telephone number and found a second number on there marked with a single letter: 'W 10267.' It was not his mother's handwriting. His heart skipped a beat. Could that be his father's number? W for Wilhelm?

He picked up the telephone handset intending to dial the number, but had a second thought when he heard the dial tone. He replaced the handset on its cradle. Then he wrote 'Max 12388' in big letters on the pad. As he went back toward the parlor to ask her whose number it was, his mother scuttled out. She disappeared into the kitchen and closed the door.

He called to her through the closed kitchen door. "I've written my number on the pad, Mother. Now you can call me whenever you like."

No answer.

"Mother, did you hear me?"

Still no response.

Max left.

When he got home, he picked up the telephone and dialed 58515.

His mother picked up the telephone after an age. "Who is it?"

"It's me, Mother. It's Max. I just rang to see if your telephone was working and to wish you a very joyous Christmas."

No answer.

"You can call me whenever you like now, Mother. I wrote my number on your pad."

"Yes, all right."

"Mother? Are you still there? Are you all right?"

"Goodbye, Max-Christian." She ended the call.

He re-ran the conversation in his mind. She hadn't sounded depressed. Was she angry about something? But what could she be angry about?

Anna entered the room, carrying a bottle of wine. "Who was that on the telephone?"

"Mother. She sounded strange."

Anna handed Max a glass of wine without comment.

"Stranger than usual, I mean."

He told Anna about how odd his mother had been on his visit.

"Did she seem unhappy?"

"No, she seemed angry about something."

"Angry about what? Was she angry with you?"

"I don't think so, but I can't be sure."

Anna responded quietly, "She's as mad as a March hare. I just hope it's not hereditary."

Max told her about the telephone number he'd found on her telephone pad 'W 10267.'

"I thought it might be my father's number. W for Wilhelm."

"What do you mean?"

"I've been wondering if he might be alive. Maybe he survived the War and came back."

"That makes no sense, Max."

"Suppose he survived the War but decided not to return to the family home."

"Why would he do that?"

"He might have been badly wounded or had shell shock. Or maybe he just couldn't face living with Mother anymore."

Anna thought about that for a few moments. "Why don't you ring the number and see who answers?"

"I suppose I could…" Max was torn between the desire to ring the number and maybe make contact with his long lost father, and the prospect that he might finally learn that his father was really dead.

"What are you waiting for, Max?" Anna picked up the telephone and handed it to him.

Max dialed 10267.

It rang three times before a man answered. "Hello?"

Max said, "Hello, who am I talking to?"

Silence.

"This is Max Noack. Is that you, Father?"

The line disconnected.

"What did he say?"

"Nothing. He broke the call."

"Did it sound like your father?"

"I have no idea what my father sounds like, but the way he broke the call suggested it might have been him. If it wasn't him, surely he would have said so, don't you think?"

Anna put her hand to her mouth. "That's creepy, Max."

"Yes, it felt like I was calling a dead man, you know."

"If only we could ask Madam Krauss. She could try to contact him. If she reached him, you'd know he's definitely dead. If not, we'd know he must be alive."

Chapter 78

January 1940

Oberassistent Fischer went looking for Schupo Officer Gretzke in Bismarckstrasse, the police station closest to St. Angar's Church. Gretzke recognized him. "What can I do for you, sir?"

"You reported a new priest in St. Angar's Church."

"That's right. Father Gunther Schlurr."

"When did you first see him?"

"About a year ago."

"And when did you last see him?"

Gretzke scratched his head. "Funny thing, but I don't recall ever seeing him again."

Fischer pulled out his notebook and pencil. "What did he look like, this disappearing priest?"

#

Fischer came into Neumann's office wearing a hangdog look. "That Father Schlurr turned into a phantom, Boss. The Schupo man says he met him only once, a year ago."

"Check with the archbishop's office. They should know where he is."

"I did that. They have no priest called Schlurr anywhere in Berlin. A wider search unearthed a Father Michael Schlurr who served in a mission in German West Africa. He died out there in 1927."

"We can't rely on their records. It is possible that this second pastor has also been murdered."

"You mean we could be hunting a serial killer that only kills religious pastors?"

Neumann ignored the question. Fischer's sarcastic tone was close to insubordination. "What about the fingerprints on the cigarette lighter, Fischer?"

"That has come up dry, Boss. We've checked every record we have. He's not in there anywhere."

"You've checked all the other Berlin districts?"

"Every one, Boss. We've even checked the files in all the other major cities in the country."

"What about Austria?"

"The Austrian police have been searching for weeks. They haven't finished yet, but we've had no success there either. I don't know what else we can do."

Neumann lit a Russian cigarette and blew a smoke ring at the ceiling. "Have you spoken to the Gestapo?"

Fischer shook his head. Neumann picked up the telephone. "Get me Jürgen Traut in the investigation department in Gestapo headquarters."

He was put though straight away.

"This is Traut."

"Jürgen, this is Erhart Neumann Berlin District 6. Good morning."

"What can I do for you, Kommissar?"

"I'd like to interview Kurt Framzl in Ethnics and Racial Affairs. But your office tells me he's been sent to a concentration camp."

"That is correct. Framzl was found guilty of corruption. He has been stripped of his rank and is cooling his heels in Sachsenhausen. Tell me why you want to interrogate him."

"I'm working on a murder case. We have found a positive link to Kurt Framzl."

"You'd better explain that."

"A member of the public complained that her grandfather's grave had been interfered with. We found the body of a priest wrapped in a carpet in the burial plot. His neck was broken. When we investigated his recent activities we came across a wedding that he conducted in March. Framzl told the registrar that the marriage authorization was a forgery."

"The name of this priest?"

"Vigo."

"Salvatore Vigo?"

Neumann sat up in his chair. "You knew him?"

"We've had our eyes on him for some time."

Neumann was not surprised. The Gestapo had their grubby fingers everywhere. "Can you say where and when Vigo was killed?"

"We know he was killed somewhere between October 5 and October 8. He was buried in a fresh grave on the night of Sunday October 8. We don't know where he was killed."

Silence from the other end of the line.

"Jürgen, are you still there?"

"October, you say. Didn't you think to alert me before now?" Traut sounded tight-lipped.

"Why should I have? It's just one of dozens of violent deaths on my caseload."

"I'll be there in 30 minutes." The line went dead.

#

SS-Sturmführer Jürgen Traut swept into the Storkowerstrasse police station and strode past the desk sergeant toward the inner offices. No one attempted to stop him. If at all possible, senior ranked police officers avoided contact with less senior ranks within the Gestapo, but such confrontations were not unheard of. They generally gave rise to tricky interagency incidents. In this case, there was no contest. A Sturmführer of the SS easily outranked everyone at the station.

Traut stormed into Neumann's office. "Tell me what progress you've made in the case since October."

Neumann rose from his chair. Traut waved at him to stay where he was.

"We found a cigarette lighter in the grass near the cemetery wall. My men took a clear set of fingerprints from it, but we haven't been able to find a match on our records. I wondered if you could check your records."

"I take it you've tried all the Kripo records in Berlin?"

Neumann offered his cigarette packet to the Gestapo man. Traut selected one and Neumann lit it for him.

"Yes, and we've checked in all the other major cities. We've even checked the Austrian police records."

Traut sucked in a lungful of smoke. He exhaled, grimaced, and peered at the cigarette. "A search of all our identity cards would take years. Do you have anything to narrow the search?"

"Not much, but you could start with Kurt Framzl. After that you could concentrate on any special records you may have, subversives, political criminals, Communists maybe?"

"Very well." He stubbed out the cigarette in Neumann's ashtray. "Let me have the fingerprints and I'll see what I can do. I'm making no promises, Kommissar, but I'll put some men on it and see what emerges."

"And Framzl?"

"I'll check his fingerprints first, and I'll see if I can arrange for you to interrogate him. Leave that with me."

#

Oberassistent Fischer called to the central office of the Reich Labor Service in Hubertus Allee and asked to speak with Max-Christian Noack. Noack came down to the lobby to meet with him.

Noack was a tall, well-built young man with a pleasant smile under a shock of dark hair. His handshake was firm.

Fischer checked his identity card quickly and handed it back. "We are investigating the killing of a Roman Catholic priest, Salvatore Vigo. Did you know him?"

Noack looked shocked. "Yes, I know him. He officiated at my wedding last year. He has been killed? How terrible. Those Brownshirts are vicious brutes."

"How well did you know Father Vigo?"

"Not well. As I said, he married us in St. Angar's Church…"

"When was that?"

"March 25 last year. I haven't seen him since."

"Do you have any connection to the Italian community in Berlin?"

Noack frowned and shook his head.

"Have you ever visited the Holy Cross Church cemetery in Kreuzberg?"

"No, I don't think so."

"What about Father Gunther Schlurr? Do you know him?"

"Never heard of him."

#

Fischer put out an alert for Father Gunther Schlurr. The newspaper carried a description: mid to early twenties, close to two meters tall, with dark hair. When Greta saw it, she contacted Peter Riese and asked him to create a new passport and a set of identity and ration cards for Max. Gunther Schlurr was dead.

Chapter 79

February 1940

Anna was preparing an evening meal in the apartment. Max was crouched over the radio, listening to the Berlin news. The Russian's incursion into Finland was going well. A new general, Erich von Manstein, had been given command of the 38th Armor Corps. Two huge trainloads of supplies had arrived in Leipzig from Russia.

The telephone rang. Anna wiped her hands on her apron and picked it up. "Berlin 12388. Who's calling?"

She handed the telephone to Max. "It's for you."

"Hello? This is Max Noack."

"Can you get to the Frederick statue in 30 minutes?"

"I think so. Who is this?"

"Meet me at the statue. I have something for you."

Before Max could reply, the telephone went dead.

"Who was that?"

"It sounded like the man I spoke to in December."

"Your father?"

Max put his coat on. "I have to go and meet him at the statue."

"Your dinner's almost ready. Have your dinner first. Did you tell him you were sitting down to your dinner?"

"Put it in the oven, Anna. Keep it warm. I won't be long."

#

To get to the statue of Frederick the Great, Max had to take two trams. He made it with five minutes to spare. The radio had said it was one of the coldest Februaries on record. Max believed it. The trees on Unter den Linden were covered in ice sparkling in the weak sunlight like natural chandeliers. The scene was all but deserted. It was dinner time and far too cold for loitering. He stood at the base of the statue, pulled his collar up around his ears and stamped his feet.

"Max-Christian Noack?" A man approached.

"I'm Max."

"Let's get in out of the cold." The man led Max to a beer cellar in Universitätstrasse. Blowing on his hands, Max pulled out two chairs and they sat at a table.

"You drink beer?" said the man.

"Yes, thanks."

The man was well covered against the cold with woolen gloves and an army greatcoat. Even so, Max reckoned he was a bulky individual under all the layers of wool. He was tall, gray-haired with a military bearing.

The man waved to a serving girl in a lacy bodice and paid her for two beers.

Unable to deny his curiosity any longer, Max blurted out, "Who are you?"

"My name is Walter Lehmann. I knew your father at the Somme. He saved my life."

"How? What happened?"

"We were under fire from a machinegun. He knocked me over, saved me."

Max took a moment to absorb that. "Was that you I spoke to in December? Your telephone number is 10267?"

"Yes. I laughed when you asked if I was your father. Do I sound like your father? Do I look like your father?"

The old photograph on the piano in his mother's house was the only picture Max had ever seen of his father. "I have no idea what my father looks like, or what his voice sounds like. I have no memory of him. I haven't seen him since I was three."

"Your father and I were close. We shared a dugout. He died at the river Somme in 1916."

"You saw his body?"

"I saw the shell hit him. He was sheltering in a foxhole. I was in another one nearby. There was a theory that a foxhole was a safe haven, that a shell couldn't fall on the same place twice."

"Like lightning?"

"The theory was just so much horseshit. The shell landed squarely in your father's foxhole. It could easily have landed in mine and killed me. It must have had his name on it, I suppose…"

Chapter 80

February 1940

The serving girl placed two beers on the table. The stranger thanked her. Max lifted his glass to cover his gloomy face. The man tapped him on the shoulder. "You knew he died in 1916. You didn't really think he was still alive, did you?"

"Not really, but we never got to bury him, and when I saw your telephone number on my mother's pad, I thought…"

"Ah, I see. I have been in touch with your mother. Your father and I had an agreement that if one of us survived he would keep an eye on the other's family. I drew the short straw." He laughed.

"When did you first start visiting my mother?"

"It was January two years ago. When I got back to Germany I had nothing. I set up a small business, made some money. Then the recession hit and I lost it all again. That was when I joined the police."

"You're a policeman?"

He opened his hand and flashed a Gestapo disk. Max's heart did a triple somersault.

"Don't look so worried. There are still some good apples left in Heydrich's rotten RSHA barrel. Not many, but a few."

"Why did you call me back?"

"The Kripo found your father's cigarette lighter at the scene of a murder. They've been searching their fingerprint records for months."

Shit! Fingerprints!

"How do you know it's my father's?"

"Your father gave it to me at the Somme in 1916, and I returned it to your mother. When I rang her to get your number, I asked if she'd passed the lighter on to you. She confirmed that she had."

"There must be hundreds of lighters like that. How can you be sure it's my father's?"

"I can't, but I thought I should warn you that the Gestapo is now searching its records. If the fingerprints on that lighter are yours, they will match them. It may take some time, but they will find a match. When they come calling they'll ask you to show them your father's lighter. If you have it at home you have nothing to worry about..."

They sipped their drinks in silence. Max could feel the bars of a trap closing around him. This man could easily have informed his superiors in the RSHA about the lighter. If he had, the Gestapo would have immediately checked Max's fingerprints on his identity card and found a match. The whole process would have taken no more than an hour. Walter Lehmann was an ally, a good friend.

"I'm grateful to you, Herr Lehmann."

"It was nothing. I owe your father a debt deeper than any man could ever repay. But tell me you didn't murder anyone."

"I murdered no one. I swear it."

"That's all I wanted to hear. My glass is empty."

Max waved to the serving girl. She came over and he paid for two more beers.

The conversation turned to Max's mother.

"How often do you visit my mother?"

"Not often. When I first visited her two years ago, she really didn't want to talk to me. I nearly didn't go back. But I tried again in the autumn. She let me in. We spoke for ten minutes."

"Ten minutes."

"She seemed uncomfortable in my presence so I left. I managed to tell her who I was, though, and the next time I called she was more amenable."

"More friendly, you mean?"

The serving girl arrived carrying a tray of full glasses. She put two down on the table and went on to deliver the others.

Lehmann took a mouthful of beer. "She's never been friendly. Your mother is not the easiest person in the world to get on with. She tolerates my presence. I usually stay for about 20 minutes."

"I'm not sure, but when I saw her in December she seemed unhappy. I thought she might be lonely."

"That's natural. She lost her husband over 20 years ago. Has she had anyone else since then?"

"Not that I know of, but she's never shown signs of loneliness before. I think meeting a friend of my father's could help her. Will you continue to visit her?"

"As long as I'm able."

"Because you gave your word to my father?"

"Yes, but that's not the only reason."

Max thought it best not probe any further on that subject. He drained half his beer and ran his hand across his lips. "Was it you that persuaded her to get a telephone?"

"Yes, I thought it might be easier to talk to her on the telephone."

"And is it?"

Lehmann laughed. "No. Your father warned me about her. I thought he was exaggerating, but he wasn't, was he?"

"Did he ever speak about me?"

"All the time. You were the apple of his eye."

"Have you ever done any work around the house for my mother?"

"A little. I fixed an annoying pipe that rattled in the kitchen and I sorted out a drainage problem in the garden."

"Wearing my father's boots?"

He grinned through the beer foam on his upper lip. "They were a snug fit."

Chapter 81

February 1940

𝐀 high degree of expectation and tension pervaded the air on the third floor of the War Office in London. All six members of Joint Forces Contingency Committee were smoking as if their lives depended on it. The chairman, Air Commodore Frank Scott had his pipe in his hand. It was full but unlit. A buzz of conversation filled the room. A rear admiral and a major general of the Army stood face to face in a corner of the room in a raging argument. The red-faced major general looked close to apoplexy.

The air commodore rapped the table with his pipe. "Please resume your seats, gentlemen. I'd like to get started."

"If I may, Air Commodore..." The speaker was Group Captain Cameron Pinkley of the RAF.

The air commodore yielded the floor to Pinkley who opened his briefcase, took out six copies of a document and circulated it around the table. Each copy was numbered and carried the heading OPERATION PIKE — MOST SECRET in large letters.

"My team at Air Readiness has been working on this plan since the last meeting. The first page contains a summary. It goes without saying that His Majesty's forces could not stand against the combined force of Nazi Germany and Stalin's Soviets. As previously discussed, the oilfields and oil refineries of Caucasia have been identified, by our French allies, as the single most vulnerable strategic asset that the Soviets possess. Analysis by the War Office proves that a carefully coordinated action from our air bases in Turkey and Iran and the French bases in Syria could destroy a large part of these assets in a series of sustained air strikes over a 3-month period."

The hubbub rose again. The air commodore raised a hand for

silence and the group captain continued, "As I've said, between the RAF and the French Air Force, we have the capacity to wipe out maybe as much as 75 percent of this strategic resource. The analysts have calculated that such a strike would neutralize the combined Soviet military forces for an extended period. In addition, it could reduce the Soviets' production of electricity, closing down large portions of their heavy industry."

Another outburst greeted these statements. Someone laughed and shouted above the racket, "I suppose they won't be able to produce food, either."

"That is correct," said the group captain. "Our analysts have calculated a reduction of 50 percent in their agriculture output. In fact, the air strike could well cause widespread famine and a complete collapse in the Soviet economy. Also, as the German Wehrmacht relies on these oilfields for much of their fuel, a strike there will kill two birds with one stone."

The red-faced major general said, "It seems rather elaborate to me, and I still question the advisability of awakening the sleeping giant."

The air commodore peered into the bowl of his pipe. "What was it the bard said about killing the serpent in the egg?"

"Julius Caesar: Act 2, scene 1," said B-S, the Assistant Director of Military Intelligence. "*And therefore we should liken him to a serpent's egg. Once it's hatched it becomes dangerous. Thus we must kill him while he is still in the egg.*"

The major general snorted. "Whatever happened to 'let sleeping dogs lie'? How can we be sure this one short air campaign will be enough to kill off the Soviet threat?"

Air Commodore Scott raised an eyebrow. "You doubt the analysis, General?"

"No, I'm sure the analysts have done a fine job. All I'm saying is we will need to be absolutely certain before we act. If the air raids miss their target or the Soviets' air defenses are more robust than we think, or the Soviets have other untapped sources of oil that we don't know about. I can think of a hundred things that might go wrong."

"Quite right, General, and that's exactly why we are warming the seats of our pants in this room. Now I suggest we start by making a list of all the contingencies we can think of, no matter how improbable, and we can proceed from there."

Chapter 82

March 1940

Max awoke with a throbbing pain in his mouth. The cyanide capsule was now a constant irritation. After a few moments of internal debate, he concluded that he was unlikely to be captured by the Gestapo, and if he was, the fact that it was the Gestapo that had inveigled him into joining the Red Orchestra in the first place should save him. He decided to get rid of it. He leapt from the bed and into the bathroom and turned the key in the bathroom door. Using his tongue, he worked the cyanide capsule loose and spat it into the toilet.

#

In Storkowerstrasse police station, Kommissar Neumann was snowed under with work. In an attempt to win over the hearts of the population, the Nazi government had initiated a new policy of prosecuting Brownshirts for their most serious crimes. To make matters worse, the Kommissar had run out of Russian cigarettes. Only the black market had them now, and no member of the Kripo could be seen buying from that source. To get over his craving, Neumann bit the inside of his cheek and threw himself into his work.

"Any word from the Gestapo on the Pastor Vigo affair, Fischer? Surely they've found those fingerprints on their records by now?"

"I've heard nothing from them, Boss. I assume they're still looking."

Neumann picked up the telephone. "Get me SS-Sturmführer Traut in Prinz-Albrecht-Strasse."

Traut picked up the telephone on the third ring and grunted his name.

"Jürgen, it's Erhart Neumann here. Have you found a fingerprint match for us yet?"

"No. The fingerprints are not Framzl's. We're still looking. I told you I'd ring if we found anything. You need to be patient, Kommissar. Have you any idea how many records we have here?"

"40 million?"

"Nearly 50 million adult records. How many do you think we can check in a day?"

"A thousand?"

"With maximum manpower, we can check 2,000 a day. That's if I put every man on it. But we have other things to do. We're checking about 250 per day. How long do you think it's going to take us to work through 50 million records?"

Neumann did some quick mental arithmetic. "A couple of years?"

"550 years! That's well past the halfway mark of the thousand year Reich."

"I thought you were going to start with the subversives and Communists."

"We have. And how many of those do you think we have?"

Neumann had no idea. He said nothing.

"Well over 200,000. That's two and a half years searching. If you have any suggestions to help to narrow the search, I'd be happy to hear them. Otherwise, get out of my ear and let me get back to work."

Chapter 83

March 1940

All through the months between December and March, Greta continued to visit Sophie at the mansion. Sophie missed her parents deeply, but she grew to love her aunt Pauletta, and she delighted in spending time with Ule. Asleep or awake, Sophie's doll was her constant companion.

While Anna kept up a steady flow of children's books to Greta's apartment, Greta spent as much time as she could with Sophie, helping Pauletta to build on the education that her sister, Matilde Rosen, had given her daughter. Greta was deeply affected by these visits. Sophie seemed to have put the tragedy of losing her parents behind her, but Greta only had to look at the sorrow etched into child's eyes to be reminded what had happened. Not that she had any details about where Sophie's parents had been taken or what had happened to them, but her imagination fed on every hint picked up from the newspaper and the radio, and ran wild.

#

Arvid and Mildred Harnack lived in constant fear of discovery. They never held meetings in their apartment or visited any of their contacts in their homes. They had no telephone for fear of Gestapo telephone tapping. All contact with other members of the network was arranged on neutral ground or by verbal messages delivered by go-betweens.

Arvid never let his guard down. He regarded any and all contact with strangers as suspicious, so when a young boy in the street handed him a plain brown envelope, he reacted as if it carried an evil curse, dropping the envelope and hurrying away without a word. It was Mildred who picked it up, gave a coin to the boy, thanked him, and sent him on his way.

In the safety of their apartment, Mildred offered the envelope to her husband. He held up both hands. "I don't want it. Throw it away."

"It's addressed to you, Arvid. I think you should open it and see what it says."

Arvid refused to touch it. Mildred fetched a knife from the kitchen and sliced it open. Inside the envelope she found a single sheet of paper with a hand-written note. Mildred read it aloud.

"How about a sailing trip? Meet me in the boathouse at 11:00 a.m. tomorrow, March 27. EvP"

Arvid plucked it from her hand and read it. "Make some coffee, dear, while I change my clothes."

"We're out of coffee, Arvid. I'll make tea." Arvid hurried into the bedroom. She called after him, "Who is this EvP?"

He emerged from the bedroom dressed in dark clothing. "Hauptmann Edwin von Pfaffel of the Abwehr, if we can believe the evidence of our eyes. It could be an elaborate trap. I need to talk with Harro."

He drank his tea, kissed Mildred and left the apartment.

The S-Bahn journey from Dahlem in the southwest to the Schulze-Boysen mansion in Pankow in the north of the city took an hour. Arvid spent the journey lost in thought. The Abwehr—Military Intelligence—was an organization cloaked in secrecy, its head, Admiral Canaris, one of Hitler's closest allies. But there were rumors about the Abwehr, rumors of foot dragging, insubordination, and incompetence. There were even rumors of active defiance. Reinhard Heydrich's RSHA had made several attempts to subsume the Abwehr, but had failed each time.

Harro opened the door, "Good to see you, my friend. I think this must be the first time you've come visiting unannounced."

"Forgive me for disturbing you at this late hour, Harro, but I need your advice."

Harro chuckled. "That's another first. Have you eaten? I could ask Libertas to fetch you something." He led Arvid into the study.

"Please don't trouble Libertas. Take a look at this and tell me what you think." He handed the note to Harro.

Harro read the note and frowned. "Is this what I think it is? A summons from Edwin von Pfaffel?"

"That's what it looks like, but it could be a trap."

Harro examined the note again. "Do you recognize the handwriting?"

"No, I've never seen von Pfaffel's handwriting. Have you?"

"Not that I can recall. Where's this boathouse?"

"We both had sailing boats on Wannsee years ago. It's quite remote. If the note is genuine, I expect that's where he means."

"What makes you think it might not be genuine?"

"Call it instinct. It must be five years since I last spoke with anyone from the Abwehr."

"If you want my advice, I'd say you've no need to worry. If the note said he wanted to discuss how best to assassinate the Führer or how to blow up the Chancellery building, you might have grounds for suspicion. This is an invitation to meet from one old friend to another."

"You don't think it could be a trap?"

Harro poured two glasses of schnapps. He handed one to Arvid. Arvid sipped it. Harro drained his glass in one swift movement. "You're being paranoid, my friend. There's no crime in meeting with an old sailing buddy."

Arvid was not convinced. "If the Gestapo wanted to entrap me, this is just the sort of thing I would expect. It's too direct. It rings too many familiar bells."

"Why don't you call von Pfaffel in the morning?"

"And say what?"

"I don't know. There must be something the Economics Ministry needs from the Abwehr. An estimate of their budget for next year, maybe?"

Chapter 84

March 1940

Arvid got up early and took his car to work. He rang the Abwehr at 9 o'clock, identified himself, and asked to speak with Hauptmann von Pfaffel.

"The Hauptmann is unavailable this morning. May I take a message?"

"Will he be there in the afternoon?"

"No sir, the Hauptmann has taken a day's leave. He'll be at his desk tomorrow."

That was all the confirmation Arvid needed. He signed himself out of the building and drove southwest toward Potsdam.

The southbound traffic was light. All the early morning traffic was heading north toward the city center. He arrived at Wannsee before 10:30, parked the car, and waited.

There were two other cars in the car park and two dinghies on the water. The lake was quiet, the flat calm water reflecting the low sun. The sight took Arvid back to his university days, when sailing was all he ever did in his spare time. It was all he ever wanted to do in those days. He might even have made a career amongst the sailing community—training youngsters or selling sailing boats or equipment—if the political situation in Germany hadn't taken such an unwelcome turn.

At ten minutes to the hour, a car arrived and parked at the far end of the car park. Arvid's heart rate increased when he saw it. He recognized Edwin von Pfaffel's old red Alfa Romeo. He got out of his car and strode across to the boathouse.

The smells in the boathouse took him back on another memory trip. There were countless outings on this and other lakes with long forgotten friends. In the early days, he had capsized more times than he could remember, and he'd nearly lost a big toe once when his foot got trapped under a sailing line under tension.

Edwin von Pfaffel appeared in the boathouse. He smiled and they shook hands. "I thought we might take the dinghy out for a spin, if you have the time."

"I'd love to, but I came unprepared." Edwin was dressed for sailing. Arvid was not.

He handed Arvid a buoyancy jacket. "That's not important, Arvid. Put this on, and we'll take her out."

Edwin climbed down into one of the dinghies and Arvid followed him. Arvid sat amidships, Edwin at the rudder. They cast off. Edwin was an accomplished sailor, and he soon had the light dinghy skimming across the corrugated surface of the water, in a light breeze.

The exhilaration of the experience resurfaced straightaway. Arvid turned his face to the wind, and the cold spray welcomed him like a lover long abandoned. After 10 minutes they were well out on the lake, the other two boats hundreds of meters away. Edwin turned her into the wind and allowed the sail to slacken.

"You've kept up with the sailing, I see," said Arvid. "It gave up on me years ago, I'm afraid."

"It helps me to unwind when the pressure of work gets too much. I've asked you here to pass on some important information. One of my agents in Britain has unearthed a Franco-British plan that could have a huge impact on the progress of the war. Generalmajor Oster asked me to pass it on to you."

Arvid stiffened.

"Since the Molotov-Ribbentrop pact was signed, we are faced with the threat that Hitler and Stalin will combine their forces. A combined force of that size would be unstoppable and would overrun the whole of Europe in a war to rival the last one."

Arvid held up a hand to slow his friend's narrative. The prospect of such a war was unthinkable. It could result in hundreds of millions of deaths. "I hope you're going to tell me that the British have found a way to prevent it."

"The French and the British have devised a plan. It's top secret, of course. They call it Operation Pike. The idea is to conduct a surprise air attack on the Soviet oilfields and refineries in Caucasia. The Wehrmacht import a lot of fuel from there and the Soviets themselves rely on the area for most of their oil supplies."

"How far advanced is this plan? It sounds crazy."

"It's already more than just a plan, Arvid. The British and French air forces have begun to position their aircraft in Turkey, Iran and Syria. The Royal Navy is transporting the bombs. They will use heavy bombs to split the oil tanks open and incendiaries to set the whole lot alight."

Arvid swallowed hard. "Have they considered the probable consequences of their actions?"

Edwin said nothing in reply. He turned the dinghy and began to tack back the way they'd come. As they tied up the boat in the boathouse, Edwin said, "We need you to transmit this information to Moscow as quickly as possible. If we can't warn the Soviets, we could be facing the apocalypse."

"Why can't you simply pass the information to the Soviet embassy?"

"We could, I suppose, but would they believe us?" He shook his head. "They need to hear it from a source they trust."

Chapter 85

April 1940

On Saturday April 6, Anna was preparing an evening meal for Max when he answered an urgent knock at the door.

"Look who it is," he said.

Anna turned to see Frau Greta, carrying a small suitcase and wearing a serious frown. "What's the matter, Frau Greta? Is it Sophie?"

Greta put the suitcase down. "No, no, Sophie's fine. She's been working her way through all those books you sent her. No, we have received some important intelligence that we need to get to the Soviets as quickly as possible." She waved her hands about as she spoke. "We want Max to take it to Brussels."

"When?" said Max.

"Right away. You must leave in the next few minutes."

"That's ridiculous," said Anna. "You can't expect him to jump on a train and travel to Belgium at such short notice."

"I've explained. The intelligence is really important. It could have an immediate and direct bearing on the War."

Anna put wrists to hips and glared at their visitor. "It may be important to you, but people have lives to lead. How many weekends has Max sacrificed since he joined your Orchestra? I'm sorry, but there's a limit to what you can ask him to do."

Max said, "I can't use my Pastor Schlurr identity card or passport. The name has come to the attention of the Kripo. Did you see the description in the newspaper?"

"We saw that. Give me the pastor's papers."

Max fetched the pastor's papers and handed them over. Greta pulled another complete set of personal papers from her handbag.

Max looked through the new set. He would travel under the name Dieter Marten, a clothing salesman from Brussels. The passport was well stamped. This was a salesman who traveled abroad a lot.

Greta pointed to the suitcase. "Those are your samples." She handed him a half-empty pack of cigarettes. "Make sure Gilbert gets these and come straight back."

"I understand, Frau Greta. When does the next train leave?"

"There's an express train in half an hour."

"I'll never make that."

"Adam's waiting outside in the car."

Max opened the suitcase and placed the cigarette pack inside. Anna peeped over his shoulder at the samples.

Max read her mind. He closed the suitcase. "You can take a look when I get back."

#

Adam drove Max to Südkreuz Bahnhof. Max bought a ticket and barely caught the 7:20 p.m. express to Cologne. The train was full. He was lucky to find the last empty seat in a compartment.

At Cologne, he changed trains. The seats on the Belgian train were harder, but there were fewer passengers. He found a window seat.

The train stopped at the border and a pair of uniformed Schupo checked his papers. "You are a salesman?"

"Yes. I sell women's clothes."

"I'll take a quick look."

Max opened the suitcase. The cigarette pack was in plain sight. The first policeman handed the pack to his companion and searched through the clothing. Max watched in horror as the second policeman helped himself to a cigarette. He put the cigarette in his mouth. Then he grinned at Max, removed a second cigarette from the pack and placed it behind his ear.

The searcher smirked. "Very nice underwear, Herr Marten."

The second policeman handed the pack to his companion who tossed it into the suitcase before closing it.

As soon as the train had crossed the border into Belgium Max opened the suitcase. There were now five cigarettes in the pack. There must have been seven to start with. So, there was a two in seven chance that the policeman had removed the cigarette with the encrypted message.

#

He found Gilbert on his usual stool at the bar in the grubby beer cellar behind the railway station. He took the seat beside the large Belgian and placed his cigarette pack beside Gilbert's.

Gilbert ordered two beers. "You traveled alone this time?"

"Vigo was killed."

"I heard. And I heard you helped with the disposal."

"I helped bury him, yes. I'm afraid the police will be looking for me soon. I will need to leave Germany. I dropped something at the scene. I've been told they are searching their fingerprint records."

"That was careless. Where will you go?"

"I thought we might come here, to Brussels, Comrade."

"We?"

"My wife and I."

Two large glasses of beer arrived in front of them on the bar. Max sank half of his in one go.

Gilbert looked sideways at his young German companion. "Are you asking me for help?"

"We will need a place to stay while we get settled."

"What do you do?"

"I work for the government, the Labor Service."

The Belgian curled his lip. "A pen-pusher. What does your wife do?"

"She's a waitress. She works in the food court at KaDeWe, a large department store."

Gilbert took several moments to think about it. "Since you're a comrade, I will be happy to arrange accommodation for two, maybe for a couple of weeks."

"It could take longer than that to find jobs and another place to live."

"Two weeks. That's the best I can do. Your wife should find work straight away, you not so easily." Gilbert sank his nose in his beer and took a long drink.

Max finished his beer and ordered two more.

#

Max told Anna about his trip and his conversation with comrade Gilbert while she worked her way through the suitcase. She liberated three items of lingerie and disappeared into the bedroom to try them on.

She called Max to come and take a look.

He called back, "Did you hear what I said, Anna? My contact in Brussels will find us somewhere to stay while we search for work. He said—"

He pushed open the bedroom door. At the sight of Anna in the lingerie, the conversation took a whole new turn.

Chapter 86

April 1940

Anna woke up with a blinding headache. She rang the department store and told them she wouldn't be in that day. She made Max's breakfast, and after he'd left for work, she went back to bed, leaving the dirty dishes in the sink.

At around noon, someone knocked on the apartment door.

She opened the door a crack. Jürgen pushed the door open and stepped into the apartment. He was dressed in his double-breasted suit.

Her heart skipped a beat. "You can't come in. I'm not well." That sounded like she had leprosy, but it was the best she could come up with.

He ran his steel-blue eyes over her. She pulled her housecoat closely around her body.

"I thought you were posted to the East."

"I was. I liberated Poland from the Poles. Now I'm back in headquarters. Aren't you pleased to see me?" He advanced, pressing her against the door.

"Please, Jürgen, I'm really not well…"

"Today you will give me what I want."

"I don't have any information for you, Jürgen. Please let me go."

"Show me your bedroom."

Anna panicked. "I'm a married woman. Please leave."

"I've spoken to the registrar. I think you'll find your marriage will soon be annulled."

"I'll scream if you touch me!"

He stepped back. "You want me to leave? I can do that. If I do, I will have to inform my colleagues that your husband is a Communist." He removed his jacket and draped it carefully over the sofa. "I will have to tell them that he murdered Salvatore Vigo, the Roman pastor." He removed his trousers, lined up the creases, and draped them over the sofa. "And I will have to tell them that he buried the priest in the Holy Cross Cemetery." He unbuttoned his shirt...

#

Max found Anna in the bed that evening. He asked her how she was and she gave him a curt reply, "I have a headache. Leave me alone."

He sat beside her on the bed. "Should I call the doctor?"

"No, I'll be fine in the morning."

#

A week after his trip to Brussels, Max got a call from Frau Greta calling herself 'Sister Bernadina' again. He was to attend an urgent meeting in Berlin's zoological gardens. The choir was assembling at the monkey house.

Max walked to the zoo. It was no more than a kilometer to the north of the apartment. Greta had sounded out of breath, distressed. Had the vital secret message been lost when the policeman at the border stole those two cigarettes? She had said the message was important, that it could affect the outcome of the War. What if it never arrived in Brussels, if the border policeman had smoked the message and Gilbert found nothing in any of the remaining five cigarettes?

He bought a ticket and made his way to the monkey house. He found Adam Kuckhoff waiting for him, the monkeys in the cages leaping about, screeching at him. Adam looked miserable.

They stepped out of the noisy monkey house onto a green area where there were groups of children rushing about making nearly as much noise as the monkeys.

"What's happened, Adam? Was there a problem with the

message?" Max was ready to explain what happened at the border. He would agree to travel to Brussels again if necessary, if it wasn't already too late.

Adam shook his head. "You played your part perfectly, Max. Gilbert transmitted the message to Moscow. The problem is that Joseph Stalin and his Intelligence chief have rejected the information out of hand. Word has come back from Moscow. They believe what we sent them is misinformation designed to misdirect the Red Army. Gilbert has been recalled to Moscow to explain his actions. And the Soviets will no longer accept intelligence from anyone in Berlin."

Max was relieved that his part of the process hadn't been at fault, but at the same time he was devastated that Gilbert would not be there to help when—if—he and Anna managed to escape to Brussels. He asked, "What was this intelligence? Frau Greta said it was of critical importance to the outcome of the War."

"I can't tell you that, but I can tell you we could be facing Armageddon if Moscow don't act on the information. No, the reason I called you here is to deliver a message from Gilbert. He says he's sorry that he won't be able to do what you discussed in Brussels."

#

Anna was devastated by the news. Every day since she'd allowed Jürgen into her bed she'd been terrified that he might come back for more, or that he might blow the whistle on Max. "We have to get out of Germany, Max."

"Don't you think I know that? As soon as the Gestapo match my fingerprints from the cigarette lighter I will be arrested and charged with murder."

"But you didn't murder Father Vigo. You helped to bury him, but you didn't kill anyone. Or did you?"

Max blinked.

"I'm not sure the Gestapo will make that distinction. At best I may be charged as an accessory. At worst I could be executed for capital murder."

As he spoke, Anna realized that she shouldn't have mentioned the name of the murdered priest. She wasn't supposed to know that. Had he noticed? She sat down wearily on the sofa.

"Oh, Max, why did you have to get involved with these people? They're murderers and Communists. And they are fighting against the Nazis. There's only one way this is going to end."

"You know why, Anna. I explained that to you. The Gestapo refused to sign our marriage authorization until I joined the Orchestra and found out where the printer is located."

"You never did find the printer, did you?"

"No, but they found it without my help. Actually, they found one of the printers. There's at least one more. I know that because the leaflets are still being printed."

Max hadn't asked how she knew the name of the victim. Perhaps he hadn't noticed. She picked at a fingernail. "When will it all end. Max?"

"It could end very quickly for us if we don't get out of Germany soon."

"But where can we go if your friend in Brussels can't help us?"

"We can still go to Belgium, Anna. We'll just have to make our own way when we get there."

Chapter 87

April 1940

Air Commodore Scott addressed the members of the Joint Forces Contingency Committee, now reduced to five members, one from each armed service and B-S, the civilian from Military Intelligence. The mood around the table was somber.

"You've all had a chance to read the final document. Operation Pike is now fully actionable. The analysts have given it the green light and the Prime Minister has sanctioned it. Our task now is to consider the ramifications."

"Perhaps you'd brief us on how far advanced are the preparations?" The air commodore addressed his question to the RAF representative, newly promoted Air Commodore Pinkley.

"The French have completed their development of several new airfields in Syria. We have committed 75 aircraft to the campaign, and the French have agreed to match that number. We have completed many reconnaissance flights over the area and worked out a detailed plan of attack. They have minimal anti-aircraft weapons in place. Many of our aircraft and much of the ordnance are already in place at our bases. The remainder of the ordnance is in transit courtesy of the Royal Navy."

"Can you give us details on the ordnance?" the rear admiral asked.

"I don't have exact numbers, but we're planning to use heavy armor-piercing shells to open up the storage tanks, followed by incendiaries. We anticipate a conflagration that could takes years to get under control."

This statement was greeted by silence.

"The port of Baku will be the main target for the first wave. The city is several feet below sea level, so we plan to destroy the sea barriers immediately after the oil refineries."

Someone said, "Won't that put the fires out?"

Pinkley ignored the comment. He sat down.

B-S lit a new cigarette from the stub of an old one with a trembling hand. "And do we have an initiation date for the plan?"

Pinkley looked flushed, whether from excitement, apprehension or embarrassment, Air Commodore Scott couldn't tell. "Operation Pike will start on May 15."

Chapter 88

May 1940

Oberst Vogel called Kommissar Neumann into his office. He invited Neumann to take a seat.

"Traut's been on the telephone. He tells me you asked for authorization to visit one of his men in a labor camp."

"That's right. Kurt Framzl in Sachsenhausen."

"You are aware that Framzl has been kicked out of the Gestapo? He's been found guilty of corruption."

"Yes, sir. I believe he may be able to help with one of our investigations."

Oberst Vogel picked up his new Meerschaum pipe and began to fill it with tobacco. "The killing of the priest."

"Yes, sir. Did Traut say when we might get that authorization?"

The Oberst pointed the stem of the pipe at an envelope on his desk. "It came in yesterday."

Neumann picked up the envelope. He opened it and pulled out the authorization.

"I need an afternoon to travel to Sachsenhausen."

"Very well, Kommissar, but tread carefully. The Sturmbannführer read me a litany of dire warnings. And you know how mud can stick."

Kommissar Neumann took the car. He traveled alone. The journey to the concentration camp in Oranienburg took an hour in light traffic. He presented his authorization three times, first at the gate, then at the door of the administration block and finally in person to the camp commander.

"What is your business with this criminal, Kommissar?"

"I'm hoping Herr Framzl can cast some light on one of the cases I'm working on, the murder of a pastor."

"You suspect him of this murder?"

"He's not a suspect, no, but he did have contact with the victim shortly before he died."

Kurt Framzl looked like a beaten man, disheveled and gaunt, with sunken eyes, his flesh barely clinging to his bones. Neumann invited him to sit, but Framzl remained standing.

Neumann said, "Has the commandant told you who I am?"

"I know who you are, Kommissar..."

"Kommissar Neumann. I'm investigating the death of a Roman Catholic priest called Salvatore Vigo. You knew Vigo."

"Yes."

"You brought him to Prinz-Albrecht-Strasse in April of last year?"

"I did, yes."

"Why?"

"It was a minor administration matter."

"I have spoken to the registrar. He told us that you claimed a marriage authorization had been forged. Is that correct?"

"Yes."

"And after speaking to the registrar you brought Vigo into Gestapo headquarters?"

"The priest married two people without following the correct procedures."

"Based on the forged authorization?'

"That's right, yes."

"You beat him up."

"That was nothing. We slapped him around a bit."

The medical examiner found the scars on his face six months later, thought Neumann.

"Shortly after that you were found guilty of corruptly demanding money as a condition for signing a marriage authorization."

Framzl's eyes lit up. "That was a lie. I never demanded a pfennig for that."

"But you refused to sign the marriage authorization?"

"I was attempting to uncover a subversive group. I was presented with an opportunity, a situation that could help to achieve my goal. I took it."

"What are you saying?"

"The woman is a *Mischling*. They had pulled strings to get their Authorization, using one of my prime suspects, an actress called Libertas Schulze-Boysen. I took the opportunity to place an informer inside the subversive group. I explained all this to my accusers."

"They didn't believe you."

Framzl clenched his fists. "What happened to me was a gross injustice. The boy, Noack, lied. It was my word against his." His voice rose a notch. "They chose to believe him."

"Are you saying you didn't demand money?"

"Haven't you been listening to me? That was a malicious lie." He was shouting, now. "Why would I jeopardize my whole future for a mere 500 Reichsmarks? It's laughable."

"You blame the priest for that malicious report?"

"Yes, I blame him. He fabricated that story to explain or excuse his own mistake."

"Is that why you killed him?"

"When was he killed? I've been in here for the past eleven months."

"Perhaps you arranged to have him killed."

Framzl's response was stunned silence, then, "As the Führer is my witness, the priest's death has nothing to do with me."

"I'm told you are a heavy smoker."

"I was. There is no tobacco here."

"Did you own a cigarette lighter?"

"No."

"Have you ever owned a cigarette lighter?"

"No. What's that got to do with the case?"

"Have you heard of a priest called Schlurr? Father Gunther Schlurr?"

Framzl shook his head. "Never heard of him."

Chapter 89

May 1940

In Gestapo headquarters, a team of three was wading through the records for government employees. It was Saturday, May 4. They had completed the trawl through the main ministries and started on the minor state services. One man gave a yelp. "I have him, sir. I have a match."

SS-Sturmführer Jürgen Traut swore under his breath. He had hoped for another trip to Kolonnenstrasse. He strode out of his office to check the man's work. "What have you got?"

"The man we are looking for is an employee of the Reich Labor Service, the RAD. His name is Max-Christian Noack, sir."

Jürgen picked up the telephone and rang Kommissar Neumann.

"We have him, Erhart. His name's Max-Christian Noack."

Neumann gasped. "We interviewed him. He's the one who forged his marriage authorization. The priest married him in his church. Do you have an address?"

Jürgen nearly blurted it out. "Not yet. We're checking that now."

A man stepped into Traut's office with a piece of paper. "I have it. It's an apartment building in Kolonnenstrasse."

#

Anna had a loaf of bread in the oven. The telephone rang. Max picked it up.

"Your fingerprints have been identified. Get out of there." It was Walter Lehmann.

"How much time do we have?"

"None. Ten minutes, maybe. Leave immediately."

"Thank you, W—"

Walter broke the call.

"Anna, we have to go."

"Go where? When?"

"Right now. The Gestapo are on the way."

"I can't leave. I have bread in the oven."

"Never mind the bread. Fetch your purse. We have to leave. Now."

"Don't we have time to pack?"

"No, Anna. I'm telling you, we have less than ten minutes."

They reached the end of the street and turned the corner as the Gestapo arrived in two black cars. They ran.

Part 5

Chapter 90

May 1940

Greta's apartment was within easy reach. They got there in 15 minutes. Max hammered on the door. Greta opened it and they piled inside.

"The Gestapo. They are in our apartment. We need a place to hide."

Greta closed the door. She went to the window and checked the street outside.

"Did anyone see you?"

"I don't know. I don't think so."

"Very well, take a seat."

Max and Anna sat on the sofa.

Greta said, "You can stay here for today. I'll find you somewhere more secure after dark. In the meantime, stay away from the windows."

Anna asked how Sophie was faring.

Greta said, "She's well. She's grown quite a bit since you saw her last."

"How old is she now?"

"She was nine last month."

Ule woke. Greta went to attend to him. Anna followed her.

When Ule was settled, Greta left the 2-year-old with Anna. She asked Max to explain what happened. He told her how he had dropped his cigarette lighter in the cemetery while helping Edmund and Bruno to bury the traitor. He didn't mention Vigo's name, as Anna was listening from the next room.

"Can you tell me which of them killed him?"

Greta blinked. "Go on with your story. Who warned you that the Gestapo was coming?"

"That was an old friend of my father's from the last War. He's with the Gestapo."

"A helpful Gestapo man. His name?"

"I'd rather not say. I don't want to get him into trouble."

"He could be useful to the Orchestra, Max. Give me his name."

Max hesitated. Frau Greta was a rock. She had been since he first met her. And he needed her help now more than ever. "His name's Walter Lehmann."

"Thank you, Max. I promise I won't get him into trouble. Now, you're going to have to get out of Germany. Where would you like to go?"

"We thought we might go to Brussels."

#

Adam arrived home after dark. He and Greta had an argument about the best course of action. Anna listened behind a closed door. She caught only a few snatches, but she gathered that Adam wanted the Communists to provide shelter for the fugitives since they were the ones that had caused the problem in the first place. Frau Greta wouldn't hear of it. She had a better idea.

They bundled Anna and Max into the back of Adam's battered old car. Frau Greta told them to lie down on the seat. She used two blankets to cover them. The last thing she said to them was, "Keep your heads down. And good luck."

Adam started the car. Anna came close to panic hiding in the dark under a blanket. And she hated the feeling of helplessness that came with being transported she knew not where. After a 20-minute journey, the car stopped. Adam came around the back and removed the blankets. "You can come out now."

Anna looked around. She recognized the mansion where she'd had her wedding reception, the home of Harro and Libertas Schulze-Boysen.

The maid, Pauletta, opened the door. She showed them into the study and went to fetch her mistress. Adam went with her.

Anna was having difficulty catching her breath. Perhaps that was from being driven at speed through the streets of Berlin under a blanket. Or it could have been the shock of what had happened. She'd had to leave everything. Her clothes, her wedding dress, her mother's willow pattern crockery, their radio, their records, the gramophone, her books, all her wedding presents, her photographs. Everything.

Her shoes!

All she had in the world now was the clothes she was wearing and the contents of her handbag—a few Reichsmarks, a handful of change, a stick of lipstick, her identity card and their two ration books.

Her job was gone. Max's job was gone. And they would have to leave the country.

Max sat on the sofa beside her. He looked pale and breathless, too.

He held her hand. "How are you feeling, Anna?"

"I'm confused." She stared into his eyes. "Did we really have to leave everything and run away?"

"We had no choice. I'm wanted for a murder I didn't commit. If the Gestapo find us…"

She was suddenly terrified. "What will become of us, Max? How will we live?"

"We'll start a new life in Belgium."

"But how?"

He put an arm around her and squeezed her shoulder. "Don't worry, my darling, Libertas can work miracles."

Dressed in a flowing housecoat and right on cue, Libertas made a grand entrance. Adam followed her into the study. "I hear you're in trouble. Welcome to my home." She pulled up a Queen Anne chair and perched on its edge facing Anna. "First, have you eaten? Are you hungry?"

"We have eaten, thank you."

"All right. Pauletta will make up a bed for you. Pauletta, give them the blue room."

Anna followed Libertas's gaze to the door where Pauletta was standing. The maid bobbed and scurried off.

"You have your identity cards with you?"

Anna opened her handbag and pulled out her papers.

Max said, "I have my Dieter Marten cards and passport."

Libertas looked pleased. "Splendid. You can travel as Frau and Herr Marten. Adam, will you talk to Peter Riese about papers for Anna?"

"Leave that to me," said Adam. He shook their hands. "We'll get you out as soon as we can. You'll be safe here in the meantime. Good luck to you both. Look us up after the War."

Adam left. Libertas opened her drinks cabinet and poured out two glasses of schnapps. She handed one to Max.

"I'm sorry, Frau Schulze-Boysen, I had to leave your book behind in the apartment," said Max.

"Don't worry about it. I never liked the book, myself. Marx is so boring." She handed the second glass of schnapps to Anna.

Anna wrinkled her nose. "Schnapps makes me sick, Frau. Do you have any white wine?"

"You've had a severe shock, young lady. Hold your nose and swallow it."

Anna did as she was told. The sensation of warmth flowing down and through her body was not unpleasant. Then she heard Adam's car start up and drive away. The sound was like an anchor chain being lifted—their last link to Frau Greta was gone.

Pauletta led them up the stairs to their room.

Anna could see immediately why it was called the blue room. Everything was blue, from the wallpaper to the curtains and the carpet. Even the covers on the four-poster bed were white with blue flowers. The overall effect was calming, if a little too much for her taste.

They got undressed. Pauletta had left one of Libertas's nightdresses on the bed. It was a little flamboyant for Anna's taste, but she put it on and they climbed into bed. Max moved close and they clung together under the cool covers. Persistent memories of her recent encounter with Jürgen flashed into her mind then, sending her close to panic, but she buried them with contempt under the weight of her love for Max. As she melted in his arms, she remembered another something that they had left behind in the bedside locker in the apartment.

Chapter 91

May 1940

Anna woke up in the morning with a headache. She had realized in the middle of the night that she would probably never see her friends again. Or her mother and father. She went looking for Libertas and asked permission to use the telephone.

"I'm sorry, Anna, but the Gestapo is almost certainly listening to all our telephone conversations. You mustn't use it. It's far too risky."

"Could you ring my parents and tell them I'm safe? You could ask them to pass a message to my friend, Ebba."

"I'll do that for you as soon as you're out of the country. You must ring me from Brussels and tell me you're safe. I'll pass on your messages then."

It was better than nothing.

Anna spent an hour experimenting at Libertas's makeup desk. When Max saw what she'd done, he stared at her open-mouthed. Anna laughed at the expression on his face. "Close your mouth, husband, you'll catch flies."

Apart from mealtimes, when they joined Libertas and Harro downstairs, they spent most of their time in the blue room. Max said it was like a second honeymoon, but Anna thought it felt more like a prison sentence. She was impatient to move on, to place some distance between the Gestapo and themselves.

On the second day, a man arrived carrying a briefcase. Libertas introduced him as Peter Riese. He took pictures of Anna. Then he took an inkpad from his briefcase and applied her fingerprints to two blank identity cards.

"Why do you need two?" she asked.

Peter explained that the extra card was a spare in case the first one didn't work out. He called her 'Comrade', which Anna found amusing. Finally, he added her date of birth and asked her to sign both cards in the name 'Anna Marten.'

After two more days, Frau Greta Kuckhoff came calling. Anna was delighted to see her again. She immediately asked for news of Sophie. They sat face to face on the armchairs in the study.

"She's well," said Greta. "She misses her parents, of course. She clings to her doll the way a drowning man clings to a piece of driftwood. She's had to stay indoors where she is and she's not happy about that. It's difficult for a child of nine to grasp the idea that the government wants to lock her up in a labor camp."

"I know how she feels. I wondered, Frau Greta, if you could make her a new identity like the one you gave Max. If she wasn't labeled a Jew, maybe she could make a life for herself."

Greta nodded. "That could be arranged, but I fear she will never lead a normal life in this country. I'd like to get her out of Germany, beyond the clutches of the Gestapo."

"Why not send her to Belgium? Max says it's a lovely place, and peaceful. It's a neutral country, and there are German speakers there..." Anna's voice faded as she realized why they were having this conversation. "You want us to take her to Belgium."

"Only if you're willing."

Anna smiled.

Greta said, "I could arrange a suitable identity. She could travel as your own child." Anna opened her mouth to respond. Frau Greta continued quickly, "She doesn't look Jewish, you must admit. You should have no trouble, and she wouldn't be a burden to you. She eats like a bird."

Anna beamed at Greta. "We'd be delighted to take Sophie with us. She would be no burden to us at all."

"Shouldn't you talk to Max before you decide?"

"Not at all. Leave Max to me. He loves Sophie as much as I do."

"I can give you names and addresses of contacts in other countries—Holland, France, and Britain—who might be willing to take her."

"We won't need those. We'd be honored to make her part of our family."

"Permanently?"

"Yes, of course, or for as long as she wishes."

It was Greta's turn to smile. "I'm very grateful to you. I will arrange identity papers for Sophie in Max's new family name, Marten, and travel permits for Brussels for all three of you. As soon as you have those, you should be able to leave."

Greta stood up, smoothing the wrinkles in her skirt. "I have a message for you from Madam Krauss."

"She's safe? They let her go?"

"Yes, the Gestapo couldn't hold her. She would have put a witch's curse on them all." She laughed. "She sends her best wishes for the future to you both. She says you should treat Sophie as your own child."

"We will." Anna's eyes were filling with tears.

"One other thing Madam Krauss said: Treasure the doll. Aschenputtel holds the key to Sophie's future."

Chapter 92

May 1940

Max was happy to take Sophie to safety with them. He made just one condition. "You must ask her aunt if she has any objection."

The next day, Anna had a word with Pauletta, Sophie's aunt. "We'll be leaving for Belgium soon. Frau Greta has asked us to take Sophie with us."

Pauletta nodded vigorously. "Frau Greta told me. I think it's a wonderful idea. The poor mite is never going to be safe in Hitler's Germany. I'm very grateful to you. But..."

Anna waited.

"It must be what Sophie wants. You must ask her. It will mean saying goodbye forever to her mama and papa."

Anna agreed.

"Is there a telephone box anywhere near the house?"

"Two streets south of here, but you don't need that. There's a telephone in the hall downstairs."

Anna thanked her.

Waiting until after dark, Anna and Max slipped out of the house through a rear door and headed south. Anna used the telephone first. She rang her parents in Dresden.

"Where are you, Anna? Are you all right? We've been trying to call you on your telephone at home. We've been worried sick."

"We're fine, Mama. We'll be leaving Germany soon."

"Where are you going?"

"Belgium. I'll ring you when we get there. Please don't worry about us."

"How can I not worry? Have you seen the newspaper? Max's

picture is in there. The police are searching for him. They want to question him about a murder."

Anna felt a lump in her throat. "He's innocent, Mama."

"Tell him to give himself up." Her father had taken the telephone. "If he's innocent he should have nothing to worry about."

Anna rolled her eyes. There wasn't time to explain to her parents the facts of life in modern Germany.

"Goodbye, Papa. I'll ring again as soon as we are safe in Belgium."

She put the telephone back on its cradle, and Max took his turn. He dialed his mother's number. It rang 12 times before she picked it up.

Hurrying back to the house, Anna asked how his mother was.

"She sounded well, much the same as she always sounds. She had a visit from the Gestapo looking for me. She was a little alarmed by that."

#

On the same day, May 8, Air Commodore Cameron Pinkley was on his feet in the War Office in London. He'd been given three minutes to make the case for Operation Pike to the two members of Neville Chamberlain's War Cabinet with primary responsibility for Britain's War Operations, the Minister for the Coordination of Defence, Lord Chatfield, and the Secretary of State for War, Leslie Hore-Belisha. Sir Kingsley Wood, the Secretary of State for Air was also in attendance, in a strictly advisory capacity.

"Gentlemen," said Pinkley, "you will see from my report that this operation has been planned down to the finest detail. Between the RAF and the French Air Force, we have 153 heavy bombers in position in airfields in Turkey, Syria and Iran. The ordnance in place consists of 1,000 tons of armor-piercing and incendiary bombs. If you turn to the last two pages you will see the analysts' estimates of the damage that the raid will inflict on the enemy…"

The Secretary of State for War spoke quietly. "I have read the analysis with interest. If it is accurate, the operation could indeed cripple a superior enemy before they have an opportunity to strike at us. But…"

Lord Chatfield continued the argument, "But we have to ask ourselves whether the Soviets are our enemy. And if we strike first…"

"Unprovoked…" from Hore-Belisha.

Lord Chatfield nodded. "…without provocation, surely this would be a serious breech of protocol. I would be interested in hearing the opinion of the Foreign Secretary on this. I can see the argument in favor, the Serpent's Egg and all that, but would we not be handing the moral high ground to the Soviets?"

The Secretary of State for Air interjected, "Hang protocol, gentlemen, and to the devil with morality. We are at war."

#

Two days later, on May 10, the German Army crossed the border into Belgium. The Belgian Army put up very little resistance, and the German armies continued on into Holland.

Belgium and Holland were no longer neutral, peaceful countries. They were now assimilated into the territories under control of the Nazi regime in Berlin.

In London, Neville Chamberlain resigned and Winston Churchill became Prime Minister of a new coalition government.

On May 12, Operation Pike landed on Churchill's desk. He read the document slowly, cover to cover. Then he stubbed out his cigar in a heavy crystal ashtray, grunted, and dropped Operation Pike into his wastepaper basket.

Chapter 93

May 1940

Ðarro Schulze-Boysen slammed the newspaper on the kitchen table. "Have you seen this?"

The front page and several inside pages were devoted to the German offensive to the west. The British Army had been encircled. 400,000 men were now corralled in a small area at Dunkirk in northern France with their backs to the sea. The Royal Navy was attempting an impossible evacuation operation.

Harro turned to page 6 where Max's picture appeared under a headline: 'WANTED FOR MURDER.'

Max read the article and passed it to Anna.

Anna read it twice. "It says they want to ask Max some questions about the murder of a religious pastor and the possible murder of another one. It doesn't say they think he had anything to do with either actual killing."

"That's police-speak," said Harro. "Trust me, they wouldn't print his picture in the newspaper unless he was a suspect."

Anna's hands closed into fists. "That's grossly unfair."

Max turned back to the front page. "Belgium is no longer an option for us, Harro. Can we get in touch with Peter the forger and ask him to change our travel documents?"

Libertas appeared at the kitchen door. "I'm sure he's already working on that."

Harro and Libertas sat together at the table opposite Anna and Max. They both wore serious frowns on their faces.

Libertas began, "We've decided it's time you moved to another location. Harro and I have discussed it, and we both feel you are no longer safe in this house."

Harro took up the argument. "I have been under the eye of the Gestapo for a long time, now. It's only my exalted position in the Luftwaffe, and Hermann Göring's superior position in the Reich hierarchy that has kept them at bay thus far."

Libertas continued, "If the house was raided and they found you here, that would almost certainly mean the end of the Orchestra."

Anna said, "Adam and Frau Greta…"

Harro shook his head. "It might take some time, my dear, but Adam and Greta, Arvid and Mildred would all be captured. Our Communist allies in Neukölln too, I shouldn't wonder."

Libertas said, "We'll move you tomorrow night." Then she looked at Harro and something unspoken passed between them.

"We'll move you tonight," said Harro.

#

Once more Anna found herself under a blanket on the back seat of a car. This time it was Harro's shiny Daimler-Benz. The suspension was superior to Adam Kuckhoff's old Horch, but the sensations of claustrophobia and helplessness were just as severe.

The journey lasted 30 minutes. Harro opened the back door and Anna and Max wriggled out from under the blankets. They were in a street that Anna didn't know with seedy-looking terraced houses on each side.

"Where are we?"

"Neukölln. Come on, get yourselves inside."

The door of the nearest house was open. They walked inside quickly and Harro closed the door. In the front parlor they found two men. Anna recognized Peter Riese, the communist forger. The second man looked stronger than anyone Anna had ever met, with impressive arm and chest muscles, like a middle-aged wrestler. Max obviously knew him, judging by the bitter look on his face.

The second man left the room. "That was Edmund," said Max.

Peter Riese opened a roll-top desk and took out a set of papers. He handed them to Anna. "These are yours, Anna. I'm still preparing your travel papers."

Anna checked the identity card. It was Belgian. It had her photograph, her date of birth and her fingerprints. And it carried an official-looking Belgian stamp. Only the name and signature were false: Anna Marten.

Max threw himself down on a chair. "Where are we going, Peter?"

"Switzerland. Zurich."

Max held out his hand, and Anna gave him her new identity card. He examined it. "This is very good work. How do you do it?"

Riese shrugged. "It's simple. All I need is a blank card and an official stamp."

#

The bedroom the Communists provided was nothing like the luxurious blue room at the Schulze-Boysen mansion. It was half the size, the bed barely wide enough for two. But still, Anna slept soundly.

She woke up to find Sophie bouncing up and down on the bed. "Sophie, what a pleasant surprise!"

"Hallo, Anna, what are you doing in my secret room?"

"This is your secret room? Herr Riese gave us the bed to sleep in for a few nights. Where's Aschenputtel?"

"She's in my bed."

Max opened his eyes. "What's happening?"

"Sophie's here. She's going to fetch her doll."

Sophie jumped off the end of the bed and ran from the room. She came back within seconds, carrying her doll.

"She looks happy," said Anna. 'Don't you think Aschenputtel looks happy, Max?"

Max rubbed his eyes. "Yes, I think she looks happy."

Clutching her doll, Sophie sat on the bed beside Anna.

Max sat up. "Have you told her where we're going?"

Anna gave Sophie a hug. "Max and I are going to Switzerland in the next few days."

"That's where all the snowy mountains are. They're called Alps."

"Yes, that's right."

"Will you be coming back here?"

"No, Sophie, we won't be back. We will make a new life for ourselves in Switzerland."

Sophie looked at Aschenputtel for a few moments. Then she looked up at Anna and whispered, "Take me with you."

Anna gave Sophie an even bigger hug and held on to her. "Of course, Sophie, of course we'll take you with us."

Sophie beamed. "Can Aschenputtel come too?"

Max laughed. "I thought she'd never ask."

Chapter 94

June 1940

By June 3, the battle of Dunkirk was over. Most of the British soldiers had been evacuated. Belgium and Holland had capitulated, and the German Army was moving south into France. The bombing of Paris began, and the French Army suffered a number of severe setbacks.

Finally, on June 13, Paris was occupied by German troops. The battle for France was over. Many of the beer cellars in Berlin declared open bars. While crowds of civilians filled the streets to celebrate Germany's triumphs, Harro was called to a top secret meeting of Intelligence chiefs from the three branches of the Wehrmacht. He emerged from the meeting with a head full of vital intelligence that simply had to be transmitted to Moscow as quickly as humanly possible. Operation Fritz, the planned invasion of the Soviet Union, had been revived and was once again under active consideration!

#

Anna did what she could to console a miserable Max, stuck indoors in the Communist safe house as the free beer flowed outside without him. She was aware that Max was antagonistic toward Edmund. His attitude toward Peter Riese was no more than cordial, but he seemed to hate the younger man, avoiding contact whenever he could. For his part, Edmund seemed content not to have to speak to Max.

A third Communist made an appearance. This man was older than Peter Riese. His name was Bruno. While Edmund hardly ever said anything, Bruno was quite talkative, but Anna could tell that Max didn't like him.

A few nights after that, when Sophie was asleep, Peter Riese gave Anna two Belgian passports in the names Anna and Sophie Marten. She showed them to Max.

Max examined them. "Does this mean we can leave?"

Bruno replied, "Soon. We need to wait another week or two."

Max snapped at him, "What are we waiting for?"

"Every policeman in the city is searching for you. And, since your picture appeared in the newspaper, everyone in Berlin will recognize you. The longer you wait the better the chances that people will have forgotten your face."

Max said, "Anna and Sophie could make the journey without me. Why not let them go now, and I'll follow later, when it's safe?"

Anna leapt to her feet. "I knew someone was going to suggest that. Well, you can forget that idea. I'm not leaving without you."

#

The very next day, Harro Schulze-Boysen arrived and told Max they would have to leave immediately.

"Why? Bruno said we should wait a week or two."

Harro handed over a half-empty cigarette pack. "We have vital intelligence for the Soviets. I want you to take it with you. When you get to Zurich, stay at the Storchen Hotel. Our contact there is called Stephan. Ask him where he was born. If he replies 'German South-West Africa' you'll know you have the right man."

#

Anna and Sophie were playing with Aschenputtel when Max came in and told them that they would be leaving for Switzerland the next day. Anna flushed at the news with excitement tinged with apprehension.

She spent some time with Sophie, preparing her for the journey.

"Max is your papa and I'm your mama."

"Like a game of make believe?"

"Yes, only more serious than that. Everybody we meet must really believe that it's true. Everything depends on that. Do you understand?"

"Yes, Anna, I understand."

Anna held up a finger. "Do you understand?"

"Yes, Mama."

Max said, "Edmund will travel with us."

Anna raised an eyebrow. "Is that necessary?"

"The intelligence is too important to risk. Harro suggested we should have a bodyguard. Edmund volunteered."

She thought that was a slightly crazy idea, but she passed no comment.

Max rehearsed their cover story with Anna. "I am Dieter Marten, a traveling salesman. I sell clothing."

Peter Riese added, "This is a holiday trip to Switzerland. Dieter is taking his wife and child to spend a few days with his parents in Zurich."

An elaborate personal history for these fictional characters sprang into Anna's mind. "Herr Marten is old. He is German, a war hero. He served his country in the last War and was wounded at Passchendaele. Frau Marten is much younger than him. She is his second wife, Dieter's stepmother—"

Riese shook his head. "Keep the story simple. They are old. They are infirm. They are looking forward to meeting their granddaughter for the first time."

Max said, "I've lost the suitcase with my samples."

"You won't need those. You're on vacation, remember." He went out of the room and came back with a suitcase. "These are your personal possessions."

Anna opened the suitcase and reeled back from the smell. It was filled with old clothing. "Why do we need all this dirty laundry?" She pulled out a brassiere, three sizes larger than her own, and a man's heavy woolen check shirt. She laughed. "Some of this stuff is crazy. Where did these come from?"

"Most of the women's garments were donated by Bruno's wife. She's a big lady. That shirt was Edmund's."

Anna rummaged about some more. "There's nothing in here for a 9-year-old girl."

"Yes, I'm sorry about that, but Sophie has some underwear you can pack, and I'm still hoping to pick up a few more items before you go."

Max held the check shirt against his chest. It was big enough for two men like Max. "When are we leaving, Peter?"

"The train leaves at seven o'clock in the morning."

#

At six o'clock the following morning, they got ready to leave. Bruno asked Max to confirm that he had the cigarette pack with the encrypted message. Max showed it to him.

They climbed aboard the red Volkswagen and Bruno drove them to Südkreuz railway station. Sophie said the car looked like a ladybug but without the spots. Max rode up front with Bruno. In the back seat Sophie clung to Aschenputtel and Anna held on tight to Sophie.

"Where's Edmund?" said Max.

Bruno replied, "Edmund will meet you on the train."

Neukölln to the railway station took 10 minutes. Bruno found a place to park the car. He told them to wait while he went into the station to buy their tickets.

They sat in the car watching hordes of office workers converging on the railway station. After five minutes, Sophie was trembling in Anna's arms. "Open the door, Max."

"Bruno told us to wait."

"I don't care what he said. We're not waiting here any longer. Get the suitcase."

Max opened the door and lifted the seat. Anna and Sophie climbed out. He took the suitcase from the trunk and they joined the crowds pouring in through the station entrance. They found Bruno near the top of a long queue at the ticket desks.

He joined them when he had the tickets. "I thought I asked you to wait in the car."

Max made no reply, and Bruno handed him the tickets. "Take the slow train to Erfurt from platform F17. It leaves in 15 minutes. Take a room at the hotel Erfurter Hof in Erfurt and catch the Zurich Express at 10:00 a.m. tomorrow. You should be safely in Switzerland by nightfall tomorrow. Good luck to you all."

Chapter 95

June 1940

The train was full, but Max found them a compartment with three spare seats, and they settled down for the journey to Erfurt.

Lutherstadt Wittenberg was the first stop, although the signs in the station still read Wittenberg.

"This is where I was born," Max said to Sophie.

"Show me your house," said Sophie. They could see a lot of houses.

"None of those, I'm afraid. You can't see my house from the train."

"Why not?"

Anna tried to explain. Some of the other passengers in the compartment smiled at the exchange.

Soon, the slow train was rattling through countryside, the acrid smell of coal smoke tickling their nostrils, the repetitive clack-aclack of the wheels on the rails lulling everyone to sleep.

They stopped at every station along the way, some little more than a bare platform surrounded by fields of grazing cattle, eventually arriving at Erfurt, their overnight destination, tired and hungry at 1:00 p.m.

#

They left the train. Making their way to a bank in the center of Erfurt, Anna used her bankbook to withdraw almost all their savings. She gave 100 Reichsmarks to Max and tucked the rest into her handbag. Next, they found the hotel Erfurter Hof and booked a room for the night.

They had lunch in the hotel and spent the afternoon like holidaymakers exploring the medieval town. Anna's ingenuity was sorely tested as she tried to explain the burnt-out shell of an ancient synagogue to Sophie.

#

Max awoke in darkness, every nerve in his body tingling. Something was wrong. Something had woken him. But what? Anna's even breathing told him that she was sleeping peacefully. Had Sophie got up to go to the bathroom? He should make sure that Sophie was all right. He reached for the lamp on the bedside locker and switched it on.

He was instantly aware of a dark figure at the foot of the bed, bent over the suitcase. The intruder looked up. Bruno!

Before Max could react, before he could make a sound, Bruno was on him, his hands around Max's neck.

Max grabbed Bruno's wrists and tried to prize them free, but Bruno was too strong. Max couldn't breathe. He thrashed about with his legs, waking Anna. She gave a cry and swung into action. Getting to her knees, she threw herself bodily at Bruno. They fell from the bed together.

Anna stood. Bruno lay on the floor, unconscious.

Max gulped a couple of breaths, rubbing his bruised neck, and croaked, "What happened?"

"I don't know. He must have hit his head on the locker. What are we going to do with him?"

"Find something to tie him up with."

Max checked the suitcase for the half-pack of cigarettes. It was still there. Then he searched Bruno and found an identical one in his pocket.

"Which one has the coded message?" said Anna.

Max shrugged. "Impossible to tell. I'll have to deliver both packs to the contact in Zurich."

#

The next morning they returned to the railway station in time to board the Zurich express, leaving Bruno in the hotel bedroom, trussed up like a Christmas goose.

Nearly four hours later, they were sitting at a table in the dining car as the train pulled out of Heidelberg station. Sophie needed a trip to the washroom, her fourth, by Max's recollection. When they returned, Anna said, "Edmund's in the corridor."

Max found Edmund's bulky frame wedged into a corner near the door.

Max hunkered down beside the big man. "You can go back to Berlin, Edmund. Tell them Bruno is their traitor. We don't need you here."

Edmund smiled. He said nothing.

#

Fischer rushed into Kommissar Neumann's office waving a piece of paper. "Max-Christian Noack has been seen boarding a train at Erfurt."

"Bound for where?"

"It's the early morning express to Zurich."

Neumann lifted the telephone. He rang the central office of the railways and asked for the senior superintendent. He gave his name and rank. "We need to stop the Zurich Express."

"I can't do that, Kommissar. Stopping one train would disrupt the timetable and cause chaos to the whole rail network. I'm sorry, what you ask is simply not possible."

Neumann ground his teeth in frustration. "There's a killer on that train. We must capture him before he escapes to Switzerland." No response. "Hello? Are you still there?"

"What you ask is beyond my powers, Kommissar. Surely you have resources you can call on. I would have thought a simple telephone call..."

"Where is the train now?"

"The Zurich Express will arrive at Offenburg in the next 18 minutes. It will depart again 5 minutes later."

"What's the next station after that?"

"Freiburg in 43 minutes, and an hour and 10 minutes after that, Basel Central."

Neumann slammed the telephone down and picked it up again. He rang the police station at Offenburg and gave them precise instructions and a description of the wanted man. "You will search the train and find this man. He will be using a false identity. He may be traveling with his wife. When you have him, arrest him and remove him from the train. He must not be allowed to cross the border, do you hear me? Make sure you use enough men for the job. Hold him until I arrive."

Fischer arrived with the car keys.

"I need to make one more call." Neumann picked up the telephone again. He rang Jürgen Traut of the Gestapo.

"Jürgen? We've found Max-Christian Noack. He's on the Zurich Express coming in to Offenburg. I've made arrangements for his arrest and detention."

"That case is no longer any of your concern, Neumann. Leave it to us."

Neumann replaced the telephone receiver and sat back in his chair, stunned.

Fischer jangled his set of car keys. "We need to get going, Boss."

"We're not going anywhere. It's in the hands of the Gestapo."

"Can we trust them not to screw it up?"

"Probably not, Fischer." He jumped to his feet. "Come on."

#

Once they'd cleared the southern suburbs of Berlin, Fischer made good time. He kept his average speed as high as he dared. By his calculations, they should arrive at Offenburg by midnight.

Kommissar Neumann sat slumped beside him in the passenger seat, his eyes closed. Fischer didn't begrudge the man his sleep. A policeman had to take his rest wherever and whenever he could. The workload had been brutal over the past two months.

Neumann opened his eyes. "Where are we?"

"We're bypassing Frankfurt."

Neumann sat up in his seat. "I'll take the wheel for a spell if you like."

"That's all right, Boss. I'll tell you if I start to get tired."

Neumann closed his eyes again. Thirty minutes later, they reached the northern outskirts of Mannheim.

Neumann woke up again and Fischer said, "I've been thinking about Pastor Schlurr. He may be connected to Noack's family in some way."

Neumann pinched his nose to stifle a sneeze. "Forget about Schlurr. There's no such person."

"What do you mean, Boss? Are you suggesting that Schupo Gretzke was dreaming?"

"No, I'm sure he met Schlurr, but the name was probably a false one. If you look at Noack's description, you'll see how similar it is to the one for Pastor Schlurr."

"So Pastor Schlurr and Max-Christian Noack are one and the same?"

Neumann's only reply was an explosive sneeze. When Fischer looked at his boss again, his eyes were closed.

Chapter 96

June 1940

The Zurich Express rolled in to Offenburg. Doors opened, passengers got off, passengers got on, doors closed. And the train sat there. Sophie stood at the window to see the guard wave his green flag and blow his whistle, but nothing happened. She tugged at Anna's clothing. "Mama, Mama, Why has the train stopped?"

Max went to the door of the carriage and lowered the window. Edmund joined him and they looked out. The platform was empty, the locomotive slowly releasing steam. And then six uniformed Schupo emerged from the station house and climbed aboard the train.

"This is not good. You need to go." Edmund pushed Max to the opposite side of the carriage and opened the door.

"I can't leave Anna and Sophie."

"You must. I'll look after them. Get off the train now."

Max hesitated. Could he trust this muscleman to look after Anna and Sophie? Did he have a choice?

A beefy fist in the back propelled him from the carriage onto the tracks. The door slammed shut. Max climbed onto the far platform. The driver of the Zurich Express blew his whistle twice and the train began to move. Max watched until it had turned a bend and disappeared from view. Then he slipped out of the station and followed the road into the town.

He sat at a table under a wide parasol in the town square. The other people at the table nodded and smiled at him. There were women and children, old men, and a few soldiers in uniform. Max was aware of curious stares from some of the people around him. As the only young man dressed in civilian clothes, he stood out from the crowd. He was sure they were all wondering who he was. Let them wonder. Unless someone asked him directly for an explanation, he would say nothing and brazen it out.

He paid for a liter of the local beer and considered his next move. Switzerland was no more than 150 km to the south—perhaps two hours by car, maybe 90 minutes by train. Anna and Sophie were his first concern. He would wait two hours. By that time, they should be safely across the border and he could look for a way of joining them.

It was a warm day, the beer refreshingly cold. He drained his first liter and ordered a second. Watching the crowd, he began to categorize them. There were housewives, grandparents, and lots of children of all ages. The schools were well into their summer recess.

A bus drew up, and a group of holidaymakers got out and sat at another table. Max got up and joined them. They all looked seriously dehydrated.

"Where are you from?" he asked a red-faced man.

"We're from Freiburg."

"You're on vacation?"

"We're on our way home after two weeks in Offenbach. That's our bus over there."

"I'm going south myself. My home is in Switzerland."

"You don't sound Swiss."

"I missed the Zurich Express. Would you have room on your bus for an extra passenger?"

The bus driver had several objections, but the red-faced man persisted and Max climbed onto the bus.

#

Max sat with his new red-faced friend, who told him of a municipal bus service from Freiburg to Basel. Max should have no trouble making the connection.

They arrived in Freiburg a half-hour later. Max's companion pointed out the municipal bus depot and the bus that would take Max to Switzerland. They shook hands like brothers and Max thanked him. He bought a ticket for the municipal bus and joined the queue of people waiting to board.

A uniformed Schupo stood by the door checking the passengers' identity cards. When it was Max's turn, he handed his card to the policeman.

The policeman ran a cursory eye over the card and handed it back. "Have a good journey, Herr Noack."

"Thank you," replied Max.

The policeman reached for his pistol and Max ran. He ducked into a maze of narrow streets. Police whistles echoed off the buildings making it impossible to tell where they were coming from. He ran, twisting and turning, doubling back when he saw police patrols.

They cornered him in a narrow laneway, put him in handcuffs and marched him to a waiting car. They opened the door and pushed him onto the back seat beside another prisoner.

"Edmund, what are you doing here?"

Edmund responded with a sheepish grin, but said nothing.

"Just tell me the others are safe."

"They are safe. They must be in Switzerland by now."

#

Kommissar Ludwig Vogel of the Offenburg Kripo greeted Neumann with a broad smile. "We have Noack safely under lock and key. We caught him attempting to board a bus at Freiburg." He handed over Max's false papers and the contents of his pockets—two half packs of cigarettes and some money.

Neumann examined the identity card. "Splendid work, Kommissar. We need to put an immediate alert out for Frau Marten."

"We did that as soon as we captured Noack, but she had crossed into Switzerland. I'm sorry. However, I have a surprise for you. It's by way of a bonus."

Neumann frowned. "I don't like surprises, Kommissar."

"We apprehended another subversive on the Zurich Express, a known Communist called 'Edmund the Hammer.' He has been on our books for some time."

"I'm not interested in subversives. You can hand him over to the Gestapo. My only interest is in capturing the killer of a religious pastor. Have you notified the Gestapo?"

"Berlin have a man on the way. I'm under strict instructions to hold these two until he arrives."

Neumann's frown deepened. "I'd like a chance to interrogate Noack before those thugs get their hands on him. Their methods leave a lot to be desired. I would have no use for a confession that's beaten out of a suspect."

Chapter 97

June 1940

A young uniformed Orpo stood by the door. The expression on his face suggested he would love an excuse to whip out his pistol and empty it into his prisoner. But Max was going nowhere. His legs were shackled together, his wrists handcuffed, the handcuffs padlocked to an iron ring welded to the top of a steel table. His papers, his money and the two cigarette packs sat out of reach on the table.

Max tested the table. It was firmly bolted to the floor, as was the chair he was sitting on. He thought about asking for something to drink, but it seemed unlikely that they would release his arms having gone to all that trouble to restrain them.

The door opened and two men entered. He recognized one of them, the Oberassistent from Berlin. The other was a stranger. They sat at the table facing Max.

"My name is Neumann, Kommissar Neumann. You may remember Oberassistent Fischer, here. He interviewed you in Berlin..."

"In January," said Fischer.

Neumann picked Max's false identity card from the table. "Do you deny that your real name is Max-Christian Noack?"

Max shook his head.

"Using a false name is a very serious offense. The country is at war, so you will be tried as an enemy agent. This false identity card alone is sufficient for a judge to sentence you to death."

Max said nothing.

"We would like to help you. We are investigating a murder. I believe you may be able to shed some light on the case. And if you can, I will do what I can to help you."

"I know nothing about a murder."

"We found your cigarette lighter at the scene, and we have linked you to the victim."

Max looked shocked. "You think I killed someone?"

"We know you murdered Pastor Salvatore Vigo and buried him in the cemetery behind Holy Cross Church. But I'm certain you had accomplices. I need their names."

"This is nonsense. I know Father Vigo. He officiated at my wedding. He is a friend. Why would I murder him?"

"We don't have much time, Noack, tell me who helped you with the murder and I'll talk to the Gestapo on your behalf."

At the mention of the Gestapo something began to crawl up Max's spine. "I'm sorry, Kommissar, but you have the wrong man."

Neumann held up a hand and listed the evidence on his fingers. "We have your fingerprints on the cigarette lighter found at the cemetery, we know the priest conducted your marriage, and we know that you forged your marriage authorization."

Fischer interjected, "Is that why you killed him?"

Neumann said, "There was also the matter of the extortion of 500 Reichsmarks by the Gestapo man, Framzl. As I understand it, Framzl agreed to sign your marriage authorization in exchange for the money. You then forged his signature…"

"…and got a Reich stamp from somewhere…" said Fischer.

"This enraged Framzl. He went back to the priest and berated him, maybe he threatened him…"

"And the registrar…"

"After that, I can only suppose the priest came back to you. He was angry. A fight broke out. You snapped his neck. Then you and your friends drove him to the Holy Cross Church and buried him there. So who helped you? Who drove the car?"

"Was it the Communist, Edmund the Hammer?" said Fischer. "Were you hoping to escape to Switzerland together?"

#

The door swung open. A third policeman stuck his head round the door. "The Gestapo man is here."

Max's heart sank. His tongue sought out his empty tooth cavity. If only he hadn't thrown away the cyanide capsule!

The Gestapo man will break every bone in my body, and I will give them every name that I know. The whole resistance network will fall.

"Last chance," said Kommissar Neumann. "Tell me who helped you with the murder of the priest and I'll ask the Gestapo to go easy on you."

Max knew the Kommissar couldn't keep to his side of that bargain. His situation was hopeless.

The door swung open again and the blond Jürgen Traut strode in dressed in his gray Gestapo uniform. He snarled at the two Kripo men. "Leave us. I will interrogate the prisoner myself."

Neumann stood his ground. "Herr Noack has information that could help to solve the case of the murdered pastor. I will sit in on the interrogation."

Jürgen roared at him, "Get out of here, both of you, and close the door."

Neumann and Fischer left the room.

The Gestapo man sat down opposite Max. He picked up the identity card. "Herr Dieter Marten, a salesman from Belgium. How inventive." He swept the money from the table and tucked it and the identity card into his left breast pocket. Then he picked up the two cigarette packs. "A heavy smoker, I see. But you have no matches, and we have your lighter in Berlin." He grinned. "I know these packs contain encrypted information intended for the Soviets. What can you tell me about that?"

Max made no reply. He tried a look of shocked surprise.

"No matter." He slipped the two packs into his right breast pocket. "I'm sure our counterintelligence men will decipher the messages when we get back to Berlin. Now tell me, at what point did you decide to renege on our agreement?"

"What agreement?"

"You joined the Red Orchestra to act as Framzl's eyes and ears.

We agreed that you would work with me to bring the Communist subversives to justice…"

"I never believed that Framzl or you would stick to your side of that bargain."

"Why were you attempting to leave the country?"

"The Kripo wanted to charge me with the death of Father Vigo."

"You are innocent of that killing, of course."

"Yes."

"Of course. I know you never killed anyone, Max-Christian. You wouldn't have the guts. Forgery and lies are your level." He stood up. "You thought you were so clever, didn't you? You thought you could outwit that *dummkopf*, Jürgen Traut. Well, let me tell you, I won that contest. I took Anna when you were away on one of your subversive trips."

"What do you mean?"

"What do you think I mean? I took her. I screwed her. Twice. In your bed. What's so difficult to understand?"

A wave of anger and revulsion energized Max. He tried to get to his feet but the shackles made that impossible. "You're lying!"

"Am I? You'll have to ask your lovely wife the next time you see her. Oh, but I forgot, you won't be seeing her again—ever—will you?"

Finally, Jürgen balled his fist and delivered a crushing blow to the side of Max's head.

Chapter 98

June 1940

Jürgen bundled Edmund and Max, both handcuffed, into the back of his car and his driver set out to the north. Max caught a glimpse of the driver. It was Walter Lehmann! Max's heart lifted. Could Lehmann be here to rescue him? After 5 km, Lehmann turned the car into a forest and switched off the engine.

"What are you doing, man?" said Jürgen.

Lehmann pulled out his gun and shot Jürgen in the head at point blank range. Blood spattered on the car window and windshield. Lehmann got out, opened the passenger door and pulled Jürgen's body from the car. Then he helped Max and Edmund out and removed their handcuffs.

Edmund was confused. "What's happening? You don't mean to shoot us here?"

"I'm letting you go. Max will explain. Now hit me and take the car. Make it look convincing."

Edmund didn't need a second invitation. He hammered a fist into Lehmann's midriff followed by another blow to the head. Lehmann fell, unconscious. Max searched Jürgen's pockets and found the two cigarette packs, his identity card and money. Then he got into the driver's seat and started the engine. Edmund tucked Lehmann's Luger into his belt and got into the back.

"Leave the gun," said Max.

"We might need it."

"We won't. Throw it away."

Edmund wound down the window and threw the gun away. "Tell me what just happened."

"The Gestapo driver is a friend."

"A friend."

"He knew my father at the Somme."

Edmund chewed over that information.

"My father saved his life."

"And we were lucky the Gestapo chose him as the driver?"

Max shook his head. "Luck had nothing to do with it."

#

Max drove south. They passed through Offenburg without incident and on to Freiburg. There were no buses in the Freiburg bus station, but a small group of people stood around. Obviously, a bus was expected.

Outside Freiburg Max passed a sign that read Basel 70 km. After 10 km a bus passed them on its way north. Another two km down the road, he spotted a group of people standing at a bus stop, obviously waiting for the southbound bus. He drove on around a bend before leaving the road.

"We get out here, Edmund."

"Why? We're nowhere near the border."

"What chance would we have of crossing the border in a Gestapo car covered in blood and brains?"

"Oh, I see, so…"

"There's a bus stop back there, people waiting for a southbound bus. We'll join them."

#

The bus arrived 20 minutes later. Max and Edmund climbed aboard behind the group of locals. Max paid for two tickets to Basel and they sat together near the back of the bus.

The bus carried them across the border into Switzerland without further incident. Edmund had Swiss papers. Max's cover of a Belgian underwear salesman got him through the checks of the guards on both sides of the border. It helped that the alert for Max had been cancelled as the police all thought he was on his way to Berlin under escort by the Gestapo.

#

At Basel railway station Max and Edmund boarded a train bound for Zurich.

"You don't need to come any further with me," Max said. "Thank you for your help."

Edmund laughed. "You'll not get rid of me that easily. I have business in Zurich."

Basel to Zurich was a 90-minute journey through magnificent scenery, with snow-capped mountains in the far distance.

They arrived at the Storchen Hotel at 4:00 p.m. Max asked for Frau Marten. The receptionist told him his wife and child were in room 103.

Edmund finally shook hands with Max. "This is where we part company, my friend."

Max was happy to see the big man leave the hotel. He'd been hanging around like a bad smell since they'd crossed the border. Max made his way up the stairs to room 103. He knocked on the door.

"Who is it?" Anna's voice.

"Room service."

She opened the door and threw herself into his arms. When they surfaced, Max looked around the suite. They had four luxury rooms. The living area had a balcony overlooking the river. Max opened the bedroom door and found a sleeping Sophie clinging to her doll.

#

The next afternoon, while Anna and Sophie went shopping for clothes, Max treated himself to a well-earned beer in the hotel bar.

A stranger sat beside him at the counter and introduced himself as 'Stephan.'

"Where were you born?" said Max.

"Windhoek, German South-West Africa," replied the stranger. "My real name is Hans Bokker. If you need anything while you're in Switzerland, I'll be happy to help. You can contact me here at the hotel."

Max handed him the two cigarette packs. "One of these carries an important message for the Soviets. Our friends in Berlin want the message transmitted as quickly as possible. Also, the next time you contact Berlin, tell them that Bruno is their traitor. He tried to stop me from delivering the message."

"Where is he now?"

"We left him tied up in a hotel in Erfurt. I expect he'll have difficulty explaining himself to the local police."

#

When Anna and Sophie returned from their shopping trip, Sophie was exhausted. Anna put her to bed.

Max closed the bedroom door quietly. "Are you hungry?"

"Famished."

"We could grab a quick meal in the restaurant."

"Should we leave Sophie?"

"She'll be fine. We won't take too long."

They took the stairs to the first floor, found the restaurant and ordered. While they waited for their food to arrive, they exchanged stories. Anna's journey had been tiring, but uneventful. His story took her through a rollercoaster of emotions, shock, fear, surprise, and relief.

They had finished the first course, and the waiter was placing their main course on the table, when the air was split by a piercing scream.

Anna gasped. "Sophie!"

Max leapt to his feet and ran up the stairs. Sophie was standing in the corridor. "Aschenputtel! The man stole my doll."

Chapter 99

June 1940

"**W**hich way did he go?"

Sophie pointed behind her and Max ran. At the end of the corridor he found a service staircase. He charged down that. At the bottom he came to an exit door. He crashed through the door onto a short pier. At the end of the pier sat a red motorboat with Edmund the Hammer on board, fiddling with the engine. He looked up nervously at Max and pulled the starter cord. The engine failed to start. Max charged down the pier. He was no more than three meters from the boat when Edmund's motor started. The boat sped away down the river belching black smoke. Max ran back into the hotel and out to the taxi rank at the front of the hotel.

He jumped into a taxi. "There's a motorboat on the river heading south. Follow him. I'll give you thirty Reichsmarks if you catch up to him."

"Make that fifty," said the taxi man.

"Fifty it is."

The taxi driver set off at speed down the side of the river, weaving around slow-moving traffic. They passed two bridges. Then the river opened up into a wide lake and they cleared the worst of the traffic. Max caught sight of the motorboat, a red dot in the distance.

"There he is!" Max cried. "We're never going to catch him. Can't you go any faster?"

"We'll catch him, don't worry, sir. Sit back and enjoy the ride." The taxi accelerated, throwing Max back into his seat.

Meter by meter they gained on the red boat until Max could make out the figure of Edmund in the wheelhouse.

They hit a built-up area with houses along the lake shore obstructing the view of the lake. A lakeside market added to Max's woes. The taxi had to slow to a crawl as he weaved past obstructing horses and carts. Max bit his tongue.

Clearing the market and the lakeside housing, Max had an interrupted view of the lake again. Edmund was closer than he expected.

The boat slowed and drew in toward the near shore. It stopped 10 meters from the bank. Edmund dropped his anchor.

The taxi man drew up at the quayside directly opposite the boat. "This is a close as I can get, sir."

Max thanked him, paid him in Reischsmarks, and got out of the car.

Below him a row of boats bobbed in the water at their moorings: Five motorboats, two with their owners tying up for the night, and several rowboats.

Max approached the owner of the first motorboat and asked if he could take him onto the lake. The man appeared not to hear him. Either that or he was stone deaf. Max tried the second motorboat owner.

"Sorry, friend, I'm done for the day. Come back tomorrow and I'll be happy to take you out."

Max jumped into a rowboat, cast off, and headed out toward the red motorboat. Little more than a ripple disturbed the surface of the lake, the only sound the creaking of Max's oars in the rowlocks.

He drew alongside the motorboat. Edmund was in the wheelhouse, his back turned, bending over the doll. Max secured the rowboat to a cleat and climbed aboard the motorboat. His weight rocking the boat alerted Edmund to his presence immediately.

Edmund turned, the doll in one giant paw. He stuck out his chest. "Come on then," he shouted. "I'm waiting."

Max stood facing Edmund, his feet planted apart. "Drop the doll, Edmund and step away."

Edmund laughed. He tossed Aschenputtel behind him and stepped out of the wheelhouse. "You're going to have to come and get it."

Max took a step forward. They tussled, Edmund attempting to

grab ahold of his younger adversary. Max kept Edmund off balance by rocking the boat from side to side. He increased the rocking motion until Edmund fell over. Then Max slipped past into the wheelhouse and grabbed Aschenputtel. The cameo brooch was still attached to the doll's clothing. Edmund threw himself at Max, but Max slipped under the big man and retreated to the stern. Edmund advanced again. Using his bulk to hold Max in place he grabbed the doll with one hand and began to push Max backward over the edge with the other.

Max swung a fist that bounced off Edmund's chest. The big man showed no sign that he'd even noticed the blow. He locked a hand around Max's throat. Max was instantly paralyzed by the pain, struggling to breathe. They were both now clinging to the doll, Max's eyes smarting from the pain, neither one prepared to let go.

Edmund laughed. "I'm going to have to crush your windpipe, little man. If I had two hands free I could show you how I break necks."

Waves of pain swept over Max. He felt the heat of the outboard engine on his back as Edmund exerted more and more downward pressure. He had seconds to act. He knew if he didn't do something quickly he would be choked to death or fried on the hot engine cowling. He did the only thing he could do. He twisted his body sideways, rocking the boat and unbalancing Edmund, pulling the doll sharply downward at the same time. Edmund toppled forward, losing his grip on Max's neck. Max tugged Aschenputtel free and tossed her over Edmund's back toward the wheelhouse.

Max got to his feet and placed himself between the big man and the doll. Edmund shouted something unintelligible. Lowering his head, he charged at Max like a bull. Max sidestepped, but Edmund's left arm caught him and they crashed down together. Max's head fell on the doll. Edmund was not so lucky. He hit his head on the gunwale. He struggled to his feet dazed, swinging a couple of wild blows that met nothing but air. Max picked up the doll and Edmund came at him again, wrapping an arm around his shoulders.

Max held the doll out over the side of the boat. Edmund stretched for it, but he couldn't reach. He leaned out some more. Max dropped, twisting his body and throwing himself backwards. As he fell, he kicked out with his right leg, catching Edmund in the groin.

Edmund sailed over Max, executed a somersault worthy of an Olympic gymnast, and hit the water with a resounding splash.

Max tossed a floatation device into the water for Edmund before starting the motorboat engine and returning to the Storchen Hotel to reunite Aschenputtel with Sophie.

Chapter 100

December 1940

Jürgen's claim that he slept with Anna preyed on Max's nerves. He suspected that it was true, that it was Jürgen who told her the name of the murdered priest. But he never confronted Anna with the accusation. He reasoned that whichever way she replied, whether she denied it or admitted it, their marriage would suffer.

The work of the Red Orchestra continued apace in Berlin. The circulation list for their monthly broadsheets grew. Arvid's spare Hectograph was taken out of its hiding place and put into production.

The NKVD set up a radio transmitter in Zurich to replace Gilbert's in Brussels. Harro Schulze-Boysen continued to expand his network of spies in the ministries, and the Red Orchestra continued to pass intelligence reports to Moscow through the Russian embassy or via the transmitter in Switzerland.

Ule was the center of Greta's life. Now nearly three years old, and eating like a horse, he was growing fast. His language skills were encouraging, too, and she planned to start teaching him to read on his third birthday.

She had heard nothing from Max or Anna, and she often wondered if they made it to safety, if they'd found work and a place to live, if Sophie had found a measure of happiness. And whether the 9-year-old was still clinging to her doll.

Then one day in December 1940, she received a letter postmarked Zug, in Switzerland.

Dear Frau Greta,

I am uncertain that this letter will reach you. I hope it does. Are you and Adam well? And little Ule, is he still growing!? We are now settled in Switzerland. We moved from Zurich to another town where they speak German. Life's no gymkhana, but Max has found work. He's paid quite well, despite being an *Ausländer*. Living on one income is proving difficult, but we'll manage until the baby is born.

I should have mentioned that earlier, I suppose. Yes, I am expecting a baby in January. Sophie's hoping for a baby sister. Max says he doesn't mind what it is, but I suspect he secretly wants a boy.

Remember Aschenputtel's cameo brooch? We took it to an antiques expert here, and he identified it. It was once owned by the Grand Duchess Tatiana Nikolaevna Romanova, one of the daughters of Tsar Nicholas of Russia. It's worth A LOT of money. But, of course, Sophie says Aschenputtel doesn't want to sell it. It was the last gift her mama and papa gave her. Max has persuaded her to put it into a bank deposit box for safekeeping.

Max says the war should be over by Easter. Let's hope he's right. If he is we'll come and visit you with the new baby, maybe in the summer. In the meantime, look after yourselves.

If you get a chance to visit Switzerland, the manager of the Storchen Hotel in Zurich has our address.

All our love,

Anna, Max, Sophie and Aschenputtel.

THE END

Thanks for reading this story. If you liked it, tell your friends. If you want to encourage the author to write more like this, please write a review on Amazon. Reviews really help.

AUTHOR'S NOTE

This is a work of fiction. However, several of the members of the Red Orchestra featured in the book were real people: Adam, Greta (and baby Ule) Kuckhoff, Arvid and Mildred Harnack, Harro and Libertas Schulze-Boysen, Annie Krauss, and Dr. Himpel. I have included these people in order to respect their actions, their bravery in the face of implacable evil, and the personal sacrifices that many of them made. They were all heroes of the German Resistance. In order to incorporate these real people in the book, I have had to imagine and invent scenes and dialog and some of the events have been moved around in time for storytelling purposes.

There were many more people involved in these resistance activities, of course. I couldn't include them all. If you are interested in reading the history of this group, I recommend *The Red Orchestra* by Anne Nelson, Random House 2009, ISBN 9781400060009

Manufactured by Amazon.com
Columbia, SC
10 April 2017